THE DARLINGS

INDIES UNITED PUBLISHING HOUSE, LLC
P.O. BOX 3071
QUINCY, IL 62305-3071
INDIESUNITED.NET

THE DARLINGS

The Darlings
Book One

VERA JANE COOK

INDIES UNITED PUBLISHING HOUSE, LLC

Chapter One

DEBORAH

1993

Deborah Darling turned her hand mirror to the side and surveyed her chin, falling more each year, each line in her once youthful face deepening like unattended cracks in concrete, covered in firming cream but still, unfortunately, duly noted and wept over and bitterly cursed. Getting older was the cruelty of life. How had Dickie remained so unchanged with his pants lying flat against his middle and his hair still thick and full, the white of age, settling foam from a turbulent ocean, wavy and refreshing, on his scalp? Still as handsome as a storybook prince, but despite the languorous stride and that prominent cleft in his chin, Dickie was no ladies' man. She wished he were, but it takes personality to attract women and Dickie had as much of that as he did the energy to mow the lawn. He always said he loved to mow the lawn, but she'd only seen him do it once in all the years they were married. Well, he also fancied himself a master bowler, bragged that he always bowled a 226 but Deborah wouldn't bowl with him; it was too noisy for her to listen to his balls plopping in the alley, and it took too much energy to pretend he was just having a bad day because she was making him nervous. Or so he said.

"In my mind, I'm a master bowler, darlin'. I think, therefore it is so," he'd tell her with one of his sly winks.

Yet, despite all that myopic self-aggrandizement, she fell in love with him, and has remained so. The first time she laid eyes on him in 1960, even though it was evening, there was no mistaking those blue eyes, same color as a blue chrysanthemum. She'd just gotten out of high school and there he was, offering her a cold beer and a Marlboro. He stuttered a bit and blushed. Must have been his shyness that melted her heart. Her Dickie was as shy as a bucked-tooth little boy about to initiate his first kiss.

But Dickie was an odd one, always had been. Well, she liked men who seemed to harbor a world of their own, secrets maybe. Most men let it all hang out, no surprises, but her Dickie was a man of few words, preferring to bite his nails rather than engage in conversation, constantly reading novels about true crime, couldn't get enough of those bullshit paperback novels, devoured maybe four or five a week. He smoked a pipe, which Deborah adored; it was so upper crust, hardly any men in Pickens smoked pipes, Pickens being Marlboro country, with draft beer and pot bellies and beards that looked like old brooms. Well, at least in the run-down sections with all the auto parts places and the taverns with cheap food. Deborah just loved the scent of Dickie's pipe, it wafted sweet air around him like some protective invocation and camouflaged any unpleasant odor he might have had like bad breath or other untoward vulnerabilities of the body.

"This is the year I get plastic surgery, Dickie. Memorize this face, it will be forever transformed."

She stood in the doorway of the den where Dickie sat propped up in his leather chair, the leather-lined and buttery like old skin that had had too much sun. The chair was near the window that framed the magnolia trees, appearing oppressively still, and the green grass beyond, looking like an emerald field with coquettish bursts of white flowers, the sun appearing like a flame, a huge, hot threat to her comfort level. The fan in the corner of the room sounded like an old man taking his last breath. Deborah put her hand on her collarbone, felt the sweat, and then loosened the top button of her dress.

"Sure enough, Sweet Pea," Dickie said. He was a man of few words, unless he was reading them.

"What crime book has enthralled you now, darlin'?" she asked.

"*Stillhouse Lake.*"

"Good?"

"Great," he said.

So be it, a man of few words. Deborah had other things to think about other than her husband's obsession with unhumorous, poker-faced detectives and gory subjects like rape, stalking and the bloody atrocities of dead bodies. But despite it all, Dickie had his charms. His magical way of attracting money for one: he simply inherited it. Deborah liked that, though she didn't marry him because he was rich. Oh no, she married him because he was an enigma, and she fell into boredom easily; Dickie would never bore her. He might infuriate her with his lack of conversation but in his silence, she found a gold mine of intrigue. Her mother always told her that it was just as easy to ensnare a rich man as a poor man, so she better put aside the fool notion of marrying for love and follow the rule of self-preservation.

Well, according to Deborah she had lucked out, had married for love *and* money. Deborah's mother was beside herself with pride. Out of a family of four daughters, her Debbie had risen to the pinnacle of success while her sisters put up with a hard life, one poor girl with a drunk for a husband, the other with a cheat, and no husband at all for Deborah's youngest sibling. Miranda fancied herself a femme fatale, one of those obnoxious man-crazy bozos who spent their money on breast enhancements and went around with no hair anywhere on their bodies. Deborah didn't even want to think about why waxing all your pubic hair was a good thing. What the hell kind of statement is that? Deborah wondered.

Deborah recognized Dickie's talents early on when he borrowed a hundred dollars from her and invested it in the stock market, in some little company called Bethlehem Steel. She kept putting a hundred dollars in that Bethlehem Steel stock every month and watched that little stock come to pay her fifteen thousand a year in access income. Dickie put his family money into stocks that took off like a speed boat demanding space on a narrow river. Dickie's talents were commendable, they sure enough were, just as his thoughts, as ambiguous as his version of reality and revealed in the curious and enigmatical facial expressions that traversed his smile. Her husband reminded her of a silent mime artist with a big frown painted on his face, interpretation of his movement lingering in the intrigue of his tenebrous silence.

Deborah was used to Dickie. He was an amusing companion when he was present, a generous husband and father. He caused no waves but was not without complexities, and

Deborah saw Dickie's unspoken secrets as deeply perplexing as Sunday's crossword puzzle, sometimes rising to the surface like a tornado with winds of enormous strength, threatening damage enough to drown her. Best to ignore a hurricane and find comfort in the delusion that it will pass right over you. Best to ignore the damn Sunday crossword puzzle, too. That just made Deborah feel dumb.

She took herself out to the sunroom, where the privacy of her thoughts were enfolded by the French doors she closed behind her. Here, she could worry over her children in the sweet silence of the room. Her son, Barnaby, for one; his wise-cracking uncensored remarks were as unpredictable as weather, so impulsive, she was always afraid he'd say something sarcastic to the wrong person and get himself beaten up. Yes, he was always speaking his mind like someone else she'd known. Hot to tell off anybody, no matter who it was. Why the president of the United States wouldn't even be able to avoid Barnaby's barrage of sarcasm. He was fiery as a July noon. July noons in Pickens, South Carolina, made her think of an inferno taking down your house and burning your lily-white skin to a crisp.

Good thing Deborah knew how to befriend those sultry summers, a little frozen daiquiri, a white lace folding hand fan, and a porch chair to put her feet up on. Deborah had a folding fan that matched the color of the walls for every room. It was her intention that no amount of sweat should appear on her peaches and cream complexion, though this day was not so oppressive as summer days were known to be in Pickens. Her sunroom, as always, was a haven shaded by trees, so much so, the Lord's blessing and the protective stance they commanded caressed her. Trees were a godsend, letting the sun in and keeping the heat out.

Bless those beautiful lofty green gods, she thought.

Though today, they just stood there, tipping neither left or right, grinning in their defiance of providing a breeze. Still, the temperature, at least, was below eighty, thank the good Lord.

Her son liked the heat and probably would have died had he been born in some cold Midwest city, where your ears fall off with the first snow and your hands grow numb with the frost, where the chill hurts your teeth and stops the flow of blood in your poor shivering body. Lord, almighty, not for Barnaby, though Deborah might have liked it. Her son would rather sweat than feel the cold. Even with a mountain of water pouring off him, wetting his dark hair and leaving rings under his shirts, he was a handsome devil. Women flocked to Barnaby, birds to crumbs thrown to the ground. The boy had matinee idol looks, enticing those sweeping birds to his scent.

Too bad Barnaby couldn't tell which of those birds wanted to be held in his hands and stroked and which were planning to peck out his eyes.

Barnaby worked with numbers, like his father, moving money around like a mad scientist. Though Barnaby didn't solve the crimes in paperback detective stories like his father, he was as good as his father with funds and stocks. Barnaby could turn a dollar into a gold piece and make you think your trust in his expertise was the smartest thing you'd ever done. He'd take home every cent you had and promise you a rich retirement in some million-dollar old-age retreat. People swore he saw into the future and trusted him with their fortunes, even though he wasn't even thirty years old. Why, her Barnaby could talk the devil into quoting the Bible and lining the pathway to heaven with gold. Truth was, though, as young as he was, the son of a gun knew what he was doing, predicting the market like some crazy seer.

But smart as he was, having an appetite for brainless women would surely put that boy in an early grave. That was his weakness, a pretty face and a witless mind, full of nothing but foolish desires. Passions of the heart make a man turn on himself, do the devil's bidding. Deborah's brow furrowed deeply thinking about Barnaby. Fool of a man, handsome but foolish. Isn't that what they say about women, too pretty to be smart? Well, could have said the same for him when it came to women. He didn't carry her genes, but he didn't carry Dickie's either. Dickie was made from gentlemanly stock; Dickie was refined and levelheaded. Barnaby was a dandy who believed that getting laid was a man's godly Bible and should be read aloud daily.

Where then did this witless Don Juan of a son originate? Had she had an affair that spurned him, like burning coal inside her belly?

Well, of course she had had an affair, doesn't every woman have an affair at one time or another? The man was Jeremiah Lennox, who had swept between her legs and stolen her vows from her, sweet words of promise she'd sworn to Dickie, *and forsaking all others, be faithful to him as long as you both shall live.* It couldn't be avoided; Jerimiah had the good looks of a fictional god; looks he'd passed on to Barnaby, both with black curls and white teeth and powers of seduction. Jerimiah had been a force to be reckoned with, a force like ticks on your dog and the tornado that might tear the roof off your house.

Protect yourself Deborah, she said to herself the first time he had looked over the hors d'oeuvre tray at her mother-in-law's gracious front parlor, looked over and met her eyes and boldly held them. She told her best friend, Lottie Lacock, "He's put a spell on me like some mighty drug, Lottie."

"Protect yourself," is what Lottie said back. "Hell, if the town finds out you're bedding down with a Black man, they'll hang you right along with him."

Well, he wasn't very black, could have passed for white on a dark night or in a dark bar. He shouldn't have been messing with her, either. She was a White woman from upstate where people paid a pretty penny for views of the Blue Ridge Mountains. Innocent, pure and clean as the driven snow, she was. Didn't stop her, though, it was a thing of passion, and she was a bit hungry for that, a bit hungry to feel she'd succumbed to a state of delirium whenever Jeremiah captured her tongue in a kiss and spun it around like a game of tag.

She hadn't been married to Dickie all that long, a little over a year, the first time she'd spread her legs for Jeremiah behind a bush in Kings Park. Dickie was sweet and mild and how fulfilling it was in the beginning. She thought she liked that, but Dickie made love like she was a follow the dots instruction sheet for putting together a table. Jerimiah was hungry and fierce, like a shark in an ocean full of fish, and he made love as though the table was already sturdy, worthy of his weight and hers, or better yet, to hell with the table — if it collapsed under them who gave a rat's ass? That's what making love should be, reckless.

Well, sex is not the reason for choosing anyone. That's what she told Barnaby when he got mixed up with Mindy Peach, sassy little girl Deborah never liked with her honey blonde hair, her Southern lilt, and those hips that never stopped swaying.

"Protect yourself," she told him, but Mindy drew him in like a long slow breath, and the stupid son of a bitch just sat back and drank in her lies like lemonade. But Deborah saw right through her: she was a liar and a user for sure. And lemonade can be bitter. Deborah nodded her head thinking, Lord, he's a dumb one. She'd tried to tell him that little Mindy Peach was as toxic as the poison used to kill mice, but who did she listen to when Jeremiah Lennox was panting in her ear like a goddamned jacked-up Casanova.

Let's see, how many years did Jeremiah get for the murder of Fletcher Smith? Deborah thought back … thirty-five to life. Hell of a sentence to pay for doing nothing but being in the wrong place at the wrong time.

Fletcher Smith was a wrung-out drunk, guilty of nothing but grabbing the wrong woman's tits at some bar at the edge of town in the fall of 1963. Halloween night it was, everyone dressed up as something or other, though the theme was *Gone with the Wind.* Poor Fletcher got drunk and stupid, and then a pistol blast to his head blew it off right in the alley behind Smith's tavern. Now we know women don't do things like that, but a woman did Fletcher in. Deborah saw the swish of a skirt fly past her for certain, but Jeremiah deserved the blame.

Deborah didn't take well to men who used her up and spat her out, spat her right back to Dickie, who was all too willing to look the other way when Barnaby came out with black hair and black eyes, shooting the same kind of bullshit as Jeremiah Lennox by the time he was three years old. But Dickie treated Barnaby no different than he treated their daughter, Robinette. Deborah always thought he even loved Barnaby more because Barnaby was a boy. He somehow saw his own image in her dark little son, dark being hair color, not skin color. Barnaby's skin was as White as hers. Jeremiah Lennox was not very dark far as Deborah could remember. But some said he was Brown, and some said he was White, but Deborah knew he was Black, 'cause he'd told her some White shit raped his great, great grandmother and all the descendants of that son of a bitch came out the womb looking as ambiguous as could be – maybe White, maybe Black, take your pick.

Barnaby had Jeremiah's wit and his impressive height, which was well over six feet. Barnaby had his lean frame and his way with women, too. But somehow Dickie didn't see that. He just saw Barnaby, his brilliant little boy who trailed behind him ever since he was a child, hanging on his every word, and Dickie liked that. Her son managed to hold Dickie up the way she couldn't. Deborah never was that kind of woman, never cared if a man couldn't take care of his own ego, so she didn't feed egos. Far be it from her to lift a man's sense of himself and pretend he was God's gift when he wasn't. Dickie was her son's world, though, the master of his misguided fate, the hero of his storybook with so many slayed dragons and so many pages of pretty little girls, the fairy tale that was supposed to end well and wouldn't, not if he were panting after Mindy. Yes, his goddamn fairy tale ended with Mindy Peach, how happy an ending could that be? Well, Barnaby kept her husband's ego 'bout as high as the stars in the sky and maybe that's what it was all about, male egos and all the crap you had to keep tossing into it. She was sure Mindy was good at that.

"Papa, Papa, build me a tree house."

And there Dickie went with his hammer and his nails, sweating in his pale blue shirt, sticking nails between his lips but he hammered and he hammered, and Barnaby watched in awe as that pile of plywood took shape, finally looking like some mighty little low-country house in a tree.

Deborah and Dickie had themselves a real low-country home as gracious as any in Charleston or Savannah. Dickie's family were all from Greenville and then moved on over to Pickens, buying up land and making themselves rich on the backs of slaves back in the days. The Civil War tore the South apart, but their home had never been destroyed by ravaging Yankees, nor their spirit. Dickie's ancestors did not succumb to defeat. They went on making money, talking sweet and owning dry-goods stores and restaurants and some even became men of God and preached the gospel. Dickie's ancestors were bankers, some were teachers he'd tell her, but mostly bankers with big cigars and slender fingers and minds that went down a one-way street to riches.

She loved her white-shuttered farmhouse with its long porch and gardens of magnolias and trellises of roses in every color. Dickie didn't like to tell people he was from a long line of slave owners. He said slavery was a sin against humankind, a black stain on the soul of our nation. Lord, her Dickie could have been born in the city of New York, where liberalism was a prerequisite for a lease and the calling card of acceptance into the Democratic party of misguided values. He was over the top, her Dickie, not that Deborah believed in slavery, she didn't think about it; she was modern, it had no place in her world. She paid her help and loved them like family. There was Deasia, their cook, big heavy-set woman who laughed constantly. Deborah didn't understand what she had to laugh about, she was so poor, but she found everything funny, including the time Deborah asked her to cook lobster and she screamed and screamed when she threw those lobsters in the pot, then laughed for days about it, said it was the worst thing she'd ever done.

When Barnaby skinned his knee as a child, she laughed, and it would make Barnaby laugh, too. She even laughed when Dickie had a car accident and came back with bandages all over his head. Deborah and the children had been horrified, but Deasia laughed so hard, she almost tripped over herself, said he looked like a monster, a funny monster who just might turn into a living mummy and kill them in the night. Deborah had chastised her for that, for scaring the children, but she'd laughed herself. "Those Negros find humor in the weirdest things, they love to laugh, those Negros," she told Dickie.

Well, Deasia was family, just like Heaven, little Black girl who came to clean two, three times a week. And then there was Héctor, the gardener and Booker, Dickie's driver, and Deborah's driver sometimes. But Deborah did like to drive herself, made her feel free driving down the highway alone without Dickie telling her she was 'bout to kill them both.

Dickie didn't know everything, Deborah thought. Didn't know or care that his son was being seduced by a girl with no brain and no future, not even for bearing children. She said she didn't want them, they were bound to ruin her figure and put her in the poor house. Barnaby just laughed and agreed. Anything the girl said, Barnaby just laughed and agreed. At times, he was as scatterbrained as Deasia.

"Time for my walk, Sweet Pea."Deborah looked up at her husband in the doorway, dressed like some movie actor with his seersucker blazer and his pleated white pants. Of course, he was, she thought. Of course, he was. No sense taking a walk that's going to mess up your clothes or put sweat on your brow, no sense looking anything other than perfect. Well, no. No telling who he'll meet in Mile Creek Park.

She smiled. "Enjoy, darlin', " she said, noticing how nicely he'd tied the ascot at his neck.

Deborah was thinking about the first time she discovered Dickie had appetites she couldn't satisfy, not with her recipes. It was right after Fletcher Smith's murder. Nothing in any cookbook on earth could muster up a sauce for 'penis' soup when there was no penis to throw in it.

"Just an urge, nothing to worry about," Lottie Lacock told her.

Uh um, she thought and went to her room to stare up at the sky for hours.

"You know men have all these weird sexual yearnings," Lottie called later to say.

Well, it *was* nothing to worry about, was it?

That was right after her affair with Jeremiah, so why should she care that Dickie was a complicated man and every now and then he liked to put a penis in his mouth. Lord, is that what they did? Lord, she just wouldn't think about it. Who knew what the hell they did? It was trivial, another one of Dickie's odd little quirks, like how he liked to birdwatch in the spring and rattle off the name of every goddamn bird in Pickens till she thought she'd strangle him, and the way he put cherry soda in his white wine and mustard on French fries. Well, why should she care about this little sideline interest; she was the only woman in his life.

She'd seen Dickie talking to the man everyone called Ginger Tea. Ginger was a man who dressed up like a woman every so often and paraded himself around town. He was married to a woman like a normal man, and Deborah had seen him several times out of his costume looking like an aristocrat, sucking on oysters and sipping Champagne. An aristocrat, that is, till he opened his mouth and sounded like a woman, a woman with a five o'clock shadow and muscles popping out of his shirt that looked as thick and hard as concrete walls. Talk about ambiguous! My God, why would any man or woman want to be as ambiguous as that? Deborah had jumped back the first time she ran into him at the supermarket, and he was wearing an orange turban on his head, several strings of beads and pedal pushers.

"Oh, so sorry," Deborah had said and jumped as if a mouse had crossed her path.

"Oh, dear." Ginger put his hand to his chest and beat it a little because he'd been startled.

Deborah stared at him. She couldn't help herself. "No bother," she said and smiled halfheartedly.

"Dearie," he said. "You best look where you're going."

Deborah shook her head and briskly walked away after she made some *tsk* sound. The bastard had knocked into her and he's telling her to look where she's going? Bastard made a weird-looking woman with his oversized tits and some long dark wig that was so full it could have had animals living in it. His face still looked masculine with his long nose and twitchy dark eyes. Just as ugly as he could be, she thought. She'd heard Fletcher's widow Rhonda had married him. What the hell was wrong with her?

Later that evening, she told Dickie about it, and he didn't say a word, just nodded his head. Then she finds out her Dickie is a friend of this she-man. There he stood on the corner of Airy Spring Road, talking to this person like they were old friends. But the kicker was the kiss that Ginger Tea placed on her Dickie's cheek.

"My God, my husband is one of those men," she told Lottie.

"One of what men?" Lottie asked.

"Queer," Deborah whispered. "My Dickie is queer. He kissed that she-man back."

Poor Lottie didn't say a word, just nodded like it was not unusual.

"Is Barnaby here yet?" Robinette asked as she came flying down the stairs from her room, from her almost a woman-cave with pictures of Martina Navratilova plastered all over the walls as if they were joined at the hip, best friends for life, blood sisters. She also had Mariah Carey's music blaring from her stereo and a million hats hanging off the walls looking deranged, like big straw Martian spaceships, headless Martians 'bout to swirl around the room and whisk her off into oblivion. Robinette didn't wear the hats, said she just liked to sketch them because they reminded her of old-fashioned pretty girls with all those long bows and little flowers on the rim. She said it made her happy that women didn't wear those silly hats anymore, 'cause women have come so far, so far that they can cut their hair short and wear caps and not have to 'fem' themselves up so much with bows and corsets and other such nonsense.

Weird thing for her daughter to say, but Deborah thought that both her children were little strangers that had slid from her belly. Her belly had been the receptacle that gave birth to these odd little people. She expected one of them to turn out like her, but then she had to accept that she was unique, and her children were not, for neither of them resembled her in any way.

"Not yet," she said as her daughter slid into the kitchen, most likely to talk Deasia into making her a tuna sandwich, so she could go out to the back patio and sit out there in the sun — without a hat — and try to tan her White body, which would most likely burn and peel and look like absolute shit inside of twenty minutes.

Robinette was a pretty girl, Deborah observed, but not pretty the way Barnaby was handsome. Robinette was cute, kind of boyish with that chestnut hair she kept short and those long, endless legs. Her small breasts were pert. Deborah took credit for that, her daughter had her breasts, but the buck stopped there. Deborah was a brunette like her daughter, but her eyes were green, like Scarlet O'Hara's. Robinette's eyes were blue like Dickie's, like a deep, blue sky at dusk. She was not tall and thin like her daughter; she was short and a tad round in the middle, used to be called an hourglass figure; now it was just called plump, like a meaty bird. When Deborah and Lottie Lacock were kids, Lottie used to tell her that she had piano legs and after Deborah cried and cried and examined her legs in the mirror for days on end, finding no resemblance to a piano leg, Deborah told Lottie she resembled

Bela Lugosi. What are friends for if not to air their cruel little personalities to each other so they could grow up to pretend they had not a mean bone in their bodies?

Deborah loved Lottie, really, she did, even though Lottie wasn't that savvy and had never married. Obviously, she never married because she couldn't hold a man's attention for more than five minutes, not talking politics and films that were made a hundred years ago and books that no one had ever heard of. Hell, with men, you got one subject: THEM — and you best know how to act stupid and not bring up things they might not have knowledge of, or even worse, beyond their intellectual capacity.

Chapter Two

Deborah

"That girl gonna burn herself to death. I tol' her, 'Put on a hat, Robinette. Get yourself out the sun.' She just smile at me from her red face. Humph."

Deborah looked up into Deasia's puffy pout and winked. "When have we ever been able to tell that girl what to do, Deasia?"

"You right," she laughed. "That girl listens to no one, got a mind of her own."

"You say that like it's a good thing, Deasia."

"Ain't no good thing, less you know better than everyone else."

"Is that Prissy back there in the kitchen. Is Prissy here?" Deborah craned her neck and spotted Prissy at the back of the house. She looked toward the dining room and watched Deasia's nineteen-year-old daughter glide through the door as if walking on puffy white clouds.

"That her." Deasia beamed.

Priscilla, *Prissy*, as she was known to the Darling family, could have been walking down the red carpet in jewels instead of the dungarees she wore, so regal and eye-catching she was. Deborah wondered where she got her looks, for neither Deasia nor her husband, Jackson, were lookers, only plain ordinary Black people who had miraculously spawned this little glamour girl. Two people who had never been outside of Pickens, South Carolina, had somehow given birth to this young woman, rivaling Dorothy Dandridge, certainly rivaling any goddess gliding down a Paris runway.

"Prissy, darlin'." Deborah held out her arms for a kiss and Prissy obliged.

"Afternoon, Miss Darling."

"Feel like you've been avoiding me, young lady. Where you been hiding yourself?"

"Behind my books, ma'am."

Swinging Prissy's hand in hers, Deborah asked. "Who does this child take after, Deasia? She's so beautiful." Deborah had asked Deasia that many times and Deasia had answered the same many times, feeling the same pride and the same apprehension, for pretty girls attract not one but many.

"She good-looking, yeah." Deasia sighed.

"Thank you, Miss Darling." Prissy had been told she was beautiful so often it had become jarring for the girl not to hear it, as if it had been purposely withheld.

"She take after my sister, Jewel. Jewel, she live

in Chicago. Prissy got her face. My sister's face get her in all sorts of trouble. She got a gangster boyfriend. I don't sleep nights, thinking about my sister. He likely to shoot her someday. Humph."

"You been telling me that for years, Deasia and she's still living, right? I think she'll be fine; she's been fine this long. Besides, gangsters don't kill their girlfriends, more likely to be their enemies, of which they have a long list, I hear. She's still on this earth, right? Fact is fact." Deborah smiled at her, somewhat condescending, for the dots added up to the obvious.

"She ain't no ganster's girlfriend, she tell me. She the girlfriend of a businessman, she tell me. Humph, that what she tell me, like I don't have a brain in my head, like I don't know truth from big fat lies. He dress in black all the time, even in July. He dress in black, like Edward G Robinson."

Deborah smiled at Prissy. "I doubt you'll wind up like Jewel, Prissy."

Prissy laughed. "Hardly, but I love Jewel, Mama. She can take care of herself."

"You don't have a weakness for gangsters, do you, Prissy?" Deborah asked.

Prissy laughed. It was a lilt and it made Deborah smile. She had known this girl since she was a baby. Times had changed in Deborah's world. Prissy had a scholarship to go to Tulane University in New Orleans and her own daughter had nothing but mediocre grades and some idea about traveling all over Europe when she got out of high school; that or join a rock band even though she sang like a hungry cat in a back ally.

Deborah sighed. "Talk some sense into Robinette, will you? She wants to travel all around like some vagabond instead of settling down and marrying."

"Robbie doesn't have a boyfriend. Hard to marry when you don't have a boyfriend." Prissy smiled and shrugged her shoulders.

"No, I don't think she does have a boyfriend, but she will. Must you call her Robbie?"

Prissy laughed again. "She likes it. Anyway," Prissy made air quote signs with her fingers, "Robinette will do what Robinette wants to do. I can't tell her a thing, Miss Darling."

"Robbie is a masculine name. We gave her such a pretty name." Deborah looked at Prissy. "Don't you think?"

"Humph, sure enough." Deasia picked up a glass bowl and examined it for fingerprints.

"I daresay you will influence my child with your sensible goals, Prissy. You're going to be a lawyer? I am so proud, like your parents, I do admire you. I doubt if Robinette could ever be a lawyer, but I think she could manage one of those shops on Main Street. She's good with numbers, like her father and her brother. That little shop on the corner of West Main, that dress shop, would be wonderful for her. What's it called?

Mademoiselle Camille's?"

Prissy laughed again, "I think Robbie's plans are a bit loftier than staying here in Pickens, ma'am, and working in a dress shop. Besides, she's an artist."

Deborah raised an eyebrow and stared at Prissy, watched her sit down in one of the big, overstuffed chairs and yawn. "Everyone fancies themselves an artist."

"She's really good, though. I don't know what she plans to do about it, but she's really good."

"Do tell what my Robinette's plans are then, Prissy?" She had emphasized her daughter's full name as she stared into Prissy's eyes. "Aside from being a famous artist."

Prissy glanced at her mother as if hoping for assistance. Finally, Deasia broke out into peals of laughter. "She goin' to New York, Miss Darling. She goin' take any job she find, long as she there. She say poverty is worth being in New York. She say better to be poor in New York than rich here in Pickens. She say all artists go to New York."

Deborah sat back and looked out toward the patio where her daughter lay in the sun, oblivious to the damage to her skin. She wouldn't last one day in New York, Deborah thought. "I daresay this is after her European journey or before?"

Prissy just smiled. "You need to ask her that, Miss Darling."

"Her answer wouldn't matter, the way she

changes her mind. Today it's New York, tomorrow, it's the moon. Wouldn't that be fine, my little Robinette on the moon?"

And with that Deasia laughed so hard she almost dropped the glass bowl she was taking to the kitchen to fill with fruit.

Deasia's laughter faded behind the slam of the front door as Barnaby walked through, holding the hand of that dimwit, Mindy Peach. Dimwit according to Deborah.

Deborah frowned but managed a fake smile as Mindy bounced over to her, her enormous breasts obliterating Deborah's glorious view out of the window. Mindy leaned down to peck her cheek with a wet kiss, and those boat paddles of hers nearly took out an eye.

"Afternoon, Miss. Darling."

"Top of the morning, Mother," Barnaby said.

Deborah watched as he tipped his straw fedora at Prissy. "You look as pretty as that sunset we are sure to get this evening, Prissy. Yep, pretty as a sunset."

Prissy smiled, showing her white, perfect teeth. Her eyes glittered, as if they were smiling at him. Deborah always thought she had a crush on her son but then again, wasn't a woman in Pickens didn't melt under Barnaby's attention. Deborah assumed he would have bedded her down if she weren't Black.

"Kind of you to say that, sir." Prissy gave

Barnaby a smile so wide, Deborah swore she could see the girl's fillings.

"Kindness has nothing to do with it. More like truth-telling." He took a seat beside Mindy on the couch, but Deborah didn't miss the lingering smile directed at Prissy.

"You must have a million boyfriends, Prissy." Deborah forced another smile as she stared at her son, a warning perhaps not to include any of the Negro help in his games of seduction.

Prissy laughed. "I'd say nine hundred and ninety-nine thousand short of a million."

"So, there is one?" Barnaby asked. "Do tell us who has captured your attention." He sat forward and grinned at her, ignoring the look on his mother's face.

"That skinny boy over at Hank's Car Parts. The one with the missing teeth?" She looked as though she was holding back a barrage of laughter.

Barnaby slapped his leg and sat back laughing. "Do tell."

"Surely you can do better than that." Deborah stared at her and wondered if she was kidding.

"Well, maybe when I move to New Orleans, but for now, that skinny boy is making money and for a Black boy in Pickens, that's something."

Barnaby and Mindy laughed hysterically, as if she'd told a joke. Deborah stared at Prissy. She must have been pulling her leg. "Lots of Black men making money in Pickens, Priss," she said.

"Oh, but they're all married, Miss. Darling. I don't date married men."

"Just skinny ones with missing teeth?" Barnaby asked, still laughing. Mindy also found that funny, hanging on Barnaby's shoulder, tears running down her cheeks. Somehow Deborah felt that she was the brunt of a joke.

Abruptly, Mindy sprang to her feet. "Is Robbie upstairs?"

Deborah made a face. "I told you not to call my daughter Robbie. She is not a boy."

"Oh, sorry. Anyway, I think it's a girl's name too. Where is she?"

"She's out in the back, sunning herself and inviting skin cancer." Deborah glared at her. "Why don't you see if Deasia will make you a tuna sandwich and you can join her out there."

"So I can get skin cancer, too?" Mindy pouted.

"Just keep your clothes on, girl." Deborah forced a smile.

"Not easy to do," she winked at Barnaby and grinned back at Deborah, "I mean, it's so hot."

Deborah let some guttural sound out of her mouth as she watched Mindy leave the room, her hips swinging as if there were music playing. She turned to Barnaby. "She's blatant," she said. "I don't wish to hear how she takes her clothes off for you."

"She didn't say that, Mother."

"It's what she meant."

Barnaby twirled his fedora around by his finger and stared at Prissy. "I think Mother thinks that Mindy is a wanton woman and will lead some poor fool down the path of shame."

"With her clothes on or off?" Prissy laughed and they sat there grinning at each other.

Deborah found her disrespectful. "The help should always side with their employers. Loose morals are nothing to joke about." Deborah tried to sound light, as if she were being facetious, but it came out haughty and condescending.

"Well, Mother, you must know that Prissy doesn't work for us, her mother does, and you have no right to talk down to her." He said it as if he were scolding a child and Deborah flinched.

"My God, Barnaby, I wasn't being serious, I was kidding. You do know I was kidding, Prissy? I know you're not our help."

Prissy smiled. "I get the art of subtlety, Miss Darling, even if your son doesn't. You were being subtle or trying to be, weren't you? But you might have been shielding your truth behind humor." Prissy winked. "A lot of people do that."

Deborah stared at her. What did she mean by that? she wondered. Had she just been exonerated or not?

Deborah nodded her head as Dickie walked through the door with a paper tucked under his arm.

"How was your walk, Darlin'?" she asked, relieved to turn her attention away from Prissy.

Dickie held the paper up over his head. "You're not going to believe this."

Deborah tried to see the headline, but she couldn't, so she sat back and smiled at him. "What aren't we going to believe, my love? Have Martians landed?"

"Jeremiah Lennox is being released from prison." He waved the paper around. "This is unbelievable." The wind knocked out of her, Deborah's whole body turned red; the heat rising, she sat there looking like a tomato. She sat up in her chair before she fainted on the floor. "I thought it was a slam dunk thirty years ago."

"So did everyone else, but apparently, they have proved that Jeremiah did not kill Fletcher, that the evidence against him was weak, that reasonable doubt was evident, and the jury convicted because he was Black, not because he was guilty."

"They proved it now, so many years later?" Deborah let her mouth hang open while she stared at her husband, who appeared exuberant. "How the hell could they prove something like that?"

"DNA, darlin'. We didn't have DNA thirty years ago, but we've got it now and it wasn't Jeremiah's DNA found at the scene of the crime, it was someone else's. As a matter of fact,

Jeremiah's DNA wasn't found anywhere at the scene of the crime."

"Whose was then?" Deborah gasped out the words; she might surely faint for sure. She turned to Prissy. "Prissy, be a dear and have your mother bring us all some iced tea."

"Who's Jeremiah Lennox?" Prissy asked as she got to her feet. "Name sounds familiar."

"He went to jail for murdering Fletcher Smith." Dickie sat in the yellow chair; the big round comfortable one that Prissy had just vacated. "I'm going to solve this one," he said to his wife. "I got myself a real live crime to work on." He grinned at Deborah, who stared back, horrified.

"Why don't you just let the police do their job, Dickie? Don't be a nuisance."

"Oh, mother," Barnaby chimed in, "let him have some fun. Can I help, Pops? I'll be your assistant."

"Of course," Dickie beamed. "No better assistant to have than my son."

Chapter Three

Leighton McArdle

Hank stood at the foot of the stairs as she came through the kitchen. If bad news was a facial expression, then she had bats in her attic.

"Bats?" she asked.

Hank nodded. "You got to get rid of 'em."

"Well, I sure as hell ain't going to live with 'em."

He shrugged his shoulders. "Sorry."

"How much?" she asked, dreading the answer.

"Going to cost you a thousand dollars."

"Shit," she said.

"You can pay it off … two installments?" He shifted his weight and stared at her.

"How soon can you start?"

"I can get over here tomorrow."

"Do you kill them?"

"No, no, can't kill bats. We just make sure that after they leave your attic, they can't get back in. They'll go somewhere else, like maybe into that cave down by your stream. That will be a good thing, they'll keep you insect free. I can build you a bat house down there."

"No, no, but thanks all the same."

"Your call, Leighton."

"Are you sure they'll leave?" She looked at him, hopefully, she was sure. He was to be her savior and she wanted him to feel her appreciation.

He nodded his head and shuffled his feet on the ground a bit before he spoke. "I'm sorry about Beau," he said as he kept his eyes on the ground. "Good man he was."

"Thanks. Will the bats leave, Hank?"

"Yep, come dusk tomorrow, they'll leave."

"Okay." She shook his hand. "What time can you come by tomorrow?"

She watched him walk off the porch after he said he'd be back at nine. Nine was good. She had nowhere to go. She couldn't live with bats, that was for sure. Even If she had had somewhere to go, she would have postponed it. She had a priority now: get rid of the bats. Priorities were good, she'd always had them, and they take your mind off things like burying your husband five weeks ago. Up until then, her priorities had been clear, Beau, her husband, her dog Aspen and then everything else, such as her job and her commitment to it. Nothing after that. No room for any more shock and loss. But her priorities kept getting hit with a dose of mind-numbing reality and were as vulnerable as a leaf in a storm. For Leighton, remembering what the hell she was supposed to be doing was as threatened as a memory in the mind of an Alzheimer's sufferer.

She walked back to the deck and stared down the stream, watched a family of ducks swim by. Aspen barked at them, wagging his tail, wanting to run after them, have something to chase, have some fun. God knows she had become a deadbeat. Aspen was sweet, though his breed was said to be nasty. Aspen would never hurt anything or anyone and Beau knew it when he brought him home from the pound, one from a litter of five that probably would be gassed if they didn't find homes.

"This is a sweet one," Beau had said, and Leighton remembers saying they were all sweet, they were just puppies. "Yeah, it's people that will make them mean." Then Beau looked sad, too sad to ignore the striking reality of animal cruelty.

They went back and took all the puppies and adopted them out themselves. It took six months to find them all a good home but who wouldn't adopt a dog from her, a detective with a heart and her husband, the chef who played Santa Claus every year at every children's hospital in and around the county of Pickens, South Carolina.

Leighton sat in an old plastic chair, weathered by rain and too many winters. It could be said that Aspen took after his human dad, sweet as Brown Butter Chess Pie. He certainly didn't take after her. She was brittle, not anyone Beau ever deserved.

She picked up the case history on Fletcher Smith with a sigh, hoping that this time she might see something she hadn't seen before. Another cold case falling into her lap because ghosts were demanding her attention, this time the ghost of Fletcher Smith. She always felt that way, that once she took a case, the ghosts were there, whispering behind her. Last time it was the ghost of Terrence White, a rich man found in a well with his throat slashed. It had been his business partner. Easy. Case closed and the ghost went away, satisfied, vindicated.

This case did not appear so easy. The DNA they'd found on a paper cup near the body had been run through a database, nothing. It wasn't Fletcher's DNA on the cup; they didn't know whose DNA was on the cup. The beer from the cup was found near Fletcher's bloody face, as if tossed or thrown at him. The man accused of the crime would be released in a week. A law-school Innocence Project had gotten him a new trial and public support was overwhelming.

Hardly anyone believed that Jeremiah Lennox had killed Fletcher. Leighton knew that the DNA on the cup did not necessarily prove the killer's identity but might uncover an eyewitness to the crime, someone who had been too afraid to come forward then; a witness who might be protecting someone. There was no apparent motive for

Fletcher's murder and that's what Leighton had to discover: who had hated Fletcher enough to blow his brains out? She heated up the barbeque and brought out a steak from the kitchen to throw on it. The wine from the previous night was in the refrigerator along with the salad she'd made that morning, covered in saran wrap, just waiting for her to eat it, the radicchio crunched, the tomatoes savored. That had been her late husband's favorite thing in the world, steak and salad with tomatoes and cucumbers. Beau had been a wonderful cook, but it wasn't the fancy things he excelled at, it was the simple things … his Southern Chili and home-baked cakes and pies. That's why his restaurant had been so popular. The food was not fancy, but it was exceptionally good and very Southern. She'd been spoiled by his Southern fried fish and his pimento mushroom omelets. She knew that no matter how hard she tried, she could not duplicate Beau's blue cheese dressing or his expertise in cooking the perfect ribs, or anything else he so easily threw on the fire, both at home and at the restaurant. It was jarring to Leighton, what vanishes with the dead. The silence haunted her most. Maybe that was the worst of it, the absent voice that once filled the silence and all the words that tumbled together in definitions of who he was. Who he was no more? Maybe. Maybe not.

She set everything on a table and promised

herself she'd have a meal without weeping. She'd wait until she was hungry, wait until the barbeque was perfectly ready and the wine had dulled her senses just enough to forget that Beau was gone. What was it that Beau always said, never insult a steak on a lukewarm grill? That memory did not make her smile; it made her sad, so sad she thought she'd just have to down a bottle of wine and sleep until it passed, the numbness of loss, the shock that rattles your soul. Leighton opened the wine and poured a glass. Yes, it was time to dull her senses. She stared out over the stream, nearly covered by the long limbs of arching trees. She wanted to think about Fletcher Smith, but Beau invaded her thoughts as he always did. She had such a clear image of her husband leaning against the porch railing, his expression serious as he gave substance to her theories, questioning her conclusions. He might have been a chef, but he understood crime, figured out who had motive and who didn't. Together they were quite a team. She didn't know if she'd ever be able to solve another crime without him. She had no one to bounce anything off except her partner, Joe Martinelli, or 'Mart' as Leighton called him, who never saw anything beyond the facts, who didn't feel the truth as a sixth sense. He never journeyed off the page of facts. He never 'felt' anything was wrong in logical conclusions, that logic could not be challenged, his mantra, "The facts speak for themselves, Leighton."

She thought about her newest ghost, Fletcher Smith. A notorious womanizer who managed to remain focused enough to run a business, countywide storage units, some large enough to store a truck. Fletcher was married but never had children. He was known to treat all women like whores, their body parts up for grabs and their rejections interpreted by Fletcher as flirtations, signals that said they wanted to be sought after and seduced, possibly even raped. Leighton didn't doubt he was guilty of rape, but not one of the women questioned admitted to that.

Well, that's somewhere to start, Leighton thought. She was sure he had come on to the wrong woman and the woman's husband or boyfriend had retaliated and that's what got him killed. A jealous husband or boyfriend. Yes, good place to start. She looked at the railing where Beau would have been standing, throwing questions at her, forcing her to look deeper. *Yes, Beau, you could be right, a woman could have killed him too. You're right, a woman could have done it.*

The man who had been accused of the crime, Jeremiah Lennox, was Black, not likely to have a hate on for Fletcher but rumor had it that he was also a womanizer. A womanizer but possibly not a killer.

"So, who would want Fletcher dead, she

whispered?" She almost heard Beau answer: "What do you know about Fletcher's wife, the gorgeous redhead he went steady with while she was still in high school, and he was what? Nearly thirty?"

Leighton thought about Rhonda Smith, questioned only once and now remarried to the town weirdo, Marshall Kram, otherwise known as Ginger Tea. The rumor going around was that Rhonda was having an affair with Jeremiah. Everyone in town knew Jeremiah was having an affair with some White woman. But right after the murder of her husband, she married Marshal Kram. Why would a woman marry a trans gender? Or was he just a cross-dresser? She wondered. Leighton would need Mart to explain the difference between the two because she had no idea what it was. For her, it was all just one and the same, a sexual dysfunction.

That night in bed, she listened for the bats, but they must have flown out; they must be eating insects by now, hanging out in caves, their myopic eyes fixed on the feast around them, their furry little bodies hanging from limbs, their wings soaring like the black span of Dracula's cape. The utter freedom of the night, a smorgasbord of insects.

Sadness for the bats crept in, their home would soon be most unwelcoming, but every creature must learn that cruelty is what we need to expect from life at one time or another and in one way or another. Cruelty is always there near the surface, easily triggered by jealousy and passion. Leighton had learned that entitled people committed murder, those who feel they have a right to take, who never consider the consequences, whose proximity to cruelty is overbearing.

She read the case history yet again. The murder was on the Halloween night of 1963. Most everyone in Pickens was all dressed up in costume over at Smith's Bar, a popular hangout for young people during the '60s. Everyone had agreed to come in costume, or told they wouldn't get in. Later that night, Fletcher wound up in the alley, wearing a clown suit, with his head nearly blown off. Confronted by someone who hated him, who might have agreed to meet him in the alley. Leighton easily saw that there was too much passion behind this murder for it to be random. It had the marks of an angry crime because the victim had a nasty burn on his hand, as if someone had stubbed a cigarette out on his flesh. It could have been self-defense, Fletcher was known to throw his weight around, to dominate people. But someone had brought a loaded gun to Smith's Bar that night which led her to conclude that Fletcher's murder was premeditated, someone planned to kill him in that alley, or she was completely wrong and there was no rhyme or reason to the murder. In any case, it had been Fletcher Smith's night to die.

Fletcher was there watching her read, grabbing at her thoughts as only ghosts can do. But they can't speak the answers, they can't call out their killer's name. If they could, she wouldn't have a job, would she? She thought about Rhonda Smith again, Fletcher's wife. She knew Beau would want her to investigate Rhonda: just how did she feel about her husband? Was she having an affair with Marshall Kram as well as Jeremiah Lennox? Had she and her future husband had an ax to grind? Did she and Marshal want Fletcher dead? Did she and Jeremiah want Fletcher dead? Do transgender women like sex with men or women?

Leighton was perplexed at that, but suspected that the tangled threads of sexuality would lead her somewhere; it was important to understand passion, all kinds of passion. As for the crime, all Jeremiah did was walk out of that alley from the opposite end to where Fletcher was murdered. Unfortunately, a woman named Deborah Darling saw him as he left the alley. He was dressed as a pirate and had worn a mask across his eyes, but Deborah recognized him enough to tell police that he had probably killed Fetcher.

Probably has no place in a conviction.

There was no proof that Jeremiah pulled the trigger of a gun they never found. She said she didn't see him kill Fletcher, just saw him leaving the alley. And he was convicted based on that evidence. Where was that gun? Why wasn't there blood on Jeremiah Lennox? Most unsettling was that Jerimiah's hands were never tested for gunshot residue. They were just too quick to convict. Did Deborah Darling want Jeremiah to pay for that crime because she had killed Fletcher? What was she doing alone in that alley at that hour? She was married. All these questions were never sufficiently answered. Jeremiah had a court-appointed attorney. A slam dunk against Jeremiah Lennox. Someone had to pay, why not that poor minority man?

A pounding noise woke Leighton the next morning. It took a few minutes for her to realize it was the bats, returning home. Do ghosts make that sound as they try to reclaim life? But, after tomorrow, there would be no entrance, no way home. She was the cruel landlord. And she felt cruel, just as anyone must feel imposing shock and loss and confusion.

Chapter Four

Dickie

Fletcher was a hateful bastard. Dickie remembered his comments about women, how he used to say that the smell between his wife's legs reminded him of all those foul early mornings before the garbage was picked up. He used to put his cigar ash in the crevice of Susan Hartford's breasts and then rub a little cross there, telling her she was as sexless as a Catholic nun. Why, he even told Dickie that Deborah must give a great blow job, her lips were so full and sensual. Dickie had been too shocked to react in the moment, but he approached Fletcher a few days later and told him that if he ever spoke about his wife that way again, he'd give him a black eye. Fletcher had been shocked. No one ever expected Dickie to come to his wife's defense, he was so mild-mannered and so even-tempered.

"Why, I thought I was complimenting her," Fletcher said. He put his arm around Dickie's shoulder. "She's a prize, Dickie, makes Rhonda look like a spinster schoolteacher with those tight lips of hers." Fletcher had laughed long and hard.

"Why, if I want a blow job, I go to the whorehouse, man."

Dickie had never really forgiven him. He didn't like Fletcher, he was crass and terribly inconsequential, like the pockets in women's clothing, always sewn up, and when you cut them open, the pockets were still so small, poor Deborah couldn't even get her keys in them. Dickie smiled, thinking about Deborah's cursing about those pockets and getting out her little scissors so she could release the threads that kept them closed and she still didn't have any room for anything but a penny, maybe.

"Hey, love," he called out. "Does it bother you that your suit jackets have small sewn-up pockets?"

Lottie sat up in her favorite vintage wing chair and laughed loudly. Lottie had such a big laugh, always made her sound so welcoming, like she was running for mayor and needed to win you over."Suit jacket pockets? Hell, they sew up women's trouser pockets too, and women's skirt pockets. Damn designers want to keep our pockets as empty as they think our heads are. You ever buy a pair of trousers with sewn-up pockets? I'll bet not."

Dickie stared at her from the other side of her lovely and airy living room which looked out onto trees with lush, green branches whispering across the sky and allowing patches of orange and blue, the flirtatious hint of a perfect day. She had a sweet little house, reminiscent of a childhood fairytale, situated like a welcoming smile on a lovely and quiet residential street. But she certainly didn't have a residential life, Dickie reflected. How long had he been coming to her sweet little house? He surmised it was way back when Barnaby was just a baby.

Lottie was a tall woman, but not nearly as tall as her laugh, but still one of those hearty Southern women you best tip your hat for, best agree with, too. He was sure she'd become a formidable old woman, certainly not one to mess with.

"So, who do you think killed Fletcher Smith?" Dickie asked her, not really expecting her to have an opinion. Lottie didn't care about some old murder that happened thirty years ago.

"Just about anybody in this town, darlin'. Could have been you, even could have been me." Dickie thought back. She was right, nobody liked the man. He was the epitome of nastiness, overcharging for his stupid storage units and burning the contents when someone couldn't pay. He'd have one of those big bonfires and there would go family heirlooms, photographs, old letters, and overstuffed settees that had graced the memory of someone's childhood with the weight of an ancestor's ass.

"Why would you have killed him, he come on

to you?"

"He did. He followed me into the park one day and made me grab his stupid hard-on."

"He made you grab his stupid hard-on? I can't imagine anyone doing that to you, Lottie."

"Your wife was there that day."

"Deborah?"

"Who else you married to Dickie?"

"He didn't make her do that, did he?"

Lottie laughed her big laugh. "He tried. But she kicked him in the shin and ran out of that park, cursing him to the devil, yelling at me to follow her. Your Deborah is quite a girl, Dickie."

"Damn right." Dickie smiled and picked up his notes. "I got it all here. Everyone who had a grudge against that awful man."

"And the list must be as long as Route 76. Who you got top of the list, darlin'?"

"I can't tell you, not till I'm certain."

Lottie popped up out of her overstuffed chair and stood before him, her nakedness like a fortress, the dark mass between her legs like a forest of crinkly little twigs hiding the luscious contents of paradise.

"What do you mean you can't tell me? What the hell are you doing here if you don't want me to help you? I thought you said you needed my brain power. Isn't that what you said, that you needed my brain power?"

"I just want to make sure of what I'm saying. I

don't want to confuse myself or anyone else."

"You don't make any sense." Lottie walked back to her bedroom, her rear end bouncing and her cellulite stretching across her backside like dips in the snow.

"I like your ass," he said.

She laughed one of her big belly laughs as if he'd said something hilarious.

"That was a compliment," he said, following behind her.

"Anyone hearing us would think we were lovers," she said and smiled, her two front teeth cutely apparent.

"Anyone watching us would think we were lovers." He walked to her and took her hand. "But we're not, right? Never were, right?" He winked and put his finger up to his mouth, shushing her.

She smiled and her lips formed a long line across her face, her dimples showing up in sweet surprise. "That's what you said years ago, darlin'. I still believe you, don't worry. You need to tell yourself we're not lovers, so you don't have to tell your wife we are. That's fine. What does being lovers mean, anyway?"

"Means there's someone in the world you can be honest with. It doesn't have to mean sex, does it?"

"Definition is in the eye of the beholder. So, Mr. Webster, what does it mean to be married?"

"*Humph.*" He turned away. "I think it's a legal term, monetary protection."

"I think it's convention, a normal conclusion to a person's life. Husband, children, you know. The whole shebang."

He laughed. "I got the whole shebang then."

"Who killed Fletcher Smith?" she asked, changing the subject. "I'd like to know so I can take him to dinner."

"Maybe Marshall Kram?"

Lottie didn't expect that. Her eyes widened. "You can't mean that," she said softly. "Why would it be Ginger?"

"Or it might have been Rhonda. She can shoot a gun." He lay on the bed next to her, as naked as she was.

"You said it was Ginger."

"Marshall. That's when he was mostly still Marshal."

"Why is life so complicated, Dickie?"

"Secrets. And because we humans are unpredictable and entirely unknowable."

"And we never tell the truth. Never."

"We hardly ever know the truth. No place in this world for the truth. There's only justice," he said. "You believe in justice?"

"Sweet justice, sweet, sweet justice. Ain't that what I'm getting now?" She kissed him long and deep. "Sweet, sweet justice," she said.

After they attempted intercourse, Dickie took a shower and carefully put his clothes back on.

"Sorry, Lottie. I'm getting too old to get it up."

"For God's sake, Dickie, you're only fifty-eight."

She stood in the doorway of the bathroom with a white sheet draped over her shoulder, her oversized feet a somewhat shocking image, a contradiction to her more feminine curves and thin waist. The image made Dickie think of trick photography.

"Well, my dick feels like it's one hundred and eight."

Lottie raised her eyebrows. "Tell Deborah to stop working you so hard."

"*Humph*," he said. Then he creamed his face just to make sure all the makeup was off. Lottie walked over and straightened his ascot.

"Still such a handsome man," she said.

"I have to take care of myself in case Deborah kicks me to the curb. Then you won't want me." He turned her to him. "You only want my wife's husband. If she divorces me, you won't want me anymore. You'll want the next man Deborah marries."

"Do you know how stupid you are, Dickie?"

"Tell me it isn't so. It's my wife you want, not me. I mean, you're obviously a lesbian."

Lottie ignored him. She picked the dress up off the chair. "Do you want me to have your dress cleaned?"

"It's got another wear in it."

"How about that form you wear that gives you tits. It's starting to smell."

"Oh, don't be vulgar. Lottie. It gives me breasts, darlin', not tits. It's my breast form."

"Who killed Fletcher, Dickie?" She didn't give him time to answer before she asked, "You know what I think? I think every woman in Pickens got together and did him in."

"Well, Ginger is at the top of my list."

She stared at him in such a way that he felt himself lose gravity. Ginger was a friend of hers. "What in God's name would Ginger have against Fletcher?" she asked.

"Rhonda, darlin'. Rhonda."

"You are simplifying the murder of Fletcher Smith. Rhonda is obvious. Agatha Christie 101. Rhonda wanted a divorce. He wouldn't give it to her, so she killed him." She shrugged her shoulders. "Too obvious. It was neither of them."

"No, he wouldn't give her a divorce, so Marshall killed him, got him out of the way and Rhonda inherited Fletcher's wealth and bought herself a new mink and a Cadillac, I believe. Or was it a Lincoln?"

"Neither. It was a Porsche. She was rich without Fletcher, you know."

"Pretentious bitch." Dickie smirked. "I don't like Rhonda. She's cold."

"I still remember your costume that night."

"Really? I don't."

"You were dressed as Rhett Butler."

Dickie smiled. "Yes, I was, wasn't I?"

"Remember what I was wearing?"

"You were dressed as Abe Lincoln. I remember that top hat, it covered your whole forehead. I remember kissing you in the alley that night, damn hat kept hitting me in the eye."

"Deborah had on a beautiful eighteenth-century dress, and she wore a diamond tiara."

Dickie smiled, remembering; his wife had been so beautiful, probably the prettiest girl in Pickens at the time. "My Deborah is so perfectly feminine, isn't she? The quintessential Scarlett O'Hara with that impetuous little grin and those green eyes."

"Can't say I ever noticed."

Dickie walked across the room like a lawyer approaching the bench. "Fletcher's death somehow gave carte blanche to Marshall to emerge as Ginger Tea and live in absolute luxury with Rhonda Smith."

"She does let him run around in dresses, doesn't she?"

"You let me run around in dresses." He smiled at her.

"You've never been out of this house in your heels and your Dior, darlin'."

He laughed. "Heavens, no, I might run into my wife."

Chapter Five

Deborah

Deborah folded the paper to cover the lead story. She didn't like seeing it: Jeremiah would be out of prison in less than a week. She'd just read he was coming back to Pickens and according to the paper, he had a job at the gas station in Powdersville. She remembered how good he was with cars. He was always fixing them, sprucing up old Chevies and Fords till the chrome shone bright as pulsars and the engines sounded like purring kittens. She'd read that he'd be staying in a halfway house about twenty minutes outside of town.

Twenty minutes certainly wasn't far enough.

Sweat broke out on Deborah's body, the way she sweats right before speaking publicly at school board meetings, or the way she used to sweat when Jeremiah stole looks at her with Dickie standing at her side. She remembered the heat rising in her, causing her to perspire so much it gave her pimples. Pimples in her late teens? My God. She used to berate him for staring at her, for being the cause of her pimples.

She wondered if she had loved him. When Deborah thought back, it was hard to remember how she'd really felt, except for the meltdown she had after he made love to her. It was as though he had caressed every fiber of her being, every fiber of her being completely spent, collapsible. She did remember that. She couldn't budge for at least an hour after he made love to her. But how had she felt about him? Passion is hard to make sense of.

Deborah was certain she'd had passion for Jeremiah — but love? Could have been, but then again, romantic love is nothing more than good chemistry bubbling up for a time and then fizzling into thin air. Real love does not bubble up and fizzle, it remains where you left it, just waiting on you, present as the air you breathe, present and welcoming, like her sweet Dickie.

Deborah was quite sure she'd be able to avoid Jeremiah: she just wouldn't go anywhere near the gas station. She was certain he wouldn't seek her out; he was furious with her for not having an abortion, convinced he'd get a double sentence for knocking up a White woman, a married White woman to boot. Barnaby was nearly a year old when Jeremiah was sentenced. But she never spoke to Jeremiah after that night in the alley, the night of Fletcher's murder by some woman he'd probably raped or otherwise affronted.

She'd insinuated Jeremiah because she could, and because Dickie's mother, Lillian, had insisted on it. Well, it gave her power over the man who was tearing her apart, leaving her for not committing murder herself. That's what abortion is, isn't it? Murder? It made her cringe to this day when she thought about it: why, she might have destroyed Barnaby before he was born, before he got to be so handsome and deliciously sweet like apple cobbler. That's what she used to call him when he was a baby, little apple cobbler. But what if his Negro features had been more pronounced, she often wondered, and he came out black as onyx. She would have insisted then that an ancestor of Dickie's had impregnated some beautiful slave girl and who knew Dickie had Negro blood? They would have joked about it with all their friends, she was sure. A gracious man, Dickie would not have cared a damn if he had Negro blood.

Lucky for Deborah, her little Barnaby was as ambiguous as his biological father: might have been Black, might have been Irish. Why she, herself, was part American Indian, some southern tribe, Choctaw, she thinks. People couldn't really tell she had any percentage of Choctaw, but if you looked close enough at Deborah Darling, you'd see her high cheekbones. She tells people that. "Look closely," she says, "before I scalp you." Then she laughs, like getting scalped by an Indian is hysterical. Dickie used to tell her that she was insensitive to their history of violence against those who were oppressed, and she'd raise her eyes at him and shake her head, thinking no doubt that he was stupid or what? Sometimes she'd say that, "Are you stupid or what?"

She was out in the garden with Héctor, pointing out some weeds that had appeared like unruly children, climbing up where they didn't belong and threatening to strangle the life out of her pink roses. She saw the car out of the corner of her eye, some plain old Black and White thing with 'Pickens County Sherriff's Office' written where the paint was white. She hunched up her shoulders and narrowed her eyes to make sure she wasn't hallucinating, but it was perfectly understandable for a police car to show up, given Jeremiah's release from prison any day now and all.

The car stopped right behind her brand-new Cadillac convertible, making that old black police car look like some lost orphan in a sea of coral reefs and aquamarine waters, those letters, 'Pickens County Sherriff's Office,' looking like a death sentence. Deborah's heart beat like butter being whipped and her skin flushed with a fever that could have killed her, or at least faint on the spot.

She knew the pretty blonde thirty-something woman who emerged from the old Ford and walked toward her. Well, she didn't really know her, she'd seen her. She'd seen her around town maybe once or twice and told by someone or other that her husband had just died, maybe by someone standing behind her at the supermarket. And the woman had said, "*Tsk, tsk*, poor dear," and shaken her head. Deborah didn't remember who it was that told her, but seeing this woman emerge now from a police car was like watching a bad movie and wanting to leave the theater, knowing you can't move because someone had glued your backside to the seat and walking out would mean ripping the skin off your ass.

"May I help you?"

The detective extended her hand. "Sorry to bother you, but I saw you from the road." Leighton looked around as if she were looking for something. "I hope you don't mind. I usually call first."

Deborah stared at the car. Naturally, she stared at the car, who wouldn't be staring at a police car showing up in your driveway and removing ten years of your life by placing the fear of God in you?

Leighton followed Deborah's eyes. "Oh, that's not really my car. My car is in the shop."

"The police lent you a car?"

"Well, I borrowed it. My car is unmarked." Leighton reached in her pocket and held out her badge. "I'm with the Pickens County Sheriff's

Office, investigative division. Leighton McArdle."

Deborah felt herself stumble. She wanted to sit, needed to sit before this woman gave her another blow and she lay flat on her back in the middle of her pink roses. She managed to laugh and put her hand to her heart. "Pray tell, what do you want with me?"

"Just want to ask you a few questions. Is your husband at home?"

Deborah released the breath she'd unconsciously been holding and laughed more loudly than necessary. It came out forced. "What's he done now?"

Leighton looked confused. "Ah, nothing."

Now it was Deborah's turn to look confused. "He just went for a walk. He does that a lot. My husband loves to walk, walks all over the place. He should be back soon."

Leighton nodded her head. "May I have a word?"

Deborah took a step back. "Why would the police want a word with me?"

Leighton cocked her head to the side and studied Deborah. "Don't worry, you've done nothing wrong, and I don't want any money for the police fund. Just want to ask you a few questions."

"About what?"

"Please, Mrs. Darling. I'm investigating the murder of Fletcher Smith and you identified

Jeremiah Lennox as being there, as committing the murder."

"Well, I didn't say he committed it, just said he walked out of the alley. I just told the police what I saw."

"Right."

"Oh." Deborah felt her head fill with something like helium and she wasn't sure she'd be able to speak. She led Leighton up to the porch and asked Deasia to bring out some tea. She observed the young woman before her. She wore large square glasses that hid a face full of freckles. Her teeth stuck out a little, but her smile was nice, welcoming. She put Deborah at ease right away as she complimented her big, beautiful house. But then she got down to brass tacks and asked her about Fletcher, how well she had known him, and this country freckled farm girl transformed into a tarantula needing the broom to it.

"Oh, I didn't know Fletcher well at all. I went to school with Rhonda, his wife." She looked at Leighton and tried to read her facial expression. Did this policewoman believe her, she wondered? "She married him the moment she got out of school."

"And how well did you know Rhonda?"

Deborah told her that her best friend in high school had been Lottie Lacock and they were still friends. But neither one of them liked Rhonda back then. "She was full of herself," Deborah said. "You know, one of those real smart girls that held their noses up to everyone who wasn't someone in their eyes. Fletcher was handsome, that's why she liked him, and he was at least thirty. Older man." Deborah smiled and winked at the same time, but there wasn't a smile on Leighton's face. "So, anyway," Deborah continued, "by the time Fletcher died, he had lost his thick wavy hair, gained more than a few pounds. He was no longer the handsome and captivating older man. That boy had deteriorated inside of four years, like the devil's own curse upon him. I imagine it was the drinking that did him in, aged him."

Deborah noticed that Leighton was not taking notes, she just sat there listening. Then she asked Deborah why she didn't like Rhonda.

"I just told you, she was full of herself."

"Any other reason?"

"I don't know, it was so long ago. She was haughty. I think Lottie and I thought she was haughty. I just told you, she was just full of herself."

"I guess that's a teenage thing."

"What?"

"Teenagers describe someone they don't like as being full of themselves."

Deborah squirmed in her seat and looked past the woman. "Well, yes."

Leighton sat forward in the white chair and

stared at Deborah through her glasses. "I want to go deeper. Feelings mature, people change by the time they turn twenty-five. Why didn't you like her when you turned twenty-five?"

Deasia brought out the tea as well as some cookies that she put on a tray before the two women.

"How are you today, Deasia?" Leighton asked.

Deborah looked up with some confusion and wondered how this woman, who didn't even look like a detective, knew her cook.

"I fine, Miss Leighton." Deasia did a little curtsey, something Deborah had never seen her do.

"How do you know Deasia, my help?" Deborah asked once Deasia had gone back through the French doors.

"Oh?" Leighton looked confused. "Her relationship to the man accused."

Deborah felt the blood drain from her body. "What relationship?" she stammered.

"Oh, didn't you know? They were neighbors back then. Jeremiah Lennox lived right behind Deasia and Jackson on Garden Drive. I guess you don't talk to Deasia much about anything other than her duties here?" Leighton smiled politely.

Unnerved, Deborah harnessed her composure and quickly put her tea down for fear it would rattle courtesy of her shaking body. How many times had Jeremiah taken her into his bedroom?

She thought back. My God, had Deasia ever seen them together? She didn't want anyone discovering her affair with Jeremiah, not even thirty years after the fact.

"Deasia was questioned around the time of Fletcher's death."

"But surely you're too young to…"

"Oh, no, I moved to Pickens from Charleston in the sixties, several months before the murder. I was five years old, so no, I don't remember the crime and it wasn't me who questioned Deasia back then." Leighton laughed. "Obviously."

"I really don't remember it all that well, Miss McArdle."

"Since we've reopened the case, I questioned Deasia, just the other day."

"Oh, she didn't mention it."

Leighton cocked her head to the side. "Why would she?"

Deborah finally felt calm enough to reach for her tea; the cup shook but not too badly. "So, any new suspects?" she asked.

"There will be several, I imagine. Now, as I was saying, why didn't you like Rhonda when you were twenty-five years old, was she still haughty?"

"Well, not so much, but she was very rich, and she flaunted it, you know?"

Leighton stared at her as she sipped her tea. "You don't like rich people?" Leighton looked around. "You appear rich to me."

"Well, yes, I am rich, but I don't flaunt it." Deborah sat back, quite self-satisfied. What in God's name was this woman implying, she wondered.

"Is that a Cadillac convertible I see in your driveway?" Leighton smiled.

Deborah smiled as well, then she sighed and then she looked off, but she didn't answer Leighton.

Leighton's smile faded abruptly. "It's okay to enjoy your money, Deborah, I'm just trying to get at your real feelings for Rhonda Smith."

"I didn't have any real feelings for Rhonda Smith. She was inconsequential to me."

"So, what were you wearing that night?"

Deborah shook her head; the woman had transitioned so quickly that there was a breeze around her like a new door opening. "Oh, yes, it was Halloween, wasn't it? Is that what you're talking about?" she stared at Leighton, who sat quietly before her. Deborah cleared her throat. "I believe I was Scarlet O'Hara that night," she said.

"And your husband came as Rhett Butler?"

"Oh, yes, he was quite dashing. He even dyed his hair black for the occasion. I told him he should have come as Ashley… Ashley was blonde like my husband, but we heard someone else was going as Ashley."

"The full cast of *Gone with the Wind*? How original." She smiled. "Who came as Ashley?"

"I barely remember that night Miss McArdle."

"Well, you seem to have had the whole cast of *Gone with the Wind* at Smith's Bar that night."

"Oh, yes, wait, I think someone came over to me and kissed my hand, introduced himself to me as Ashley Wilkes. I do remember that now."

"Why?"

"Why? Well, there was something off about him. I don't know what, so don't even ask me that."

"Who was he?"

"I'd never seen him before. He was pretty though, a natural blond. He could have been a girl."

"Hm, that's interesting. Do you remember anything else about him?"

"No, not really. His uniform looked authentic, it was grey, and I remember he had an old-fashioned-looking pistol in his holster."

"That's an interesting thing to remember."

"Well, I had joked with him and asked him if his gun had bullets."

"And he said?"

"Oh, he pulled it out of his holster and pulled the trigger. No bullets."

"Do you remember Belle Watling?

"What? Who's Belle Watling?"

Leighton sat back. "I see it's been a while."

"Been a while what?"

"Since you've seen the movie or read the

book? Belle Watling was the prostitute in *Gone with the Wind*. She ran the cat house. You recall the main characters?"

"Oh, someone dressed up as Belle Watling that night? No, I don't remember. The prostitute in *Gone with the Wind*? I thought I was the only woman there in a dress from the Civil War period."

"Do you remember who dressed up as Belle?"

"I really don't know what Belle looked like."

"Well, she probably had red hair done up the way it was in the film, I think. And she'd have had a very seductive bodice, I would imagine."

"Oh." Bewildered, she didn't remember anyone else dressed like that. She was sure she would have noticed.

"There were a lot of witches and clowns that night," she told Leighton. "Someone came as the Grim Reaper, or was that the year before? I swear, it's hard to remember these things. The bar was packed wall to wall. Oh, wait, yes, Lottie came as Abe Lincoln and looked ridiculous. Her hat kept sliding down on her forehead."

Leighton stared at her, waiting for her to say more.

"Well, who came as Belle Watling that night? For it was so long ago, I don't remember. I swear, I had a lot to drink that night."

"That's the thing," Leighton said. "Everyone but you, it seems, remembers her being at the bar but no one seems to know who was behind the mask. Her identity was never discovered, or at least not remembered. I think it's because she left the party early."

"We all promised we wouldn't remove our masks until the end of the evening. It was like that every year. We don't do those parties anymore, but we loved them back then."

"Belle's mask must have really covered her face then?"

"Everyone's did."

"Well, I guess once Fletcher's body was discovered, the party broke up."

Deborah laughed. "Of course. I was outside, but everyone inside the bar left. I know that because Dickie came to get me, but the police didn't let me go for a while. Interesting. Maybe Belle Watling killed Fletcher Smith?"

"Maybe." Leighton smiled. "Or maybe she just left the party early."

Dickie walked up from the road and removed his hat when he noticed his wife on their front porch with Leighton. Even from where Deborah sat, he looked as if he'd had something sour for lunch.

"You're peaked, Dickie, are you feeling well?" she asked as he all but dragged himself up the four steps onto the porch. "Oh, this is Leighton

McArdle. She's a policewoman."

"A detective, Deborah. I'm a detective but that's alright."

Dickie smiled as he took her hand and shook it. "Can't very well kiss the hand of a detective, can I?"

"I would forgive you, Mr. Darling."

"I assume you're here to question us about Fletcher Smith? I know they're letting Jeremiah out of jail, reopening the case."

"As long as you're here, Mr. Darling, would you mind a few questions?"

"Didn't it all come out in the trial? Fletcher was a womanizer that men and women alike despised. He was not a nice man. No surprise he got bumped off."

Leighton sat back and stared up at him. "Who came to your little party that night as Belle Watling?"

Deborah noticed her husband's face reddened a bit. She wondered if he was fevered.

"Do you remember, Mr. Darling?" Leighton asked him.

Dickie sat back and removed his handkerchief from his pocket and wiped his brow. "Belle Watling was Rhett Butler's friend. Yes, I had a few words with her that evening." He sat back and laughed. "I was Rhett Butler, after all."

"Who was under that costume, Mr. Darling?" Leighton moved in closer to him. "Do you remember?"

"No, I'm afraid not," Dickie said. "But we spoke in character, and I told her not to tell Scarlet I was at the whorehouse night before." He looked at his wife impishly.

"Oh, Dickie," Deborah laughed. "How could you remember that?"

Dickie hunched up his shoulders and smiled at Leighton. "I don't forget a pretty woman, especially not one I had to pay for." He laughed and took his wife's hand. "Just kidding, darlin'. I have no idea who Belle Watling was, maybe Marshall Kram."

Chapter Six

DICKIE

She had blonde hair, the color of a golden sun at the height of noon, with freckles sprinkled on her face like haphazard drops of sand. One crooked tooth in front always made her look mischievous, like she was up to something, a 'going to get you good in a prank' look. She wore a cap to school and when she put her hair up in it, she looked like a boy. He didn't see her much in dresses except when her mother insisted she wear them. She'd complain to him about her mother and how she should be allowed to dress any way she chose. She'd complain all the way to school in that big yellow bus that stopped at the corner of her road. He was always there, waiting for her, saving her a seat. Dickie would never let anyone else sit next to him but her.

She used to slap his arm when she sat. He knew it was her attempt at affection but sometimes it hurt, and he'd scream out *Ow!* She never apologized though, and she never stopped slapping his arm when she saw him, not even when they got to Junior High School and started kissing by the lake, behind the weeds where they couldn't be seen. His feelings toward her changed when he turned fifteen, they matured, and all he thought about was what it would be like to have sex with her. He was obsessed with those desires because of all the movies she'd dragged him to, and he'd have to sit there staring at all the men and women on the screen who were obviously doing it with each other. He'd been feeling a lot of desire lately, most of it very confusing. As for love, that was a given.

"I love you," he said behind the weeds, his right hand on her breast while her hand slipped between his legs. Their foray into sex was quick but tender. He knew she was the only girl in the world for him. There was just something about her that drew him to her like a lightning bug to a night sky. He instinctively felt she understood him like no one else ever had or would and because of that, he trusted her, he trusted her with all his secrets.

The weekend his parents went up to Greenville to see his Uncle Laurel, he told her he had a surprise for her and invited her over to watch *Perry Mason.* He had put on his sister's skirt and cardigan sweater, and was sitting on the couch with his legs crossed in his mother's nylons and high heels when she came through the door. His palm up to his cheeks, he smiled at her, hoping she wouldn't run screaming out of the house. "Just a joke," he'd say if she did that. His red lips as perfectly painted as the rouge sweetly dusted across his pretty face — the quintessential picture of a young lady waiting on the love of her life.

She walked in slowly, her mouth open wide, and she stared at him while he prayed she wouldn't start laughing, but she didn't laugh. She just stared, incredulous.

"Dickie?" she said. She studied him as if he were something she'd just painted on canvas. She ogled every inch of him.

"Do you like me like this?" he asked with a coy tilt of his head.

"Wow," she finally said.

Dickie let his breath out. He'd been so afraid she'd have hysterics after the initial shock passed. But she sat beside him and took his hand, then she kissed him in a way she had never kissed him before... an aggressive kiss and he melted under the weight of it.

"Do you want to be a girl or a boy?" she finally asked when she came up for air.

"Both," he said.

"Me, too," she said. "Don't know which one I want to be more."

"I'm not attracted to boys." He looked at her sheepishly. "I want to sleep with you."

"I like boys." She touched his cheek lightly with her finger and they wound up on the floor rolling all over each other. She made love to him as if she were the aggressor, gently pulling down his nylons, opening the buttons on his cardigan. She straddled him, professing her love for him while they slowly fornicated to exhaustion.

"You going to tell anyone about this?" He hoped he could trust her. He couldn't bear to be the brunt of someone's nasty joke.

She hugged him close. "I feel your pain," she said. "It makes me love you so much."

She became pregnant in their senior year, and he would go out to the weeds and sit there staring out over the lake and wishing he were dead because he would be sure to lose her when her parents found out. Well, obviously her parents found out and he kept expecting them to break down his door and lynch him in his own backyard.

But her parents never confronted him, and they never told his parents he'd made their daughter pregnant, not so far as he knew anyway. She and her family just left town, never to be heard from again. He assumed she'd never told them who the father of her baby was, and he was grateful for that. He assumed she'd had an abortion but hoped she'd had their baby. He finally heard that her family had moved to Charleston, but he could never get an address;

they all just disappeared. He thought about her all through college and he thought back to their love-making a million times. He wondered if she were laughing at him, thinking back, and laughing at the freak she'd gotten to impregnate her. He wondered if she were afraid that their baby would be a freak as well, *if* she'd had the baby, but he guessed she probably hadn't.

Then, in 1963, when he was a grown man with his own business and a wife named Deborah, she returned to Pickens, and he heard she'd bought the old Victorian everyone used to say was haunted. She lived there with her husband; a man named Walter McNeil. He saw her Halloween day on East Main Street with a little girl about five years old and a boy that looked to be a teenager, maybe fifteen or so.

He approached her slowly. "Hello, Leah." He watched her eyes as she stared at him. He saw a moment of recollection but only for a moment, soon replaced by embarrassment, a deep reddening of her skin. It had to be the memory of them together, how passionately she made love to him when he was dressed as a girl. Once they got into high school, he didn't remember a time when they made love that he didn't wear female clothing.

"Dickie," she said. "How are you?" She stepped back and looked him over. He was sure he saw her blush even more deeply. He wondered just how mundane she'd be after the passion of their youth.

"Welcome back to Pickens," he said.

"Yeah, good to be here." She stared at him, as if the act of conversation had escaped her.

"Going to the Halloween party tonight?" he asked, and she nodded her head.

"Yes, a friend of mine invited me."

"Is this your daughter?" he asked as he bent down to the little girl's level.

"This is Leighton," she said. "Leighton, this is Mr. Darling."

He studied the girl a long time and then he looked up at her. "And the boy?"

"Oh, this is Kenny, my husband's son."

"It's easy to see which one is yours," he said.

Tears came to his eyes as he stared at the little girl with strawberry blonde hair and red eyelashes. He searched the woman's eyes. "I'm never going to forget you," he said. "Nor you." He bent down and kissed the little girl's cheek. "She's mine, isn't she?"

Leah didn't answer him right away. "My husband adopted her. I married Walter right after I moved to Charleston, so she's his, she's his daughter since the day she was born. I prefer she not know anything other than that, Dickie. Walter and I decided not to tell her."

"Alright," he said with a lump in his throat. He wanted to claim her right in that moment. He wanted to take her hand and lead her off.

"I'm never going to forget you, either." Leah smiled and reached out to touch his face. "But I've changed."

"I haven't," he said as he waited for her to say something else, something like "I love you" or "It's so good to see you, when can I see you again?" But she remained as silent as a hot day by an ocean without waves and a sky without wind … eerily quiet. He walked away, the lump still in his throat. The empty hole of rejection smoldered and he swallowed the impulse to start yelling at her.

Dickie never did forget Leah. He thought about her, obsessed, for months after that meeting. It was hard not to, he saw her everywhere he went now, on the corner of West Main Street and Jewell, in front of the new wine store on Pumpkin town highway. Sometimes they spoke briefly, and his heart flipped, and one Sunday, at the Episcopalian Church they both went to, he introduced her to Deborah as an old friend.

Later that evening, Deborah said, "She's an odd one, isn't she, what kind of lady wears pants to church? She should be in the freak show. She's not setting an example for that young daughter of hers. I hear her son gets into all sorts of trouble. Is it any wonder? How well did you know her, Dickie? She struck me as being a freaky one. I mean, she's just so unfeminine."

Dickie remembered how he looked at his wife after that. Her opinions and her judgments sickened him. But he didn't say anything. Something withered in his heart for Deborah in that moment. He looked at her after that as someone to tolerate, sometimes amusing but never accepting; no, never accepting. His affair with Lottie seemed so much deeper than his relationship with his wife. Lottie understood him and welcomed him in a way Deborah never could or would. Lottie was his lover, and his wife was just a ritual he performed every day. Kiss her hello and goodbye, tell her how wonderful she looks and walk through the rooms like someone's husband, specifically Deborah's husband. He might have left his wife, but his life was too perfect, and he had a son who was just a baby at the time, so what would be the point?

Lottie didn't really want to marry him, she just liked the idea of the intimacy, one so much deeper than Dickie shared with Deborah and Lottie knew that, and maybe she took some sort of odd pleasure in knowing that, for she had him in a way Deborah never could.

Dickie didn't want anyone else but Deborah, not really. It looked like a picture-perfect marriage on the outside. There was no tug of war here between Lottie and Deborah. Lottie was a woman with an open mind and Deborah was not.

For Lottie, the adventure was so much more rewarding than some conventional commitment like marriage, so why even entertain that option. Besides, a divorce would hurt her friend Deborah, the shock of her betrayal would be devastating and besides, marriage, even to Dickie, would only cause Lottie a maddening claustrophobia. Dickie continued to see Leah every now and then and he continued to harbor the same longing for her, but he brushed it aside. Her name had been Leah Warren, now she was Leah McNeil. Her husband was a distant cousin of Fletcher's but far as he could tell, Fletcher didn't know Walter existed. Leah lived in Pickens now, but she didn't live close by, so it wasn't as though Dickie saw her often. He noticed that he rarely ever saw her with her husband. Dickie never went out of his way to speak to her, either, not since that first time. She was, after all, a married woman and he, of course, was a married man. And she said she'd changed, which probably meant she was no longer the girl who had once adored him. She would no longer find his proclivities fascinating and charming. More than likely she'd find him freaky, a cripple taken to bed out of pity.

Funny thing is Leighton resembled him, if they stood side by side, lots of people would wonder if they were related. She looked more like his daughter than Robbie did. Robbie was dark like her mother and Barnaby didn't take after anybody. He was himself, unique. Dickie smiled as he picked up his pipe and watched Deborah stare out of the window, thinking about God knows what, maybe beating Lottie later at canasta or Checkers. His wife's thoughts were often so inconsequential. After a while, he stood up and gazed at himself out in the hall mirror.

"Going somewhere, darlin'?" Deborah asked in her sweetest drawl.

"Yes, dear, won't be gone long. I need some aimlessness, like a thoughtless walk through a loblolly pine forest."

He listened to her laughter as he strolled out of the door. He knew exactly where he was going. He had to let his detective daughter think she knew who the killer of Fletcher Smith was, and he would help, with a smorgasbord of lies.

Leighton McArdle lived out by Upper Springs Road, he knew that much, an area with rather impressive gardens dotting the landscape. Dickie didn't get to that part of town often and he'd forgotten how lovely it was with its winding, narrow roads, many of which looked out onto Sassafras Mountain. He parked in front of the local realtor's office, the one that was selling Beau McArdle's restaurant and he told the realtor that he might know people who'd be interested in what had been a successful little business, but he had another matter to discuss with Leighton of a personal nature. He needed her address so he could approach her in private.

"I can relay the message, Mr. Darling. Just leave me your phone number and I'll pass it on." The realtor was clearly possessive about the property.

"It's an urgent matter. I really need to speak with her; if you'll just tell me where she lives." He smiled his boyish smile and let his eyes dance into hers. "I rarely get out this way and Leighton and I are old friends."

The middle-aged and pleasantly plump realtor acquiesced after gazing back at him. Who could resist his dancing blue eyes, as Deborah always said when she was about to forgive him for something or other?

"Well, I know how long your family has lived here, Mr. Darling, what would be the harm?" She giggled as she wrote Leighton's address on a piece of notepad paper. "We all just drop in on each other in this neck of the woods. I'm sure she'll be delighted to see you."

"I would never dishonor your contract with Leighton, and I will be sure to notify you first if there is any interest in the restaurant among my many friends and clients."

The realtor beamed after that. She knew Dickie. She knew he knew everyone. "I do not doubt for a moment you will do that, Mr. Darling."

Dickie was impressed by the small, charming house nestled between enormous dogwood trees, more of a cottage than a house. It made him think of Hill Top Farm, Beatrix Potter's studio, more English than Southern but just as enchanting, though not nearly as large. Her house was tiny, really, and almost smothered in purple flowers. The driveway had two cars, a large plain Ford, and a Corvette. That was impressive, Dickie thought, a Corvette, most likely owned by her dead husband. If she were selling the Corvette, he might be interested. Dickie had a thing for Corvettes; Deborah thought they were impractical. Deborah hated cars with only two seats. Dickie smiled to himself: his Deborah had so many strong likes and dislikes. Maybe he could talk her into this one though; it was cherry red with rich tan leather seats, close in color to a cashew nut.

Dickie had kept up on news of his daughter over the years. He knew when she graduated high school, what college she went to, and he was there at the day of her wedding. He stood at the back of the ceremony with tears in his eyes, as if he had raised her. He went to Beau's restaurant often and got to know the man she married. He was there, unnoticed, at Beau's funeral, shedding tears like everyone else. He was proud when she became a detective and he saw her around town often but never approached her. He kept his distance from Leighton, but it wasn't by choice, it was out of respect for Leah, who wanted it that way. Besides, Leighton had no idea that Walter was not her biological father. Leah had told him that. It angered him but there was nothing he could do about it.

Walter was something of an enigma. He was rarely seen anywhere with his family. Rumor had it that he had a mistress in Spartanburg and that's where he spent most of his time. It was obvious that the raising of the children fell to Leah, who pretty much kept to herself and who was, according to Deborah, a bit of a recluse. "She is some sort of strange eccentric," Deborah would say. "I think she locks those doors of hers and does God knows what behind them, dances in the nude maybe and chants like a loon."

A dog barked. Too close for comfort, he thought, a large dog and sounding as if it could work for the police force sniffing out narcotics and giving hardened criminals heart attacks. His nerves rattled a little as he got out of the car and walked to the front door, carefully screening the area for the dog. Naturally, she had a watchdog; she was a woman alone now.

He was just about to put his finger on the

doorbell when he felt something on his backside and a snout that attacked his crotch. He put up his hands. "I don't have a gun," he hollered.

"Aspen, down," Leighton called out forcefully. She looked at Dickie oddly as she walked from behind the house. "What are you doing here, Mr. Darling?" The dog ran around in circles as though chasing something or other but at least, Dickie noticed with some relief, he was no longer of interest to this mutt with a mouth like a tractor.

"You both snuck up on me, scared me to death."

"I didn't sneak up on you, Mr. Darling. I was working in my garden."

He gave her his sweetest smile and held up his notes. "These are going to be of interest to you," he said.

"Oh, really? Why is that Mr. Darling?" She stood before him in an almost challenging way with her hands on her hips.

"Call me Dickie." He attempted a smile that she didn't reciprocate.

"What can I do for you?"

"May we sit somewhere?" He looked around. Most of the house was hidden, just a little peaked roof sneaking through the branches of dogwood trees like a smile, a rather playful one he thought, not to mention beguiling, like little girls in sun bonnets.

She took off her garden gloves and walked the

path that led to the front door. "Come in, *Dickie*."

Dickie liked that she was snarly, and he assumed as opinionated as his other daughter, who thought American politics would become more and more corrupt in years to come, and too, in years to come, we'd lose our landscape to environmental disasters. Dickie chuckled at that; Robinette was a certain pessimist.

Leighton's house had a delightful charm. She liked the colors yellow and blue, and her white curtains were so white they made him think of sour cream. She led him out to a sun porch with striped chairs and large white lamps with lavender shades. He wondered where on earth she ever found lavender shades.

"Sweet little cottage you have here, Leighton."

"Have a seat, Mr. … Dickie."

Dickie looked out of the screen porch and admired the gardens. She must have a green thumb; her eupatoriums were rich in color and surrounded by irises and daylilies. An interesting choice, he thought. The flowers seemed to dance with one another or to kiss and sway. That was it, her house was musical. He realized with some amount of pride that she was very much like him; she had his talent for creating lively and spectacular gardens.

"Beautiful," he said. "My wife has a thing for roses, but I prefer more common and uncomplicated flowers, like camellias and hydrangeas. Oh, I just love hydrangeas, but we have roses all over the place, in every size and color." He laughed. "Deborah loves them. They smell good, though they are difficult to care for."

"What do you want to talk to me about, Dickie?"

Dickie leaned forward in his chair and found her eyes. "After you left, I got to thinking … Look, Leighton, I want to help you solve this crime, the murder of Fletcher Smith."

She gave him an odd look. "Do you have any information for me?"

"Yes, I do." He handed her his notes and patiently waited while she scanned them. "I know everyone in this town and not a man, woman or child in this town liked Fletcher," he told her as he watched her expression.

"Not liking someone is not cause for murder. Anyway, that's old news." She handed him back his notes.

"Aren't you going to read them carefully?"

"No. You can tell me what's in them."

"Well, blackmail is new news."

Now it was Leighton's turn to sit forward in her seat and stare at him. "Blackmail?"

Dickie nodded. "Fletcher was being blackmailed for an affair he was having."

Leighton shook her head. "I heard he had many affairs."

"Rumor," Dickie said and stared at her. "This

was serious."

"So, who was the woman?"

"I didn't say it was a woman."

Leighton was surely puzzled as he knew she would be. "A man?"

"That remains to be seen."

"What in God's name are you talking about? Stop being convoluted, Mr. Darling."

Dickie stood up and walked away from her but then he turned abruptly. "Oh," he said, scratching his forehead. Thinking of Columbo and the way he staged his accusations, the way he paused right before he was about to drop a bomb. He stared at her. "One more question," he said.

"But you haven't asked me any questions, Mr. Darling."

"Once we find our Belle Watling, we find our murderer." He perused the notes she had given back to him while she drummed her fingers on the arm of her chair. "You've come to that conclusion too, haven't you?"

"Is that your one last question?"

Dickie looked at the dog at her feet, snoring loudly. The beast had quickly fallen into a dreamlike stupor but still appeared to have one eye on Dickie, partially closed, fluttering and still threatening.

"Aspen is friendly," Leighton said, gauging Dickie's facial expression, one of apprehension. "He won't hurt you."

"I like dogs, I'm just not used to them. Deborah would never allow the children to have dogs. They were raised feeling terribly deprived. I mean, everyone has dogs." Dickie laughed.

"So, Dickie, what is your opinion. Who was Belle Watling?"

"Oh? Well, I think Belle was Marshall Kram. I hadn't remembered for sure when you first asked me, but I thought about it and, yes, it was Marshall. I do remember that now."

"Rhonda's present husband?"

"Yes, Ginger. He's a master with makeup. Have you questioned him?"

Leighton sat back and stared at Dickie. He could tell she was trying to make sense of it.

"If I'm following you, I think that you think that Fletcher made a pass at Belle and when he found out that Belle was really a man, he got furious and the two had a fight in the alley which culminated in Fletcher's death?"

"Perhaps it was Belle Fletcher was having the affair with."

Leighton sat back and let a short laugh emerge that hit Dickie's heart like an arrow. "Can you please explain to me, Mr. Darling, what a womanizer, a notorious womanizer, even a dangerous womanizer would want with a cross-dresser? Doesn't compute."

"Marshall Kram is not a cross-dresser, he's a drag queen. The two are quite different."

"Let me rephrase the question then." She leaned in toward him. "What would Fletcher have wanted with a man who dresses up like a woman?"

"I see you don't understand the nature of men who like women like that."

"Women like that? They aren't women, they're oddities. They're neither here nor there." She grinned at him.

Dickie felt as if he'd just been slapped. "Well, then let me *rephrase* that question, the nature of men like that?"

"You're saying Fletcher Smith was gay?"

"I am saying that the man under Belle's costume that night was not a biological woman. If a man were attracted to her, would that man be straight or gay?"

"I'd say gay, but what do I know. I don't like men in women's clothing." She sat back without removing her eyes from his. "You're telling me then that Marshall thought of himself as a woman scorned perhaps by the man he loved?"

"It was blackmail, I told you that."

Leighton looked puzzled. "Who was blackmailing whom and for what?"

"What if I told you that Fletcher was having an affair with Ginger, alias Marshall and Marshall threatened to go public with it if Fletcher didn't leave his wife."

"Fletcher refused and Marshall shot him?"

"Precisely. I see you've caught on."

"Did he own a Smith & Wesson?"

"What's that?"

"A gun, Mr. Darling. An antique gun to be precise. Probably manufactured in the 1800s at some point. Did anyone bring a gun into the bar that night?"

Dickie stood up quickly. "I don't remember anything about finding a gun. I know he was shot but there was no gun, right?"

"No, there was no gun but there was an old lead bullet found … it was removed from Fletcher's head. Most likely, it was a bullet from an old Smith & Wesson, but the gun had disappeared. Someone testified that they saw a Smith & Wesson at someone's waist. It does fit that it may have been the gun that killed Fletcher."

"The person who saw the gun does not remember on whose waist it was?"

"No, unfortunately not."

"Aren't guns supposed to be registered?"

"Yes, but we don't have the gun, so it doesn't matter, unless we recover it. An antique gun, not meant to be fired, I would assume. It probably came from someone's collection of antique guns."

"A lot of men in this town have guns," he said as his mind raced, trying to remember whose gun collection had contained an antique Smith & Wesson. Obviously, it was not someone he knew well, but he had a vision of it, oddly enough.

"Any thoughts, Mr. Darling?"

"Could the bullet have come from a new gun?" he asked her.

"Yes, could have. But a collector would not have put an old bullet like that in a new gun."

"I guess that without the gun you have no real suspects?"

"We have several suspects but no witnesses and no definitive motive."

"Want me to find out if Marshall Kram owned a Smith & Wesson back then, an old one?"

Leighton looked at him as if he were crazy. "Thank you for your theories, Dickie. I'll consider them, but it's highly unlikely we'll ever find that gun."

"So, you'll look into it? Into Marshall, I mean?"

"I will. By the way, do you remember who came as Ashley Wilkes that Halloween night?"

Dickie thought hard. *What would be the harm, it was common knowledge she was there.* "Leah McNeil."

"My mother?"

He heard the surprise in her voice. Dickie stood up; "Yes, I believe so."

"This is getting odder every moment. I didn't know that."

"Why would you? You were a child." Dickie smiled. He realized he had to put an end to this meeting. She was not going to offer him tea and crumpets and she was not going to ask him about his childhood in Pickens. That kind of talk was only for people who were interested in each other. Sharing a crumpet and tea meant friendship, like Lottie and Deborah, who chatted aimlessly about nothing. He stood to his feet and held out his hand.

"I was sorry to hear about Beau. Good man."

"Thank you," she said as she opened the door and waved him on like a pesky neighbor … but then he heard her call his name and he turned.

"Yes, Leighton?"

"Wouldn't owning an antique gun collection be an odd hobby for a drag queen?"

He smiled awkwardly. "I suppose so," he said as he walked through her door.

Dickie felt sad. He sensed his daughter had a certain distaste for him. Maybe she thought he was aggressive, just showing up on her doorstep with his crazy theories. He'd wanted to embrace her in the worst way, put comforting arms around her. For God's sake, she'd lost her husband, a forty-year-old man whom fate decreed would drop dead of a heart attack in the kitchen of his restaurant with a soup ladle in his hand.

Well, in any event, he had achieved his purpose and given his daughter a bunch of bullshit to ponder over. Obviously, the gun was registered to someone who may have collected guns. Did that mean that the murder was premeditated? He had a vague memory of seeing an old Smith & Wesson in someone's gun case, but he couldn't remember whose. His thoughts were too muddled. As for Ginger, he had a solid alibi that night, so he would never be seriously accused. Dickie himself could vouch for Ginger, for Dickie could swear under oath that he heard Fletcher's voice in the alley, long after he'd seen Ginger leave, telling Dickie she was off to her 'all girls only party'. He'd merely mention to Leighton that he'd forgotten that tidbit.

It was so long ago, he'd tell her. People forget.

Chapter Seven

Barnaby

Barnaby lived in an old guest house on his parent's property. It was set back behind the main house, the private road, draped in birch trees, long limbs that harbored the music of Carolina chickadees and the tufted titmouse's song from its curved black bill. One had to know exactly where to turn to find the dirt road. Barnaby always told his friends to look for the curve sign on the main road. He told them to not even think about it, just make the turn and follow the road for another second or so and the house would magically appear. Barnaby had lived there since he'd convinced his mother he needed to live alone, which wasn't the whole truth. He'd needed a place to take women, specifically one woman, one woman he couldn't let his mother see him with. Not yet anyway, not until his grandmother's ring was on her finger and he'd told his parents that he didn't give a damn about their prejudices.

His mother had refurbished the guest house years ago and it was olde-worlde attractive, filled to the brim with stunning antiques and large windows that let in the sun. It wasn't much smaller than the main house but only had two bedrooms. The main house had five, not nearly enough for guests when the holidays rolled around, so the guest cottage was an extra treat with its beautifully adorned rooms for aunts and cousins, and many visiting relatives had stayed there over the years. Now they all stayed in the main house — his grandparents, on his mother's side, usually took over Barnaby's old room and Lillian, his father's mother, offered the guest rooms in her house to any extra family members.

Barney's guest cottage was now off limits to all the tedious distant aunts and uncles who seemed to bring nothing with them but stale memories and redundant complaints about the atrocities of getting old. The floor-to-ceiling windows looked out over acres of land and the bay windows off the living room looked out onto the front drive. He could easily see anyone approaching the house, except for his father, who walked everywhere, undetected as he tiptoed through the trees and into the back yard, and then, in through the kitchen like a cat seeking prey.

Barnaby kept a sharp ear on any sounds, for his father was liable to show up at any time during the day, possibly even at night, which had happened only once when Barnaby had some friends over, so Prissy wasn't obvious, just one of five others.

He never got annoyed with his father, but he had to be cautious, he knew that. His mother drove up the drive when she paid him a spontaneous visit. That's what she'd always say, "Just being spontaneous, honey." That gave him time to hide Prissy in the upstairs bedroom or send her home out the back way where her car was parked under the Jacaranda trees, or as she would say, "*hidden* under the Jacaranda trees."

There would come a time when he'd have to tell his parents the truth. He and Prissy were planning to marry after she got her law degree and settled back in Pickens. She wanted to work as a public defender and open a practice in town to help Black citizens get legal justice and they only wanted one child, hopefully a girl they would name after Prissy's mother.

Barnaby didn't have any objections, Deasia was a beautiful name, but he could just see his mother's face, another humiliation, she'd think. It was bad enough her son had married the help's daughter, but then he goes and names their daughter after the help, not after his mother or his grandmother Lillian, which was a name his mother loved. His mother always hinted how his first girl should be named Lillian, after Dickie's mother. He laughed out loud. His mother always made him laugh, not necessarily when she was present but when he thought of her in hindsight. She reminded him of some cartoon character who said outrageous things and had no idea she was being ignorant or prejudiced, that her thoughts were simply outrageous. His mother had no idea that she appeared ignorant.

"I'm not prejudiced," she'd say, "I think the Negros are a joyous group, they can sing, they can dance but their brains aren't as large as ours, honey. Plain and simple. Science tells it like it is. Intelligence is based on brain size, I think. You know what I'm saying, honey, Negros just aren't as smart as us. I think our own *Post and Courier* had an article about that very finding."

"No comment, Mother," he'd say, as his mouth closed and the shock passed.

He traced her shoulder with his finger. Well, she was the smartest person he knew, White or Black. Her skin felt like velvet. He moved his mouth down her arm and he heard her voice ever so slightly, "Feels so good."

"Your skin is softer than any flower petal I've ever held in my hand ... softer than a baby's behind."

"What do you know about a baby's behind?"

"Nothing yet, I'm waiting on our child so I can find out."

"No children till I'm through school, Barney."

"And no sex until this evening." He winked.

She laughed and got up slowly. She put on the

silk robe at the bottom of the bed and walked to the window. After peering out, she looked back at him. "I heard whistling."

"A bird?"

"Not whistling 'Suwanee.'"

Barnaby rolled over and sighed. "Oh, my God, is one of my parents invading my privacy?"

She squinted out the window. "Your father has just passed your Juneberry bush and is now approaching your barbeque grill, still whistling 'Suwanee,' I might add."

Barnaby sat up quickly and ran to the window. "We don't have to answer."

"Your car is in the drive, sweetheart. Besides, he'll just let himself in."

Barnaby grabbed his pants from the floor and slid into them as quickly as he could. Then he grabbed his shirt and ran to the door. Stay here," he said.

"Do I have a choice?"

Barnaby ran down the stairs and back to the kitchen. He opened the door quickly and watched his father glide across the lawn. His white fedora down on his forehead and his light blue shirt opened three buttons. He wore white Keds that Barnaby could clearly see in the meandering stroll toward his house, as if he were about to lie under a shady tree with a copy of one of his favorite crime books.

"Son." Dickie tipped his hat and waved with it.

Barnaby leaned against the doorframe. "Hey, Pops."

"Hope you don't mind, son. I was just passing."

"Hard not to pass when you're out passing." Barnaby laughed. "On foot."

Dickie walked into the living room where the large doors were open, and the sheer drapes moved in the breeze like a seductive woman doing a belly dance. "I'm always on foot. You know that."

"If Mother would let you buy a sports car, I doubt that would be the case."

"I'll give you your inheritance early if you can convince her."

"So, Dad, have you solved it?" Barnaby took the chair opposite his father and sank down low. "Is that what you're here to tell me?"

"Where's your shoes?"

"Who needs 'em?"

Barnaby noticed his father's quick glance up the stairs but then his eyes returned to his son's nervous expression. "You don't have to work on this case with me. I know you have better things to do, Barney. I know you're busy."

"Yes, I'm busy but I already have a theory. I realize that I love this stuff. Isn't it like predicting the market? You know, will it go up or down, sort of like who killed Fletcher Smith, his wife, or his lover?"

Dickie sat forward. "Neither."

"Well, Fletcher seduced someone into that alley and then made a pass at her, but the woman's boyfriend or husband followed her out there and shot Fletcher. Hey, by the way, did you see Fletcher go into the alley that night?"

"I did not. Are you questioning me?"

"Um." Barnaby sat back. "Makes sense, though, doesn't it? It's a crime of passion. Has to be."

"Then check it out. See what you can dig up. I've got to go." Dickie stood to his feet.

"You just got here."

"I was just passing, like I said." he winked. "A bottle of water would be nice. He put his hat back on and smiled at his son. "You're on my way home."

"Sure, Dad, come by anytime but giving me a heads up would be nice." Barnaby walked back into the kitchen and emerged a moment later with a bottle of Evian. "That way, I could have a bowl full of pecans or something ready for you."

"Hey, you know anyone in this town with an antique gun collection?" Dickie asked.

Barnaby stared at him. "I don't think so. Everyone I know has regular guns, not antique guns."

Dickie glanced up the stairs. "Got a woman up there?"

Barnaby felt the flush come to his face. "Of

course not."

"Right." Dickie said. He walked back out the front way and admired the property. He didn't think Barnaby would be much of a threat. He was all wrong about the murder and would probably lose interest in a day or two. He whistled 'Suwanee' on the short distance home, trying to remember where he'd seen that gun collection.

Barnaby climbed the stairs. Prissy was fully dressed and staring out the window.

"I better go," she said.

He walked behind her and kissed the back of her head. "That murder seems obvious to me. Some jealous boyfriend shot the bastard."

"That what he came to talk about?"

"I don't think he came to talk about anything. He was on his way home. The guesthouse was in his sightline and so he came by. He was thirsty."

"Knowing somebody shot someone is not enough, you have to know *who* shot him." She kissed his nose, something she always did when she thought he was being silly.

He smiled and grabbed her fingers and put them to his lips. "Well, sure, we'll know soon enough. My Pops is on the case." He smiled wide.

"You two don't have any suspects. To solve a murder case, you have to have suspects."

Barnaby laughed. "Just trying to please my

father. He loves this shit."

"Ask your mother for suspects."

"What?"

"She's the one who fingered that guy, Jeremiah Lennox."

"My mother?"

"Of course, didn't you know that?"

"Who told you that?"

"My mama."

"What else your mama tell you?"

"That it used to be a joke in town about Deborah Darling putting the finger on Jeremiah Lennox 'cause he was Black. And then the rest of those bigot jurors convicted him 'cause he was Black, and they wanted closure."

"Do tell."

"I'd forgotten Jeremiah's name until today. Mama hasn't really talked about him for years."

Barnaby stared at her. It wasn't computing for him, and he'd never heard that before.

"Everyone knows how prejudiced your mother is, Barnaby. She assumed Jeremiah killed that guy cause he was there, and he was Black, but Jeremiah said he was meeting a woman in the alley, but she never showed up, so he left. My mama said he was always meeting women, so it makes sense."

"My mother fingered him that night?"

"Yes, Barnaby, our very own Mrs. Darling."

"Well, I'll be damned."

"You should question my mother about that crime as well."

"Deasia?" Barnaby looked at her as if he thought she was crazy.

"My mother was always talking about that murder when I was a little girl, then it became old news, you know? But I remember she always said White people didn't know shit about what goes on in this town. She kept saying they convicted an innocent man." Prissy made a face and scowled. "White people don't know shit," she said and laughed. "I can still see my mama's face, her brows all furrowed. 'White people don't know shit.'"

After Prissy went home Barnaby sat in front of the television, eating the leftovers his mother had brought him the day before. He tried to remember if his parents had ever talked about that murder and he doesn't think they ever did, at least not in front of him. Something about this guy being released was making it the talk of the town. So, his mother had been a witness? He'd had no idea. He wondered what Deasia would have to say about it.

Chapter Eight

Dickie

Dickie watched his wife and Lottie as they sat at a card table deeply engrossed in a game of Checkers, their expressions intense, as if they were plotting to overthrow the government. They sipped on Margaritas and smashed out so many butts in the ashtray that you couldn't see the tray, just the ash. They had just finished a game of Clue, that Dickie had won, Professor Plum had done it in the kitchen with a pair of scissors.

"I don't believe it," Deborah had said as she tossed the little pieces of the game to the floor with a grunt of disgust, sore loser that she was.

"How the hell did you know it was Professor Plum, Dickie?" Deborah scowled at him. "We were only playing the game for five minutes."

"He knows everything if it involves murder." Lottie didn't lift her eyes from the board. "King me, Debs," she said.

"My Dickie knows how to reason," Deborah said as she placed a checker onto the checker that had finagled its way into being kinged. "Did you cheat, Lottie?" Deborah sat back and raised an eyebrow.

Lottie glared at her. "Sore loser, Deborah. You've always been a sore loser."

"I took my eyes away from the board for a few minutes when I got up to get us drinks and you could have cheated then."

Lottie raised her eyes to the ceiling. "I'm sure I could not have gotten away with that. If I were a cheat, I wouldn't be a careless one. Dickie would have seen me do that and I'm sure he would have told you. Now stop being ridiculous and make your move."

"I need to think now, this is going to take some time."

"Take all the time you want, Deborah. You have never beaten me at Checkers and tonight will not be the night you do."

Dickie sat in the yellow leather chair pretending to read the paper. He didn't want anyone to notice that he was deeply disturbed and ask him what was wrong, and he'd have to lie, think of something to say, but he'd talk about it later with Lottie. God, he had to talk about it with someone.

"You see her cheat, Dickie?" Deborah blew the smoke toward the ceiling and winked at him.

Dickie wanted to get his mind off what he had just seen up in his daughter's bedroom. He looked at Lottie, hoping she'd say something controversial so he could argue with her and get wrapped up in the present and not the immediate past. He was trying hard to erase the immediate past, send it back to a moment that he could alter somehow.

He put his head back and thought about Deborah, back to that time when he first met her. He loved thinking of that day. Reminiscing should occupy his thoughts for a while. He smiled to himself. He could have called it love at first sight back then. He wouldn't call it that now but back then, he felt as if she'd thoroughly ensnared him forever and he would never feel his feet on the ground again. She had a certain way of lowering her eyes and then raising them back up again to his, her long dark eyelashes fluttering, her beautiful emerald eyes making him weak in the knees.

He had met Deborah and Lottie at the same time in 1959. They had all met on a football field where a bunch of young people were sitting around drinking beer. Deborah told him several months later that she thought it was Lottie he found attractive. "When you asked me out on a date, Dickie, Lottie was so pissed." Deborah had laughed and batted her eyes at him. "She's a sore loser, Dickie. She's mad at me for winning you."

Dickie grinned to himself. He remembered feeling lucky to be the reason two women were fighting over him but at the time, he hadn't given Lottie a thought, though she was lovely to look at, very idiosyncratic, like a poodle-dachshund mix. She had dark curly hair that always struck him as unruly, and lips that turned up as if she was perpetually smiling, and a thousand opinions about everything, from politics to the best sun sign to be born under. Her dark eyes were intelligent, like the poodle mix. He remembered noticing that right away and maybe that put him off, her probing eyes. Back then, his mind was more focused on sex than some woman with opinions. He was busy ogling Deborah's pretty face, not Lottie's big mouth. Lottie was going to some community college to study business and Deborah was remaining behind in Pickens to get married, "and make someone happy just like the song says," she'd said. He'd found that so cute.

Dickie remembered grinning at her words as he felt her small hand in his, tracing her thumb on his palm and sending tingles through him. He didn't want a woman who would go off to college and come back knowing more than he did, if that were even possible. He wanted Deborah and her beautiful smile and her helpless expression and the way she melted in his arms as though he was the world holding her in its vortex, never letting go.

Lottie was there at their wedding in 1961, back from college and just as opinionated as ever, throwing Nietzsche around like some people quote the Bible. After she graduated, she landed herself a job at a bank, managing the small local branch in Pickens. She bought herself a house and a car and he used to see her at Smith's Bar playing pool with the best of them. She was independent and strong and at the time, Dickie did not find that attractive. As a matter of fact, he found it intimidating. Lottie later told him, after they were sleeping together, "I intimidated you, Dickie."

Truth be told, he'd never thought of Lottie one way or the other except as Deborah's childhood friend whom she hated one day and loved the next. He didn't understand their relationship; they were always fighting, obviously intensely jealous of one another even though Deborah could not imagine working for a living like Lottie, and Lottie thought marriage was an archaic union to subvert women and poor Deborah wasn't smart enough to see that. However, Dickie doubted that their spheres could spin in the universe with any great distance from the other.

When Deborah put down Leah for wearing pants to church, Dickie thought it was the most ridiculous thing he'd ever heard, and it bothered him for days that Deborah had that opinion. It infuriated him that she was so small-minded. He wondered what she'd think of him when he'd snuck off to the guest house and put on women's clothes in those early years. He'd spend hours dressed as a woman and sometimes he'd cook, or he'd listen to music. Sometimes he'd sit by the window pretending he was a young woman dreaming about love, about a prince.

But Dickie was not gay: he just lived in a fantasy world of his choosing. He didn't want to sleep with men, though he would have welcomed a man's attention, not sexual, of course, but gentlemanly. He could never figure out how Lottie discovered that world, that world of his imagination where women were so alluring, so worthy of impersonation. His secret desires, somehow laid bare under the perceptive dark eyes of Lottie's observation, and so soon after his marriage to Deborah. His wife was eight months pregnant with Barnaby when she made that comment about Leah, and he realized the constricted opinions that stifled a broader sense of the world. Just a few months later, sitting in Lottie's car, he'd driven her home after one of Deborah's dinner parties and she'd had too much wine.

"What do you think about women in pants?" he'd asked her.

Lottie had laughed. "Have you noticed what I'm wearing tonight, Dickie? My God, it's 1963. What should we be wearing, corsets?"

"Yes, but would you wear pants in church?"

Lottie looked at him as though he'd lost his mind. "Not likely to offend a God I don't believe in."

Dickie leaned his head back and smiled. Had Deborah heard Lottie say that, she would have stormed out of the car, slammed the door, and the two of them would have been at odds for weeks.

"Not sure I believe in God either but don't tell Deborah." He winked at her.

They sat in the car silently for a while because it had started to pour, with lightning streaking the sky in front of them like cannon fire. She'd looked at him and suddenly said out of nowhere, "You're so pretty, how does Deborah stand being with a man prettier than she is?"

Dickie remembered how her words affected him. He was melting, everything fell away, all inhibition, and he began to cry. The tears rolled down his cheeks and the harder he tried to stop crying, the harder he cried.

"Sorry," he said.

Lottie slid over in the car seat and held him, and then he felt her fingers down his shirt and on his nipples. She slid her hands all over his body, and he sighed, as if he were a woman. He sighed like a woman, and she did not reject him. She made love to him there in his car in the pouring rain with the cannon fire lightning making his heart pop. He felt alive for the first time in so long, not since Leah.

He went back to Lottie's the next day and they

just stared at each other on her doorstep. Then she took his hand and led him inside. She dressed him in her clothes and made up his face. She made love to him in his female identity, the one in which he called himself Deedee, and he felt reborn. Finally, someone he could be himself with again.

They never discussed his leaving Deborah and marrying her because they understood each other, it wasn't what either of them wanted. He continued to make love to his wife and Robinette was born in 1976, so it was clear he was still sleeping with Deborah, but he saw Lottie more than he saw his wife. Lottie was family, Aunt Lottie, as the children grew up calling her, and that's just the way she wanted it. It was also the way he wanted it.

Lottie's raucous laughter startled him back to the present and he looked over at the two women glaring at each other across a Checkers board, arguing over something. They were always arguing. He frowned at his daughter as she suddenly came down the stairs, followed by Mindy Peach and his stomach did a flip, the immediate past roaring back. Deborah looked up.

"I didn't know you were in the house, Mindy," she said.

Mindy looked at Robinette and smiled. "Oh, I

guess you didn't hear me come in. It's these new sandals, they don't make a sound."

The girl was flushed, as if she'd had too much sun. Robinette stood behind her on the stairs.

Deborah sighed. "Well, at least you're not with my son."

Dickie flinched and smiled half-heartedly at his wife. He had gone to the bathroom at some point. At the top of the stairs, he heard his daughter giggling. He knocked on the door to her room, but perhaps knocked too softly, for no one answered. So, he walked into his daughter's room to find out what was making her giggle so much, which he felt he had a right to do, especially if she was smoking something she shouldn't be smoking.

He'd meant no intrusion, but it had been an intrusion. There was his daughter half under the sheets and there was Mindy Peach fully under the sheets and there was only one place his daughter's head could have been. He turned sharply and walked out, hoping he hadn't been seen. Apparently, that had been a very pleasurable giggle.

"My God," he whispered. "My daughter is a lesbian?"

"Deep in thought", Deborah said. "Solving crimes?"

Dickie laughed. "Sure enough."

"Drive Lottie home," Deborah kissed his forehead, "she's had one too many."

They sat in his car as they had that first night so many years ago, when she'd made love to him. He stared out of the window and Lottie asked him what was wrong, why he was so lost in thought.

"My daughter is gay," he said, turning to her sadly.

"Really? Well, I'm not surprised."

Dickie turned away and stared out of the window. "You're not? I am."

"It's not the end of the world, Dickie."

He stared back at her; his eyes wide. "You don't get it. Robinette is gay. Deborah thinks she's going to get grandchildren."

"You have a son, Dickie. You'll have grandchildren."

"I mean her daughter's grandchildren."

"Look, to hell with Deborah. Robinette is her own person. I don't think there's anything wrong with it."

"You wouldn't."

She sighed. "You should talk."

"I saw her taking pleasure with Mindy Peach."

"What? Mindy Peach is Barny's girl, isn't she?"

"My son is in love with Prissy." He slapped his head back on the car seat. "You know Prissy,

Deasia's daughter. You'd have to be blind not to see it."

Lottie looked at him. "Of course, I know Deasia's daughter."

He peered into her eyes. "That's all you have to say?"

"What more is there to say?"

"My daughter is gay, Lottie."

Lottie shook her head, smiling all the while.

"My son is in love with a Black girl."

Lottie sighed. "It's no big deal, honey. Neither issue is a big deal."

He sat there a few moments but then he laughed quietly. "No big deal. Life is life. This is Pickens, South Carolina, Lottie. This is not Los Angeles or New York City. You just have to let it be. Is that what you're saying? You don't even believe in God, why should I listen to you?"

"You hypocritical bastard. You're worried about such bullshit. Your family would put you in the loony bin if they knew about you."

Dickie closed his eyes. "It's not turning out the way Deborah wanted it, none of it."

She took his hand. "Why do you think your children avoid telling her anything? It's because it's all about what Deborah wants, not what they want, or what you want. What's real for others is above Deborah's realm of understanding, Dickie."

Dickie sighed. "I don't really care about any of it. I care only because it's going to hurt Deborah.

But they are my children and I love them the way they are, whoever they are. That is the truth."

She took his hand. "Love is about acceptance, Dickie. Tell Deborah that, will you?"

"I can't tell Deborah anything."

"Then be prepared for her finding out on her own and blowing the roof off your house."

Chapter Nine

Barnaby

Barnaby entered the kitchen through the back door. Deasia was at the stove watching a small television on the shelf above her while she fried potatoes. It was the same soap opera she always watched, *Days of Our Lives*. Barnaby smiled as he tiptoed behind her and grabbed her around the waist.

Deasia screamed as Barnaby made a face. "You get me every time. You a bad boy. You 'bout to stop my heart."

"Can't help myself." He grabbed a potato that was draining on a paper towel. "Oh, my God, this is the best damn potato I ever had." He grabbed another one. "I am the baddest boy the South has ever seen because I am going to eat all of these potatoes and leave none for my mother. I tell you in advance." He reached out and grabbed another potato.

"You put that potato back, young man. Your mama says I never make enough potatoes. I'm going to tell her you steal my batch and that's why there's never enough." She slapped his hand.

"Don't you take no more potatoes."

"You're the potato lady, Deasia, and the pot roast lady, and the chicken lady, and I could go on and on. You should buy Beau McArdle's restaurant and cook for this entire town. They don't know what they're missing. Say you will."

"Save your breath, Barnaby. I is nothing but a good cook, but I is tied to this kitchen and this kitchen only."

"The hell with this kitchen. Buy that restaurant and share your talent with the world. Pickens needs to smell more like brisket and less like Pluff Mud."

"When it rain money, I'll catch me some. Anyhows, Pluff Mud smell good, smell like home."

"Yes, ma'am." He grinned. "Where is everyone?" He looked through to the empty living room.

"Mr. Dickie went to his office; Miss Deborah went shopping."

"And Miss Robinette?"

"Sleeping her silly head off. That child came home stinking like beer. She smell so bad I snuck her upstairs 'fore her Mama smell the stink and punish her ass for the next twelve months."

Barnaby laughed. "She's almost eighteen."

"Almost eighteen ain't eighteen."

"Bah Humbug." Barnaby winked at her.

"You just as bad as she is."

"You know I'm going to marry your daughter,

don't you?" He kissed her cheek. "So how bad can I be? I know a good thing." He put his fingers in front of his mouth. "Shush. Don't tell Miss Deborah."

Deasia turned her back on him and started heating up shortening for the chicken but not before he saw her grin. She wasn't saying how she really felt about her daughter marrying him, but she did grin.

"In a few years, Deasia, we'll get married in a few years. She has to get through college."

"*Humph*, Miss Deborah get wind of you marrying my daughter, she fire my ass and burn my house down."

Barnaby laughed. "My mother will do no such thing and if she does, I'll buy you a new house. And I'll ride my Prissy off on a white charger to a better land. You can come, too."

"*Humph*."

"Speaking of murder."

She turned to him sharply. "I wasn't speaking of no murder."

He wondered if he was skating on thin ice. The help in Pickens didn't talk about their business or their gossip, except amongst themselves, but it was the way Priss had hinted that her mama knew things. He'd be a hero to his father if he solved this murder. He doubted if his father would be questioning Deasia. He decided to jump right in but with caution.

"What do you remember about the murder of Fletcher Smith?"

He noticed the twitch in her shoulder, it was slight, but it was still a reaction.

"Nothin'."

"Oh, come on, everyone in this town was talking about it and now it's new news again because Jerimiah is coming back from prison."

"He's already back," she said.

Barnaby's ears pricked up. "He's back?"

"Yep."

"Did you know him?"

"I knew him."

"How well?"

Deasia leaned up and turned the volume up on the television. "You leave me to my show now, Barnaby. I been waiting on this scene. Jessica goin' to get a proposal."

Barnaby watched as Deasia turned down the flame and sat on the stool.

"Where's he living, that Jeremiah guy?"

She turned to him sharply. "Why you want to know?"

He shrugged his shoulders and looked off. "I want to question him about the murder, that's all."

"He didn't do it."

"I know. You think he knows who did?"

Deasia scrunched up her face. "You stay away from that man."

"Look, my Pops and I are working on this case together. We're going to solve it. We'll be the talk of Pickens." He grabbed her around the waist again. "Split the reward money if there is any."

"I don't know where he live, but he work at the gas station in Powdersville and you the last person he want to see, so you stay away from that man, or I'll tell your mama and she make short work of you."

"Do tell," he said and grabbed another potato from the towel. "Why would I be the last person he'd want to see?"

"You or anybody would be the last person. He angry. Wouldn't you be if you in prison for years for something you didn't do?"

"Who did it, Deasia, who killed Fletcher?"

"Shoot, I don't have a crystal ball. Now you stay away from him."

"What's he gonna do, shoot me, beat me up?"

"More likely he'll just pick you up over his head and toss you in the river. You nothin' to him, Barnaby, you mind your business or someone tan your hide. Hear? He got no reason to talk to you, you just a little pipsqueak to him."

Barnaby smiled at her. "Pipsqueak?" He pinched her cheek. "I take what you say to heart, Deasia, don't I always?"

Barnaby wondered if he should be driving out

to Powdersville to talk to a man who might want to put his mother six feet under for accusing him of killing Fletcher and might want to toss his nosey ass in the river just like Deasia said. He didn't know what he would say to the man either. Maybe he shouldn't tell Jeremiah he was Deborah Darling's son. He had no set plan; this would be purely improvisation. He started thinking up questions he could ask: *You see anything? You hear anything? Who do you think killed him?*

He pulled into the gas station and parked his car near the convenience store. Two men were pumping gas, they both wore striped uniforms with the name "Pete's" over their hearts. But neither of those men was Jeremiah Lennox and he knew that because they were both White men. He knew Jeremiah was Black because he'd been told that. Prissy said that's why they convicted him; Black men got to be guilty of something. If there was a crime, then a Black man did it.

Barnaby walked into the garage where cars were up on lifts and two or three men were working on them. One man in the back was polishing a spiffy Mustang and Barnaby admired the shine. He thought the man was ambiguous looking, maybe Black, maybe White, could be Jeremiah. Then someone called out to the man, called him 'Jeremiah' and he turned. Barnaby watched him hand the man something, some tool he had asked for and then he went back to what he'd been doing.

He looked at the man rubbing down the chrome. He didn't have any doubt he was Jeremiah Lennox now, but he was surprised because he didn't altogether look like a Black man.

"What you looking at?" Jeremiah asked him as he stood and wiped off his hands.

Barnaby searched his face for a few seconds before he spoke. He noticed the ease with which Jeremiah stood before him, not frowning but not smiling either.

"You did a great job on that car. I can see myself in it." Barnaby walked closer and admired the car.

"Can't do it right, don't do it at all. You got a car you want me to wash?"

"Sure, sure I do."

"There's extra charge for the wax but I recommend it if you want it to look like this." Jeremiah leaned down and went back to rubbing down the hubcaps.

Barnaby walked up close to the man. "Nice looking Mustang," he said.

The man turned sharply and looked up at him. He stared at Barnaby for a second before he said anything. "Yeah, it's nice."

Barnaby laughed. "Is it yours?"

Jeremiah gave him a scowl "Why do you want to know? You want to buy it?"

"Might."

"Not for sale."

Barnaby stepped back. "Are you Jeremiah?"

"Are you Jesus?"

Barnaby laughed; the man smiled.

"Who wants to know?"

Barnaby held out his hand, but the man didn't take it. "I wonder if I could ask you a few questions about the Fletcher Smith murder?"

"I'm done with that, son. Got nothing to say."

Barnaby shook his head. He was a bit shocked at the look of this guy, he was neat as a pin except for a bit of grease on his jumpsuit. His hair, black as tar and streaked with silver, was waved like a White man's. He was tall as Barnaby and built slim, hard muscles and a soft look to his expression. He hardly looked like a murderer either, with that easy smile and facial features that might have been found in Hollywood. His eyes were almost black but soft. His beard was short and mostly grey. Handsome dude, Barnaby thought to himself.

"You are Jeremiah Lennox, right?" Barnaby asked.

"No other name to claim, mister. I am Jeremiah Lennox, known for the way I can make a Mustang shine and the fact that I can sing better than Willie Nelson."

"Really?" Barnaby grinned at him.

Jeremiah took a stance in the middle of the

garage and pretended to be strumming a guitar. Then he started singing, foot-tapping, country boy twang. It was hysterical to Barnaby, but he held the laughter back. He thought Jeremiah might take it the wrong way.

> *Just can't wait to get on the road again,*
> *The life I love is makin' music with my friends,*
> *And I can't wait to get on the road again.*
> *On the road again*
> *Goin' places that I've never been*
> *Seein' things that I may never see again,*
> *And I can't wait to get on the road again.*

Barnaby finally let his laughter out. He knew his smile was cracking his face. He was thinking that he liked this guy, he was a bit of a character. "I sure do like Willie Nelson," Barnaby said.

"Good White, country music." Jeremiah smiled. "Who are you anyway, Magnum PI, or maybe, Mannix?" Jeremiah rubbed his hands on a rag and stared at Barnaby.

Barnaby laughed again. "Neither. Barnaby Darling." He held out his hand.

Jeremiah stood there looking as if he'd had a sudden heart attack. He leaned against the car he was cleaning and breathed in deep. "Deborah's kid?"

Barnaby's head snapped back. "Yes, my mother was the one who saw you that night. We all know you didn't do it now. I'm sure my mother feels terrible. My father and I want to solve the crime, find out who really did the murder, really vindicate you."

"I live in the present, not the past. Let it go. Anyway, bastard deserved to die. I'm sure you've heard that."

"Well, justice wasn't done."

Jeremiah threw the rag inside the Mustang and then wiped some sweat from his brow with a handkerchief. "Your mother still living?"

"Why, you fixing to kill her?" Barnaby laughed self-consciously. "Fingered you, didn't she?"

"Can't kill Deborah Darling, she'll just come back to haunt you. Anyway, she didn't finger me, just said she saw me there."

Barnaby gave him a short, sly smile, "Not even going to ask you what you mean by that, that my mother would just come back to haunt you."

"You're a fine-looking boy, but you don't take after your mother."

Barnaby's eyebrows came together. "No? I always thought I did."

"Glad she never did it." He stood close to the boy and stared in his face.

"Did what?"

"Well, feel badly about being the one that fingered me. She doesn't, does she?"

"Never talks about it."

"So, what you want to know, am I going to

seek revenge on those other Southern bigots that sent me to prison?"

"Were they Southern bigots?"

"You don't look stupid."

"Did you see anyone that night? I mean, you were there in the alley, weren't you?"

"Sure, saw a lot of people." Jeremiah looked around nervously. "I can't speak to you here; my boss could show up any minute. I'm not supposed to be making small talk on his time. Want to take me to dinner? I'll tell you everything I saw and everything I heard that night?"

Barnaby smiled, savoring the thought that he was way ahead of his father. "Has my father been to see you?" he asked.

"Who's your father?"

"Dickie Darling."

"I remember him. Pleasant guy."

"A bit of a crime buff." Barnaby smiled self-consciously. "He'll probably want to question you."

"Well, let's just say you've got the exclusive."

They shook hands, they were eye to eye; Jeremy Lennox had something familiar about him, but Barnaby had no idea why; he'd never seen this man in his life.

Barnaby drove home after making dinner plans with Mr. Lennox. He liked the guy. Must be still in pain over the time he spent in jail. He'd have to tell his father that Jeremiah Lennox was a nice guy, but far be it from him to mention it to his mother.

Chapter Ten

Robbie

They say having sex is like floating to heaven, an all-consuming euphoria. It's losing your mind and smiling over the loss. It's a surrender you welcome and it settles in your blood stream, lulling your heightened senses, filling you, filling the moan that emerges from your soul, and the pleasure you feel is a drowning, an absorption so rich in its entirety, it holds you captive in its endless embrace. Is it love, she wondered? Does it matter?

"I'm not giving you money to move to New York, Robinette. I'm only going to support you if you go to college. If you marry some fine young man who will take care of you, we will put your inheritance into a trust fund for your children. Now, what will it be, marriage or college?"

Robbie smiled at her mother, so disillusioned. "Neither, Mother."

Deborah sighed and slammed her cup on the saucer.

"Dare we shatter a Delft China cup over it, Mother?"

Deborah stood up. "You're insufferable, Robinette. Don't you date, for God's sake?"

"I do, Mother. I do." Oh, how she wanted to blurt it out, the union of two hearts beating and throbbing in the throes of passion, the long languid reach of a lover into the unknowable, unthinkable drowning of satisfaction. The collapse of total delirium in her drug of choice. Still, she shouldn't have told her mother she dated. Now she'll never leave her alone.

"Is there someone special, Robinette?" Her mother almost danced on her toes, almost leapt like a ballerina, an entrechat performed in a moment of heightened skill. Robbie stared at her, into her eyes which must surely be staring into hers, which were glowing in tears of satisfaction. How could this woman not know she's been to paradise?

"Perhaps." Robbie said.

This made her mother happy, and she rose to her feet. Another entrechat was entirely likely. "Oh, we must meet him then. I'll throw a dinner party next weekend and you'll bring him. You're such an attractive girl, Robinette. There must be hundreds of boys pursuing you."

"Only one is necessary, isn't it? According to you, that is."

"For God's sakes, yes, one special boy."

"I did say perhaps, not 'certainly' didn't I?"

"I know you're teasing me. I always know

when you're teasing me."

"My love is an undesirable." Robbie smiled as she noticed the jolt with which her mother fell forward. But she caught herself on the arm of a wing chair.

Deborah's mouth hung open in disbelief. *My daughter is dating a Black man? Oh my God*, her expression read. "Undesirable is an ambiguous expression, honey. I will be open to Catholics and Democrats. You know that."

Robbie threw her head back. "Oh, boy."

"I insist you bring him for dinner." Deborah forced herself to smile.

"I'm sorry, but I won't subject my one and only to your prejudices. I will not parade my special human in front of your disbelieving eyes and the hatred you harbor toward unnatural acts of passion."

Robinette knew that look. Her mother was wondering what the hell her daughter was talking about. She'd have to ask Dickie, is what she was thinking. The children favored their father. Robbie knew her mother did not understand why both of her children seemed to look upon her with scorn. *Because there is no other reaction to you, Mother.*

"You are being unfair to me, Robinette. I insist on meeting the boy you are dating."

"Then I risk being disowned."

"I don't care if he's Black, my darlin'. I mean

there is Black and there is Black. There's Denzel Washington Black and then there's Poor White Trash Black. How Black is he? Is he a poor boy? Oh, I don't care about that. You're not marrying him, are you?" Deborah laughed. "I'm sure with your good taste, he gives Denzel a run for his money."

Robbie smiled. "A poor boy is better than no boy, isn't that right, Mother?"

Deborah gave her a weak smile. Her daughter left the room quietly, mumbling something under her breath that Deborah did not hear but sounded like a cuss of some kind.

Robbie slammed into the guest house and flung herself into the soft cushions of the couch. Barnaby came in from the kitchen crunching cold cereal and Prissy sat at the kitchen table sipping coffee.

"She's intolerable," Robbie screamed.

"What did she do now?" Barnaby asked.

"She insists I bring the boy I'm dating to dinner."

"Why did you tell her you're dating anyone?" Barnaby took a spoonful of cereal and stared at her.

"She forced me into it. You know how she is." Robbie looked at her brother and shook her head. "She's so disillusioned. She'll never leave me alone."

"Well, look, let's bombard her with the truth. We can all gather around her and insist on playing a game of 'Secrets'. We'll tell her that each of us has to reveal something very personal about ourselves that no one else knows." Barnaby looked at his sister forlornly as he sat next to her on the couch. "Come on, sis, I'm game if you are. We'll spill it all then. Winner of the worst secret gets a hundred bucks. You and Mindy, me and Prissy, and ole Mumsy will have to eat it, after she reveals her own secrets, that is." He raised his eyebrows. "If she has any."

Robbie gave him an easy smile. "Oh, yes, then we'd be responsible for our Mother's heart attack and poor Pops would be alone and miserable."

"I doubt if your Pops would be alone for long," Prissy said as she handed Robbie a mug of coffee and noticed their startled expressions. "I just mean he's so handsome and engaging."

Barnaby sighed. "That he is and devoted to our mother. The truth would be sure to kill her," he looked sadly at Robbie. "I don't even think she's aware of women who like other women." Barnaby put his fingers into air quotes, "That way."

Prissy sighed. "Sure to kill her."

"Then where would Pops be?" Robbie took a sip of her coffee and slid back into the couch.

"No doubt with Aunt Lottie," Barnaby said,

and they both laughed.

"Who thinks all men are creatures from the Black Lagoon," Robbie giggled a bit hysterically. "She'd kick him out on his ass with all his mysterious walks and his crime paperbacks."

"Well, at least we got a smile out of you," Prissy said as she slid beside Robbie on the couch and took her hand. "You need a beard," she said.

Robbie raised her eyebrows and stared at Prissy. "What the hell is a beard?"

Prissy and Barnaby laughed. "You don't know what a beard is?" Barnaby asked her.

"What is it?" She looked at Barnaby because he usually had all the answers.

"Someone who will pretend to be your beau," he said.

"You mean like Mindy pretending to be your girlfriend?"

Barnaby nodded. "Yes, Mother makes a lot of assumptions. Unfortunately, they are never the correct ones."

Prissy stood up and tapped her head. "I have just the boy."

Barnaby and Robbie stared at her. "He better be capable of keeping the secret," Barnaby said.

Prissy shrugged her shoulders. "Well, you tell me. I wouldn't trust a teenager. I was thinking of Kenny McNeil. He's mature enough not to say anything."

"Mature? Kenny McNeil is like forty years old,

maybe more and he's short. He's no boy." Robbie nearly jumped out of her seat.

"And that's why you didn't want to introduce him to your mom. I mean he's so much older… and shorter." Prissy giggled. "This is perfect. I know Kenny, he owns the Chrysler dealership. He'd make a great beard. He's mature, won't screw it up."

"Kenny Mcneil is a criminal. God, don't you remember, he got in all that trouble?" Robbie glared at her. "Didn't he rob the gas station and shoot the owner when he was young?"

"Well, he didn't kill him. Anyway, that was years ago." Barnaby grinned at her. "When he was young. You weren't even born yet. He's paid his debt to society."

"I can't believe the poor guy can't live his reputation down." Prissy looked at her with a raised eyebrow. "Where did you hear about him anyway?"

"Kids at school make fun of his son. They call him the son of Jesse James." Robbie hunched up her shoulders. "Jesus, he has a son my age. It's obscene."

"Nothing Mother needs to know," Barnaby said. "Short people look younger than they are. He's got dimples and all his hair, and all his hair is still brown."

"Well, I guess that's perfect. I told Mother he's an undesirable. I wasn't far from the truth."

"He's respectable now." Prissy smiled at her. "He's an upstanding citizen."

Barnaby took his sister's hand. "Don't worry, Sport, we'll get Mother off your back. Kenny is okay. We all do things when we're young, stupid things."

Chapter Eleven

Leighton

As Leighton drove up the drive toward Rhonda's house, she recognized the old Antebellum-style home from magazine photographs she'd seen of Southern mansions, like the mysterious and haunting plantations she used to pass on her way into Columbia. Rhonda's mansion was rich in history, its pristine and stately personality loomed before her, reeking of privilege and olde-worlde manners, and she realized she had been wrong about Rhonda, thinking of Rhonda Smith Kram as rich but that was not so, she was *extraordinarily* rich.

"Can't stop thinking of the Civil War," she whispered to herself.

Leighton didn't know what she expected of Rhonda, she had pretty much internalized Deborah Darling's account of her as being "full of herself" and that's what she expected. But as the redheaded woman approached Leighton, she judged right away that Rhonda was not what one would call full of herself. She was simply a presence in the room that one could not avert one's eyes from. She was beautiful, and commanding, clearly grounded in her wealth, an imposing figure, not terribly approachable, but certainly not a cute, flirtatious female with bouncing breasts and alluring dimples, who was full of herself, as Leighton had somehow expected. On the contrary, she was striking, as only the rich can be.

"Right this way," Rhonda said as she led Leighton into what could only be described as a drawing room out of the opulent past of the South's great plantations. The scent of magnolia trees and honeysuckle wafted in through the large open windows.

"What a magnificent home," Leighton said.

"I had it restored as close to the original as I could," Rhonda told her as she walked beside Leighton. "It was built by my family in the early eighteen hundreds and we've never let go of it." She laughed lightly. "We refer to it as 'The Plantation'. Not a terribly pleasant nickname but fitting."

Leighton could not picture this woman married to a creep like Fletcher Smith, much less a man who ran around town in dresses. Rhonda Smith was certainly an enigma.

They sat in beautiful, upholstered love seats that faced each other on opposite sides of a marble table. The tall deep-blue vase between them was filled with the most beautiful pink flowers Leighton had ever seen, pink like the sky at dawn, poetically streaking the sky. "What beautiful peonies," Leighton said. "I've never quite seen that color before, pale pink and so delicate."

Rhonda smiled. Leighton noticed she had long, slender legs. She wore Bermuda shorts and a man's tailored white shirt. Her red toenails peeked out from the straps of her sandals.

"I'd like to ask you a few questions about Halloween night, 1963."

"I don't remember that far back." Rhonda laughed as she summoned a maid and asked for two glasses of sweet tea to be brought to her. "You do like sweet tea?" she asked Leighton.

Leighton nodded and smiled. "Your husband was murdered that night, surely you remember it?"

"Oh, yes, of course. Fletcher's murder. I remember. I'm so sorry. One of the many things I try to forget."

"Were you seeing your present husband at the time of your then husband's death?"

Startled, Rhonda regained her composure quickly. "No, of course not."

"Would you describe your marriage to Fletcher as a happy one?"

Rhonda paused only a moment. "No," she said.

"And why was that?"

"He was a brute. He slept with other women. He left bruises all over my body. Obviously, I no longer loved him."

"Had you ever?"

"I met him when I was a junior in high school. He was older, very sure of himself, handsome. I was young and I found those things attractive. But those attractions were short-lived."

"Were you planning to divorce him?"

"I was."

"Did he know?"

"Yes."

"And he reacted how?"

"Like Hurricane Hugo when it hit South Carolina."

The sweet tea served, Leighton asked her questions, followed by brief answers as Rhonda waited patiently for the next imposition, the next absurd bombardment of her time, her opinions readily apparent in her expression, most particularly her eyes, as languid as a beautiful grey rain cloud.

"I've been told that Fletcher had a lot of enemies." Leighton sat back in the colorful upholstered couch with pale orange flowers against a silky beige background.

"You're correct. My husband was not a nice man."

"Anyone in particular who might have wanted to harm him?"

"Everyone wanted to harm him." Rhonda laughed softly. "But no, no one in particular."

"Did you go to the party that night as Belle Watling? I heard '*Gone with the Wind*' was the theme that night."

Rhonda made a play of thinking back. "No," she said. "But I believe Marshall did."

"Were you in costume that night?"

"Yes, I was Jack the Ripper?"

"Really? You were dressed as a man?"

"I was. It wasn't mandatory to come as a character from *Gone with the Wind*."

"I can't imagine you dressed as Jack the Ripper. You seem so proper."

"Old Jack was certainly not proper, was he?" Rhonda laughed almost hysterically. "More like a variable psychopath. Anyway, I'm not so proper," she said, her dimples showing and making her seem less austere.

"Did you wear a pistol in a holster on your waist?"

Leighton heeded a slight reaction, some intake of breath. "No," she said. "Jack's weapon of choice was a knife."

Leighton let that sink in. "You left early?"

"Oh, that I don't remember."

"Is your husband at home? I wouldn't mind asking him a few questions as well."

"No, Malcolm is at work."

"And he works at Cassidy & Lowe

Accounting?"

"Yes."

Leighton was about to step into deep waters, but none of it made sense, and had to make sense in order for her to understand it, and to discover motive. She took a deep breath.

"Your husband is a cross-dresser?"

"I don't see where that's any concern of yours or what in God's name it would have to do with Fletcher's murder." Rhonda snapped, indignant, certainly a bit angry. "But he is not a cross-dresser."

"Does he go to work in female clothes?"

Surprisingly, Rhonda smiled at her. "No, of course not."

"It's common knowledge that he cross-dresses." Leighton held her eyes and registered the stubbornness. "Though I was corrected the other day and told he was a drag queen? Is that more precise? I mean to me, there is no difference, but I guess technically there is."

"My husband has interests outside of our family that is completely his business. Being a drag queen is an art for some."

"Well, you must admit, it's strange to be married to a drag queen."

"My relationship with my husband is none of your business, to put it as politely as I can."

"Well, it's just that your husband was pretty undercover in 1963 and if Fletcher was blackmailing him, he'd have cause to shut him up."

"My husband is not a murderer. He is many things, but murderer is not among them. And now I think I've come to the end of our time together, Miss McArdle."

Leighton smiled as she stood to shake Rhonda's hand. The woman was tall and familiar, but Leighton could not place her.

"You don't know my mother by any chance? I feel we've met before."

"I do know your mother, Leighton. You used to come here as a child. You don't remember?"

"No, I don't recall that at all, but you do look familiar."

Rhonda searched her face with an odd tenderness, then she nodded her head but said, "You were so young and then you became a teenager so quickly. After that, you didn't notice anything other than boys. But yes, I know your mother. We're still friends."

"I must pay more attention to my mother's friends," Leighton said and held out her hand. "Thank you for your time."

Leighton and Mart had their feet up on the deck as they downed beers. Aspen lay beside them, snoring rhythmically, as if he were playing a musical instrument.

"How does a woman like Rhonda Smith marry a guy who runs around in dresses? I don't get it. Am I supposed to get it, am I missing something here?" Leighton turned her head to stare at Mart with a perplexed tilt.

"Well, look, Leighton, you don't know the intimacies of their relationship. Maybe it's platonic between them and they're close, like girlfriends." Mart laughed.

"Rhonda knew my mother, knows my mother. I didn't think my mother had any friends."

She looked at Mart, his boyish features, the dimple in his left cheek and the mustache that fell below his lips, his rusty brown hair that fell past his neck, way too long for a cop.

"She told me I used to play in her house."

Mart looked up. "Really?"

Leighton shrugged. "My mother is full of surprises."

"Well, Pickens is a small town. Everyone knows everyone, at least on sight."

"I guess." Leighton took a swig of beer. "Why would any woman want that?" she asked.

"Want what?"

"A drag queen for a husband."

"I don't know, maybe she's not into men."

This got Leighton's attention and she sat up straight. "Well, okay, let's say maybe she isn't, what would that mean exactly?"

Mart shrugged his shoulders. "I think you

need to find out if she's sleeping with her husband. Some women like men who cross-dress or don't mind if they do. I heard most women don't even know their husbands cross-dress."

"How the hell am I going to find out if she's sleeping with her husband?"

"Well, I guess you could ask her."

"I think I'll just assume she isn't."

"I wouldn't assume it." Mart shrugged his shoulders.

"Malcolm is a drag queen, not a cross-dresser, Mart. It's highly likely he's gay."

"Oh. Well, that certainly means she's not sleeping with him, I would imagine."

"Bingo. But then why marry him?"

"I don't know how deep we can get into people's sex life, but I don't know if we can solve this crime without getting into it."

"Maybe Fletcher had a secret life." She looked up at him. "Forget I said that. His life was out there, the guy was a cheating, lying, wife-beating brute, and everyone knew it."

Mart stood up. "Okay, what do we have?" He went back into the kitchen and brought out two more beers.

"Suspect number one, Malcolm Kram. He could have shot Fletcher for threatening to expose him as a drag queen," Mart said as he popped open the beer and sat down.

"Personally, I don't think Malcolm would care

if he were exposed. I mean everyone in this town thinks of him as a professional accountant, not a professional drag queen. He's respectable. He's married to Rhonda, so people accept him. They go to his drag shows and look the other way when he shows up in town in a dress. I think people think it's hysterical."

"Well, it is kind of funny."

Leighton gave him a strange look and raised her eyebrows. "Okay, this doesn't compute. Why would Rhonda marry a drag queen?"

Mart grinned at her. "Companionship?"

"She was only in her twenties when she married him. She'd want a sex life with someone."

"Perhaps she had a lover she couldn't marry. So, let's just say she married Marshall as a beard. Maybe he did it out of friendship for her."

"To keep her other relationship undercover because the guy was married and maybe he was some big muckety-muck." Leighton raised an eyebrow.

"Let's see, who was the Governor of South Carolina back then?"

"Let's say Fletcher threatened to divorce Rhonda when he found out about her affair. She had a lot to lose... I've seen that house she lives in... the woman is loaded. Maybe she stood to lose a lot in divorce, but she'd get all of it if Fletcher were out of the picture, as in dead. So, she and this mystery man, possibly Marshall, conspired to kill Fletcher."

"Rhonda didn't need Fletcher's money. He was wealthy but she comes from real wealth. The woman's family is Old South, established and very well off. That house has been in her family since before the Civil War and it came with quite a trust fund."

"You don't say? She didn't kill Fletcher for his money?"

"Exactly. She's got a house in Charleston, too. Goes there a lot. Probably lives there more than she lives here."

"Alone?"

"No, she travels with another woman. I haven't been able to find out who yet, it's just a matter of time."

"My mother goes to Charleston a lot. I keep thinking she has a boyfriend there."

Mart swigged his beer and winked at her. "She never told you about him?

"No, I never asked." Leighton stretched out her legs and let them hang over the deck. "I still don't know Deborah Darling's story. I mean, does she have a story, did she have any reason to have killed Fletcher?"

"We've still got a lot of digging to do,"

"You'd think Rhonda would have been the main suspect back then. I mean, he beat her. She got fed up and shot him."

"And over fifty people or so saw her at the bar

at the time of the gunshot that killed Fletcher."

"She wasn't wearing a mask?"

Mart shrugged. "Couldn't hide her voice or that deep red hair, I guess, or those long red fingernails. Besides, she was in an argument with Custer Hodge over whether or not to tear down the old movie theater."

"Well, if she was against it, she won," Leighton laughed. "it's the highlight of Pickens County."

They sat in silence and stared out at the stream. Mart finished his beer and looked over at Leighton. "Hey, how you holding up?"

"As well as I can, but I miss my husband."

"I know what you mean, I miss my wife." He reached out and held her hand.

"I'm glad we have each other," Leighton said as she brought his hand to her lips and kissed it.

Their relationship was strictly platonic. They had known each other for years and joined the police force together. Mart's wife, June, had died a few years earlier from cervical cancer and she and Beau nurtured him as they would an orphaned child. Beau cooked for him, and Leighton spent her free time hiking with him and fishing down by the river. He was like a brother to both, and June had been her friend from high school. Now she and Mart had two deaths in common, two premature, horrible deaths.

"Look into Deborah Darling's past as much as you can, will you? I need to eliminate her. She was in the alley that night. We've got to consider that. She might be lying about something."

Mart looked at her. "You don't really suspect her, do you?"

"I don't know yet. I'd just like to get past any vendetta she might have had against Jeremiah. Did she have a reason to frame Jeremiah because she killed Fletcher?" Leighton looked at Mart and raised an eyebrow. "You questioned her maid?"

"Her cook actually, but yes, I have, and she's not telling me everything she knows but she intimated that Deborah had secrets. She was evasive and she was nervous. She was afraid of saying something she shouldn't."

Mart nodded his head and took another swallow of beer. "Okay, I'll look deeper into Deborah. And if it's okay with you, I'll question her cook again."

Chapter Twelve

Dickie

Halloween 1963

"I've never gotten over you." Dickie laughed as he said it, as if it might be a joke. Leah stared at him expressionlessly. The night was dark, he could barely see her. He reached out to touch her but then he'd seen Fletcher walk toward them. He stumbled and stepped back.

"Do you think we can meet now and then?" Dickie quickly reached for her again and pulled her to him. He whispered the words close to her ear, repeated what he had just asked her. He was a bit drunk and if Fletcher had not shown up, he might have tried to kiss her.

Fletcher grabbed Leah by the arm. "We need to talk, he said."

"Can't you see that the young lady and I are talking?" Dickie stared him right in the eyes.

"Faggot," he said. "Saw you humping Abe Lincoln in a doorway." Fletcher laughed and pushed Dickie back, the beer in Dickie's paper cup spilling to the ground. He wanted to tell

Fletcher it was Lottie under the Abe Lincoln outfit, but he couldn't betray her.

"Didn't you hear what I said? Get out of here." Fletcher shoved him again and Dickie tossed the whole cup of beer at him. What was left in the cup spilled at his feet.

Fletcher wiped the beer off his face and glared at Dickie. "I could fucking kill you with my pinkie finger, asshole. Now get the hell out of here."

"What do you want with her?"

"None of your fucking business." He stood close to Dickie and scowled. "C'mon," he said as he turned back to Leah and grabbed her arm again. Dickie pulled her back.

Leah looked at Dickie. Her eyes were pinched together, and she looked angry.

"Go home to your wife, Dickie," she said. As angry as her expression was, she'd said that gently, with affection.

"Do you need my help?" he asked.

"I do not," she said.

"Okay. I can take a hint." He turned from her and walked away, wishing her well and promising himself he wouldn't ever bother speaking to her again. But as he stood in the alley, he paused at the back entrance to the bar to listen to what she and Fletcher were saying, but the noise from the bar was so damn loud. "I'm calling the cops on you," he heard her screech and he heard Fletcher's laughter, heard him say something about owning the police.

Dickie turned to enter the bar, but as he did, Leah was still screaming at Fletcher, calling him a bastard. She said she'd get him arrested; her voice rising to fever pitch. Then Dickie saw Malcolm in the darkness where Fletcher and Leah were standing. The screaming stopped for just a second. He heard voices, unable to see who stood in the shadows.

After a moment, Malcolm skipped toward him, laughing, his high heels making clicks on the cement. He said something about being late for an all-girl's party. So apparently Malcolm hadn't stopped to speak to Leah, to find out what was wrong, to ask why she was so angry. Once Malcolm passed in his most flamboyant Ginger Tea drag, Leah screamed at Fletcher again. He thought he heard her threaten to kill him. But it didn't sound like Leah at that point. Dickie realized someone else was with them, hidden in the darkness of the alley. Whoever it was, threatened Fletcher, told him to back off, or something to that effect.

Dickie fretted over what Leah was so angry about as he entered the crowded bar. He wondered if he should be chivalrous and go back outside and break up their argument, but it sounded more as if Fletcher needed the protection. He wasn't doing all the yelling, she was.

He looked for Deborah at the bar but didn't see her. He spotted Lottie talking to people he didn't recognize behind their costumes. She waved at him. About ten minutes after he'd finally found a seat at the bar and ordered another beer, he heard something like a backfire, but no one paid attention to it. He'd almost finished his beer when he heard sirens outside the alley. Someone ran in and said that Fletcher had been shot. Everyone started talking about Fletcher lying dead in the alley. Dickie assumed Leah had killed him, at least he thought she might have. He hadn't seen anyone else out there except Malcolm. However, he thought he'd heard another voice, one he didn't recognize. Dickie knew Leah sounded angry enough to kill somebody and Fletcher was the obvious target. Malcolm hadn't killed Fletcher because Malcolm had left the alley as Ginger Tea while Leah was still screaming.

Dickie shot up in bed and looked at the clock. It was eleven-thirty and he'd been lying there for an hour, unable to sleep, disturbed by what Leighton had told him about the old antique gun earlier that day, the gun that had most likely killed Fletcher Smith. He'd seen a gun collection in a mahogany case somewhere, but where? Where had he seen it? It was probably a long time ago, but he remembered staring at it. Was it in Leah's house?

He thought back to that night in 1963, he thought hard on the memory, but it was all so difficult to recall. He held it in his mind until something finally materialized, and images surfaced, his memories of that evening expanding. Then, abruptly, he remembered visiting Leah the day after Fletcher's murder. The memories fuzzy — he'd been so hung over after the night before — but he was finally able to recognize what he was looking at. He was finally able to materialize exactly what he was trying to remember. Apparently, he'd been correct, he'd been correct all along. Leah had committed that murder. She had killed Fletcher. He had seen that antique gun in her gun case.

Dickie remembered now, he had gone to see her the day after the party, the day after Fletcher was murdered. He wanted to ask her if she needed his help. He figured she must be so terribly frightened, for certainly, it was she who had shot Fletcher, must have been. Dickie decided he would help her, even lie for her if he had to.

She had been pleasant that day, yet impatient. She had led him into the library, and he kept staring at the gun case. He wanted to bring up having seen her in the alley the night before and apologize for acting like an ass. He wanted her to trust him, to turn to him.

Yes, it was becoming clearer. He had been to see her the day following the murder. His memory was disjointed but he was remembering. Quite suddenly, he decided that he had to protect her now, as he had wanted to protect her then. So, instead of going for one of his usual early morning walks, he dressed quickly and got into his car before Deborah awoke. He drove the thirty minutes it took him to park in front of Leah's house. He walked up to the front door. He was nervous. He didn't know exactly what he wanted to say to Leah, but he needed to warn her, to have her hide the gun.

She answered the door in an old shirt, gardening clogs and shorts that went to her knees. She gasped when she saw Dickie. It was as if she'd seen a ghost.

Dickie looked her over and smiled. "She gets it from you, I see."

Leah shook her head. "What?"

"Leighton," he said. "She loves to garden. Quite good at it."

"Yes, she is. How do you know she loves to garden, Dickie?"

"I spoke to her about Fletcher's murder. She came to see my wife," he said, observing the strange expression on her face. "I thought of some things that might help Leighton solve the case, so I drove by. Charming house she has."

"I had no idea you knew anything at all about

Fletcher's murder."

"You don't remember?"

"Remember what?" she asked, seemingly a bit startled.

"We spoke that night in the alley."

"I don't remember." She put her hand to her forehead. "We did?"

Dickie cleared his throat. "Can I come in?" he asked.

"Sure." She opened the door a bit further and stepped aside.

Dickie noticed how charming the house was; this spooky old house stood solid and welcoming and smelled of lavender. Or was it Leah that smelled of lavender? Dickie smiled as the memory of lavender oil filled his senses. She'd always worn it as a teenager, dabbed behind her ear where he used to nestle his head in her hair.

"You have done such a fine job with this house. Your renovations don't fight the charm but enhance it, rather." Dickie forced a smile as she led him into the parlor, and he sat in a wing chair that faced a large fireplace. The mantle was made of Turquin Blue marble.

"Is this 19th century?" he asked as he stared at it, recognizing the marble from his knowledge of 19th-century furnishings.

"Yes." She said. She sat opposite him, near a window bursting with sunlight. She offered him coffee. "Do you normally call on people so early in the morning?”

“No to both questions.” Dickie smiled.

“Do you want something from me, Dickie, or were you just passing by?”

“Passed this house a thousand times over the years. Always wanted to drop in. Just didn’t feel welcome, I guess.”

“There was no reason for you to feel that way.”

“Remember our conversation the day after Fletcher’s murder? I came by that day.”

Leah put her hand to her forehead. “I don’t remember. I’m sorry.”

“I remember you had a gun collection back in that library room.” Dickie pointed with his finger at the doors to the library. “We sat in there to talk because there was a breeze in that room, and it was so hot here. The sun was just pouring in.”

“That was a long time ago.”

“Still have the gun collection?”

She nodded her head and Dickie recalled that day in her library. He had said he wanted to see her again, as he had said the night before. Now she says she doesn’t remember. Well, maybe she doesn’t. She had told him she wouldn’t see him anyway, so what difference did it make whether she remembered or not?

Dickie shook his head as if to clear it. “You also have a son,” he said. “I remember.”

“My husband’s child. Kenny. He was barely a

teenager when I married his father."

"Yes, Leighton's stepbrother."

"That's right, they were raised as brother and sister."

"Bit of a juvenile delinquent when he was young. I remember that."

"Yes, he might have been. I'm immensely proud of him now. He owns his own car dealership."

She shifted, as if uncomfortable, and he smiled. He didn't want her to feel that way. They looked at each other awkwardly until they both spoke at the same time. Dickie stopped talking quickly.

"What do you want, Dickie, surely not to see me again after all these years?"

"No, no," he said. "I just want to ask you a few things."

"Like what?"

"Did Fletcher know that Leighton was my child? I mean, Fletcher was Walter's cousin."

Leah seemed startled and she looked at him oddly. "As far as I know, Fletcher didn't know."

"Well, Walter and Fletcher were cousins, so I just thought he'd know."

"Distant cousins, Dickie. No, he didn't know. I'm quite sure of it. Why?"

Dickie leaned forward in his chair. "Our daughter is looking into Fletcher's murder." He noticed a slight twitch in Leah's lip and wondered if she was telling the truth.

"What are you insinuating? That Black man did it, didn't he?"

Dickie told her that Jerimiah had been released from prison and watched her expression. She looked unsettled, as if she'd eaten something sour.

"Look, Leah, Fletcher could have tried to blackmail you to get you into bed. We know how he was. Fletcher was a pig. Did he threaten to tell your daughter that I was her father?"

Leah got to her feet and stared him in the face. "I was not being blackmailed, Dickie. What are you accusing me of?"

"You have that gun collection?"

"I do. I told you that."

"Any antique guns in that collection.?'

"I wouldn't know an antique gun from a banana," she said.

Dickie locked eyes with her. "Did you ever have an old Smith & Wesson?"

"We might have. My husband liked guns. I didn't. He didn't take the collection with him; his present wife doesn't like them either, but maybe he kept one or two."

"Yes, I heard you were divorced."

"Yes, we're divorced. We have been for years."

"You never remarried?"

"No, I did not."

Dickie let that sink in and then decided he was

done questioning her. If she did kill Fletcher, she certainly had years to get rid of the gun.

"Well, your daughter isn't going to come and arrest you." Dickie laughed.

"Why would she do that?" She stopped and scowled at him as if he had horns.

"Well, I hope we can be friends," he said as he walked to the door. "I've been happily married for years, you know. Pretty much right after you moved to Charleston. I have two children."

"Yes, Dickie, I know. I've met your wife a few times through mutual friends, and you introduced us once … at church."

"That so? Well, take care, Leah. I'm sure I'll see you around."

Leah's demeanor was one of ill ease; Dickie didn't know if it was because she was guilty of something or she was just annoyed.

Dickie stopped at the door and turned to her. "I would have liked to stay friends," he said. "It's a shame we didn't keep our friendship going."

"We should have remained friends, yes."

"Yes," he said as he left. "I would have liked that."

Dickie got back in his car, the desire to cry overwhelming. She was so distant. He was sure she was protecting someone, but who? Her husband was no longer in the picture. His emotions remained the way he'd felt years ago when she'd made love to him. He lamented that her feelings had to change, had to disappear, when his remained, soft, and deep, a memory he cherished and she, obviously, did not.

He drove to Lottie's and let himself in with the key she'd given him years ago. She was in the kitchen making coffee. Startled at first to see him, then her face relaxed.

"Morning sex? My God, Dickie, we haven't done that in years."

Dickie laughed. "My good woman, let's have a walk. I need to listen to your chatter as it lands like music inside my head and distracts me from the convoluted world around me. I need the wind in my face, your hand in mine."

"Not a good idea."

"I know, we might be accused of being lovers."

"*Tsk. Tsk.*"

"I hardly get it up at all anymore, not even for Deborah."

She slammed down her coffee cup and glared at him. "Not *even for* Deborah?"

"Well, darlin', she demands it of me every now and then, not too often. You know how she can be. She pulls on the damn thing until it takes on a life of its own."

"How sweet of you to share that with me, Dickie."

"Sex means nothing to me, you know that."

Some odd sound came from her mouth as she raised her eyebrows. But then she smiled. "Next Saturday night, we are going to a bar in Greenville. You are going to let your hair down, my love," she said.

Dickie shook his head. "Can't. Deborah is having a dinner party for Robbie's beau."

"Robbie doesn't have a beau, unless you mean Mindy."

"Heaven forbid." Dickie smiled. "Deborah is clueless."

"Can you get out after the dinner party?"

"Where do you want to take me?"

"Ginger is performing her Judy Garland act at this new bar. It's called Red Lady. You're coming as Deedee. No one will know you."

Dickie stood very still. "I can't do that."

"Believe me, Deborah will not be there."

He shook his head. "I can't."

"Don't you want to show your beautiful Deedee to the world?"

"Not the world, no."

She put her hand between his legs and rubbed until he grew hard.

"C'mon, sweetheart, do it for Lottie. I want to show you off."

He pushed her back into the counter, their sex was quick and what might even be called passionate.

"We've never done that before," he said

breathlessly as he zipped up his fly.

"You must come for coffee more often," she said as she closed her robe and pulled up her underwear. "that was like relieving myself of a pesky itch, hate to say."

Dickie sat on one of her kitchen chairs and grinned at her. "I'll do it, I'll sneak out. Deborah goes to bed early and she sleeps like the dead. She'll never know. That quickie you gave me has filled me with courage."

"Bless your sweet Southern soul, Miss Deedee. I'll make you up here and then we'll go. Ginger's show is at midnight, gives us plenty of time."

"I can't wait. My first night out." He put a napkin up to his lips and giggled.

Chapter Thirteen

Robbie

Robbie looked across the booth at Kenny McNeil. He was grinning at her as though she'd just allowed him to feel her up. His curly brown hair fell into his eyes, and he kept wiping it back.

"You're a dyke?"

The comment wounded Robbie as if she'd just been insulted. Yes, she was a dyke, but maybe it was the way he said it.

"Yeah," she said.

"Your mother doesn't know?"

"Nobody knows."

"And you want me to pretend I'm sleeping with you?"

"No. I want you to pretend to be going out with me. Like my boyfriend."

Kenny sat back with a thud. "I have a wife and a child, a son about your age."

"I don't care. It's not important. You just have to pretend to be my boyfriend on Saturday night when you come to dinner."

"What if it gets back to my wife?"

"Well, tell her what it's all about, that it's a

favor."

"I thought you didn't want anyone to know."

Now it was Robbie's turn to sit back with a thud. She hated this. She hated this enormous lie she had to tell. She had to pretend to like Kenny McNeil, who was probably not even five foot four. Cocky little bastard. That's what she'd always thought of him. Now she'd have to pretend that she likes men who have a brain the size of a peanut and are so old they have lines in their forehead.

What the hell was wrong with the world when her beautiful Mindy had to pretend she was leading Barney down the path of no return, when the truth was that both she and Barney were deliciously in love with the right people. My God, she thought, the heart attack her mother will have when she learns she's about to have a Black daughter-in-law and a lesbian daughter-in-law, so to speak.

Robbie passionately believed that one day it was all going to change. Gay people would be able to join the military, run the country and most importantly, marry. But for now, she was stuck in a lie, and she hated herself for telling it, for concealing the truth. She really wanted to tell her mother to go to hell. Well, so be it, the truth was all going to come out at some point. It had to. Then she'd be disowned, for sure. Her father would be so disappointed that his pretty little girl wasn't the least bit interested in boys. They were jerks, most of them, except for her brother. He was interesting and charismatic, and he loved her, no matter what. She couldn't even say that about her father. She had no idea what her father thought about anything, except for his liberal politics, which Robbie gave him a lot of credit for. She was quite sure her father would accept her, if she told him, but he was under her mother's thumb. If her mother said "Get out of this house and don't come back, you pervert," she was sure her father would keep his mouth shut and let her go.

"What do I have to do, hold your hand?" Kenny looked at her with a wink.

"Just pretend to think I'm the living end." Asshole, she wanted to add but didn't. "And get my mother off my back."

Chapter Fourteen

Leah McNeil

Leah took the back roads as she always had and followed a rocky path to the back of Rhonda's gracious home. She entered through the large kitchen as she had been doing for years. Grayson asked if she wanted coffee, which she always asked, and which Leah always accepted. Leah took a chair at the old pine kitchen table and watched Grayson work her magic, a magic Leah always tried to replicate, but failed at miserably. Her coffee was not nearly as strong and not nearly as aromatic as the steaming cup of java placed before her that hinted at a taste of pecans.

"Thank you, Grayson," Leah said. "Tell me, do you chop up pecans for the filter?"

Grayson laughed. "You ask me that every single morning and every single morning, I'm telling you the same. No, ma'am, just chocolate, not pecans."

"Chocolate? Really?" Leah took a sip, "Smells like pecans. I'm going to keep asking you till you tell me the truth."

Grayson shook her head and laughed. "No

pecans. I think you think I'm hiding something from you. There's no secret to the coffee, just make sure the beans are from the cliffs of Jamaica."

"Jamaica, huh? You never mentioned that."

Grayson shook her head from side to side. "You don't listen, Leah, too busy thinking your next thought. It drowns out all my answers."

Leah smiled. "Miss Julia Sugarbaker still asleep?"

That was their private joke, referring to Rhonda as 'Miss Julia Sugarbaker' from the only television comedy Leah loved, *Designing Women*. She watched it with her son, who thought Julia Sugarbaker was the quintessence of femininity. The similarities between them were the large Antebellum house, Julia's striking looks, and maybe just more than a hint of the liberal politics she often pontificated about, as if she were running for office, so much like Rhonda.

Grayson laughed. "She is as knocked out as a piece of veal under my mallet, soon to be a cutlet on your plate. Where'd you two go last night, how many bars?"

"Now you know we are never seen in public together."

"Then you two had your own party. Lord, that woman can drink."

"Lord, that woman can sleep." Leah grinned at her. "I think I shall pay a visit to Miss

Sugarbaker and breathe some life back into that pretty head."

"Miss Sugarbaker's coffee, Leah?" She held out the cup. "You forget Miss Sugarbaker's coffee, she'll lynch you from that tree out there even though you ain't Black."

Leah laughed. "Ouch."

Grayson handed her the bone china cup and saucer. The bone china cup being the only cup Rhonda would allow into her bedroom, certainly she'd cringe at ceramic or, God forbid, plastic. The steaming latte would be received like rubies from a Burmese mine, but only in its china cup.

Leah took her two cups of coffee and walked through the house and up the familiar stairs to Rhonda's familiar bedroom. She placed Rhonda's coffee on the bedside table. She went to the windows and drew the drapes, revealing the very naked body of her lover, wearing only night shades and rings with the glitter of diamonds.

"Rise and shine, darlin'."

Leah knew only too well that one "rise and shine" would not produce the desired effect, that it would take at least three more clarion calls and one very wet morning kiss, but it would be the ear nibbles that would do it, would finally tempt Rhonda's beautiful grey eyes to open, resembling the sky after a storm, settling their ominousness on hers.

Rhonda had the most resplendent view from

her bedroom windows of the greenest grass and most musical trees, swaying limbs like accepting arms. Honeysuckles and Magnolias were everywhere, as picturesque as the dawn with its dappled hues of pink and blue.

She watched Rhonda turn onto her back, one of the three body movements that led to the full-body mouth-opening yawn. That was when she awoke, eyes open with an almost startled look as she gazed upon Leah, as if wondering who the hell she was when every morning — well, nearly every morning — Leah was there, one way or the other.

Leah sat on the edge of the bed and stared at Rhonda, remembering how easy it was to throw caution to the wind so many years ago and allow this beautiful woman to mount her like some warm, sensual goddess, despite Leah's protests of "I'm not queer, get off me", and then finally feeling her body go limp under Rhonda's. She'd been limp and then tense and then limp again, as if an ocean had provided waves of passionate swells, terribly frightening and ferocious. She hadn't been able to control her sexual moaning and ecstatic indistinct murmurs. It was a ride like no other she had ever taken.

Leah was working as a waitress in Charleston practically up until the moment she gave birth, and there was Rhonda by her side. Then Walter showed up to offer the conventions of marriage, to convince her, to tell her why it made sense, to insist that their children needed homes. To lament that his wife had left him without a forwarding address — he was devastated and his son was devastated — poor little Kenny needed a mother and, naturally, Leah's daughter would need a father.

It was weeks after Walter proposed, and the baby was born, that Rhonda made love to her, suddenly and with great passion, so much so that Leah resisted at first, confused as she was by something so foreign as another woman finding her attractive. But at some point, she could not resist the magic of the ride she was on, the altitudinous drug she had taken. The drug was Rhonda herself, professing her love, her body, and her emotional allurement, all of which swept Leah up onto the avenue of no return.

Leah married Walter and persuaded him to move with her to Pickens to open his hardware store, where both she and her secret lover, Rhonda, were perfectly acceptable in the Southern small town in which they lived, with its conventional laws and its aversion to all things considered "unnatural".

Rhonda's husband, however, was a monster and left so many bruises on Rhonda's body that Leah often fantasized about killing him, or at least praying for his demise in some horrific car accident in which his body would be torn to shreds in the wreck. The son of a bitch beat his wife for what he suspected she did, none of which she did: there were no other men, just Leah. When Fletcher found out his wife engaged in unnatural sexual acts, which he was bound to discover, he was so stunned, he had stayed away from her, not understanding this peculiar madness. But, unsurprisingly, he went back to beating her, threatening that if she didn't stop seeing Leah, he would kill them both. He avoided bruises on Rhonda's beautiful face, but her body was not as apparent. So, the purple, and black sores on her body were covered in pancake makeup, if not long pants, and long sleeves, even in the heat of summer.

Fletcher told Walter his wife was a lesbian and poor Walter put two and two together; it explained why Leah shunned his advances so much of the time. He took his own lovers and eventually divorced his wife. Leah was happy, happy too, after Fletcher's head was blown off that night in '63. She and Rhonda saw each other as much as possible after that, avoiding rumor by never letting anyone see them together, at least not in Pickens or any neighboring town. Not even Leah's children knew of their relationship. They were able to be much more open in Charleston, where they kept a second home, for their histories there were of little interest to most. No one knew either of them well. Rhonda was regarded as that poor widow, and her friend, Leah, dismissed as an unfortunate divorcee. Just two more unfortunate women without men. No one knew how to include them, so they were both pretty much avoided.

Leah was the first thing Rhonda saw when she opened her eyes. She reached out her hand and pulled Leah close.

"Good morning, darlin'," she said.

Leah bent to kiss her cheek. "Dickie Darling has been to see me," she said.

"Dickie? What did he want?"

"He asked me if I had an antique gun."

Rhonda sat up and reached for her coffee. "What did you tell him?"

"That I did not have an antique gun."

Rhonda sipped the coffee and sat back. "Don't worry," Rhonda said. "We're safe. There is no antique gun." She looked into Leah's eyes, her own wide and unblinking. Then she smiled.

Leah looked at her over the rim of her cup. "My daughter is on Fletcher's case, a 'cold' case she calls it. She'll solve it. She's incredibly good at what she does."

"Yes, she's been to see me."

Now it was Leah's turn to raise her eyebrows. "And?"

Rhonda put her cup down and brought Leah

back into her arms. "It's all going to be perfectly fine. It can't be solved. Witnesses?"

Leah shrugged her shoulders. They sat sipping their coffee for a while and then Leah moved to the chair opposite the bed.

"He's still in love with me, you know."

"Who is still in love with you? Certainly not Walter."

Leah laughed. "No, Dickie Darling."

"Oh, the cross-dresser, your old beau."

"Very old beau, but I think he believes he's protecting me from something."

Rhonda put her coffee down and stretched out her arms. "Good. He owes you for never blabbing about his idiosyncrasies to anyone."

"Except you." Leah smiled. "Oh, yes, and Ginger."

"I wish we could live together and to hell with rumor and conjecture. It's as if we were ugly. Just two poor celibate creatures who can't attract men."

Leah stood up and returned to the bed. "We could live together if we moved somewhere else, where no one knows us, where no one would murder us for being queer as frost flowers."

Rhonda laughed and took her hand. "We have Charleston."

"We don't live in Charleston," Leah said. "We just visit there. I want to live somewhere together."

"We have set up a house in Charleston."

"The whole town thinks we're gay, I'm sure."

"They don't even know what the word means, except in terms of 'happy.' So, they think we're happy, do they?"

Leah's eyes were sad, filmy the way they got when she was about to cry. She looked away.

"Leah, I can't sell this house," Rhonda said. "It's my history. Charleston will have to do. We have a life there, be it part-time or not, it's still a life.'"

"I'm not asking you to sell this house, but we could let someone live in it. Let Grayson have it."

Rhonda laughed. "I would like nothing more than to give this house to Grayson so her family could get out of that rickety old shack they live in, but the historical society of the South's most historic homes would have me murdered. They would kill me if I let a family of Negros live in one of the South's most coveted historical plantations."

Leah laughed. "You can afford to keep it maintained and we could live somewhere else."

"I love it here, Leah. I refuse to run away. Besides, I think we have a perfectly fine life."

"We have a fine unauthentic life." Leah sighed. "Let's pretend then, pretend we move to Charleston or Savanah, or some other wonderful place. How about Chicago?"

Rhonda made a face. "You've got to be

kidding. Chicago?"

Leah scurried up to the pillow next to Rhonda. "Will we take Ginger with us when we move?" Leah asked, and they both started to laugh.

"'Bout time I divorced her. No, we will not take Ginger. But we best stay close enough to get wind of any pillow talk she might decide to whisper to some hunky fag she finds on one of her late-night strolls through the park."

"Then I guess we'll have to shoot her. Big mouths need to be shut."

"You think she's been silent all these years?" Rhonda asked.

"I think if she hadn't been silent, my daughter would be beating down our door."

Rhonda smiled and pulled her close.

"Will you just consider it, Rhonda?" Leah asked.

"Consider what?"

"Moving to Charleston full time."

She heard Rhonda sigh, which she assumed was better than nothing.

Chapter Fifteen

Leah McNeil

Halloween Night 1963

Ginger swept through the room looking like Lauren Bacall, a glamour girl with a cigarette in her hand and a wise-cracking expression on her face.

"The bastard is dead? Girls, is it true?" She stared at Rhonda, who was on the couch holding Leah's hand. "Has justice finally come to Dodge City, Kansas?"

"It's three in the morning, how did you get in?" Rhonda looked at her and scowled.

"Your door was ajar. You must have been so upset, you raced home in tears." Ginger threw her hands in the air and shook her head. "Poor dear. Anyway, your house is all lit up from the road. I knew you must be up tonight singing your praises to the devil that took him."

"You look beautiful," Leah said through her sniffles."

"Thank you, honey." Ginger sat beside them on the couch. "What happened to you?" She looked intently at Leah. "That bruise on your face looks like an eggplant."

"It's nothing, really, I must have fallen..."

"He's dead," Rhonda interrupted.

Ginger sat back. "Yes, I heard, and I didn't rush over here to say I'm sorry, either. Well, one more bastard off the earth." She stared at the two of them and finally asked the inevitable question. "Who did it?"

"He was shot through the head." Leah put her hand on Ginger's, "The bullet went through his forehead."

"I didn't ask you how, I asked you who?"

Both women shook their heads. "Who knows?" Rhonda looked up at Ginger. "Do you really care who killed him?"

"No, girl," Ginger said. "Of course not."

Rhonda sighed. "I still find it hard to believe. I have to bury the son of a bitch."

"That Black guy, Jeremiah Lennox, was in the alley. Someone said he did it." Ginger looked back at Leah and Rhonda on the couch. "Least, that's what I heard. Isn't that ridiculous? Jeremiah couldn't hurt a fly. He's too pretty for violence. That boy would look gorgeous in drag."

"They're going to have to blame someone," Rhonda said. "No one liked Fletcher, but money talks. They respected him even though there was nothing to respect but his bank account. He was a bastard, but they'll blame the first person they can think of for this."

"Well then, I'd say that the bastard has met his maker and let his maker deal with him. What say we celebrate?" Ginger went to Rhonda's bar and poured herself a drink. "C'mon, girls, the witch is dead."

"Where were you?" Rhonda asked.

"An all-girl's party," she said and laughed. Ginger looked at their baffled expressions. "Oh, you know, I went as Belle Watling to Smith's but me and the girls had planned our own party, so I had to leave. We were just hanging out, working on some routines and then Sylvia, you know Sylvia? She wears those short skirts up to the slit in her ass, what a slut that girl is. Anyway, she comes busting in to tell us someone put a hole in Fletcher's head. C'mon ya all, smile. It's party time." Ginger held up her glass. "Don't ya think?"

Leah sighed loudly and then started to cry again.

"Jesus, Leah, what are you crying about? This leaves you two free to do your thing. You should be dancing in the middle of the room." Ginger got up and put on music. "Enjoy your good fortune, ladies." She started to twirl to 'One Fine Day.' "Me and the girls are working up a Chiffons' routine." She did a few steps and turned back to them. "What do you think?"

Rhonda put her arm around Leah and hugged her while Leah continued to cry. Ginger stopped dancing and turned to them. "Good God, one of you did it… which one of you bitches did it? Was it you, Leah, that what you're crying about? He give you that eggplant on your cheek?"

"Go home, Ginger," Rhonda said.

"I saw Leah and Fletcher arguing out there." She walked over closer to the couch and peered down at them. "Remember? I passed you in the alley and, yes, now I remember, it was you, Leah. You were threatening him to death. Jesus, do I have to tell the police that? They'll arrest you. Oh my God, I can't incriminate you. You're my best friend."

Leah did not respond, just held on more tightly to Rhonda. "You going to tell the police that, Ginger?" Rhonda asked. "You want to see Leah arrested?"

Ginger put her cigarette out. "I just said I couldn't do that. No, of course not, I couldn't. You're my best friends, both of you. I won't say anything."

"Until you get angry at one of us and change your mind," Rhonda said as she stared into Ginger's eyes. Then she turned back to Leah. "At the slightest provocation, she'll blab to whoever will listen. She'll say you did it."

Ginger jumped up. "How could I say that? I didn't see her shoot anyone?" Ginger put her hands on her hips and rolled her eyes.

"You tell the police she was arguing with

Fletcher and that's the assumption they'll come to." Rhonda glared at her.

"Motive?" Ginger asked. She looked from one woman to the other. "Well, what the hell would she shoot him for?"

"For threatening to kill *me*," Rhonda shouted.

"Yeah, then the whole damn town will put it together and surmise that Rhonda and I are wrinkling up the sheets together." Leah glared at her. "There's motive for you."

"Oh, who cares what a bunch of bigots think?" Ginger made a face and lit another cigarette. When she looked up, Rhonda and Leah had gone off to the other room and were huddled together, obviously something they didn't want Ginger to hear. She smoked the whole cigarette before they walked back in.

"What was that huddle about?" Ginger asked. "You're making me feel like a traitor. You going to shoot me, too?"

"How can we assure your silence?" Rhonda handed Leah a tissue and she blew her nose. "We don't want to shoot you, Ginger."

Ginger jumped back. "Jesus," she said. "I guess I should say thank you."

"Only kidding, but we don't need someone spreading a rumor like that about Leah." Rhonda met her eyes and held them as she said it. "They're likely to torment her children and torch her house. Not bad enough she killed a man, she's also a dyke."

"Oh, come on now." Ginger took a chair and sat back and blew the smoke out of her mouth and through her teeth. "Clear case of self-defense. Look at that bruise on her."

"You think Leah killed Fletcher?" Rhonda glared at Ginger.

"I saw the two of them arguing with my own two eyes. Sure sounded like she could have."

"She didn't do it," Rhonda said and stood over Ginger, her hands on the arm of her chair.

"Have the police been here?" Ginger asked.

"Yes," Rhonda said. "They have been here with their bad news. They left after ten minutes."

Ginger didn't say anything for several seconds. She sat back and looked at both women, who had the most serious expressions she'd ever seen on either of them.

"Buy my silence," she said to Rhonda. "I'd rather marry you than be shot by you." She grinned. "Then I won't say anything about the argument you had with him moments before he was shot." She pursed her lips and stared at Leah.

"Be serious," Leah said.

"I am serious." Ginger glared at Leah.

"What will that prove?" Rhonda asked.

"Marry me," she said as she looked back at Rhonda. "And prove that I am worthy."

Rhonda threw herself on the couch, her mouth literally falling open. "Are you crazy? You want it all, is that it? Anyway, I can't prove you worthy."

"I need credibility," she said. "No one takes me seriously. Not that I care, but I need to make a living. No one wants to hire me. I graduated college suma cum laude, but people still think I'm an idiot, think I'm strange. If I were married to you, not one man, woman or child in this town wouldn't respect me, wouldn't step aside for me, wouldn't offer me the best job they had because you think I'm an okay man. They'll just think you have a taste for eccentricity, that's all."

"You're serious?" Rhonda looked back at Leah who was just staring at Ginger like she'd lost her mind. Then Leah stood and walked over to Rhonda. "I think this is blackmail, don't you?"

"Oh, c'mon, Ladies, blackmail? Oh no, I won't tell the police anything, you don't have to marry me, Rhonda." Ginger put her head in her hands. "Sorry I even brought it up."

"What will it take to assure you never tell the police that we were arguing with Fletcher in the alley?" Rhonda glared at him.

"We? I just saw Leah arguing with him."

Rhonda smiled at her. "Maybe you were too busy dangling your bracelets in the air to see anyone else."

Ginger was visibly trying to remember but obviously couldn't. "So, you did it, you shot him?"

"C'mon, what will it take to shut your mouth?"

Rhonda came close to her face as she spoke.

"One hundred thousand dollars and your hand in marriage. In name only, of course. I don't want to sleep with you." Ginger looked at her with her lips set, as if she wouldn't take no for an answer. "My lips are sealed if you agree. If you don't, I just might get loose at the lips and bring more suspicion on your head than you can imagine. There, how's that for blackmail?"

"You bastard," Leah said.

"Self-preservation, dear. I need to be legitimized."

Rhonda laughed. "Yep, you're quite correct, married to me, you'll go from freak to eccentric in a minute. Southern towns don't bat an eye at eccentricity."

The three of them stood there looking at the floor until finally, Rhonda broke the silence. "We need to protect each other." She looked at Leah. "I don't want the police interrogating me, or you."

"They're going to interrogate you, you were his wife," Leah said.

"But I don't own the gun that shot him. No one saw me in that alley. Besides, I was out on the patio where the barbeque was when we all heard what we thought was a backfire. I was with five or six people."

"They'll figure you had a lover who shot him. They'll go to great lengths to find out who that person is. I can see the headlines now, 'Love Triangle Ends in Tragedy.'" Leah sat back and sighed. "We'll be found out."

"I don't think it's possible for them to discover who my lover really is …" Rhonda said.

"Well, they'd have to prove you had a lover," Ginger said. "How they going to do that?"

Leah went to Rhonda and took her hand. "I'm not so sure no one knows. God, they could interrogate poor Grayson and she might let it slip."

"Grayson would never tell them anything. Look, the police don't need to know we were the last people to see him alive, do they?" Rhonda turned to Ginger. "You are the only person who can tell the police you saw us arguing."

"My lips are sealed." Ginger smiled as she put her finger to her mouth and zipped it. "Besides, I never saw *you*."

Leah nodded. "If she marries you, you'll make a fool out of her showing up in drag all over town."

"She's above gossip. They'll just think of her as eccentric, the way they think of me. I'm out of drag more than I'm in it, anyway."

Rhonda looked back at Leah, "See how much I love you, darlin'," she said. "I'd do anything for you, and this most certainly is doing anything for you."

Ginger played with her hair while she waited

for a response. Finally, Rhonda walked to her. She leaned down to her eye level. "You can live in the south wing of the house. It's the old servant's quarters, but it's been renovated. There is a private entrance. I will transfer one hundred thousand dollars into your account but no more, so get a job, Ginger. There will be a prenup. I will protect Leah. If I die, Ginger, you won't benefit all that much. You keep your fucking mouth shut and it's a deal."

"Marriage to you is benefit enough," Ginger said.

"And if we ever find out you sang to the police about Leah's little disagreement in the alley with Fletcher, or anyone else for that matter, your reputation won't hold up anywhere in the state of South Carolina. Your bank account will disappear. You'll never work again, except as a drag queen who make what? Fifty dollars a show?"

"Oh, girls, you two are my best friends. I would never say anything to anyone."

"Then watch your drinking," Rhonda said.

Ginger laughed loudly. "You think I'd mess up a marriage like this?" She laughed. "Malcolm will not only be safe, but he'll also be envied. You are rich and beautiful, what more could a girl ask for?"

Leah leaned over and kissed Rhonda on the cheek. "Thank you," she said.

"Everyone knew he beat you up, don't you think you'd get off, self-defense?" Ginger said. "I feel just terrible asking you to marry me. I think you'd get off. If you did it, that is. You can afford the best attorney in the county."

"I didn't do it, Ginger. And I'd prefer not to go through the emotional roller coaster of a trial, and I don't want Leah to go through that, either." Rhonda smiled at Leah and took her hand. "Everything will be alright now. No one has any reason to suspect us of anything."

Chapter Sixteen

Robbie

Robbie had no doubt her mother was about to have a heart attack as she glared at her jeans and man's tailored shirt, Robbie's favorite, with light blue stripes. On her feet, she wore her high-top Nike's.

"My Lord," her mother gasped. "You're not going to wear that?"

"What would you have me wear, Mother, ballerina slippers and a tutu?"

"You're going on a date… don't you want to look feminine?"

"Not particularly."

Deborah stormed off and a moment later, dragged Barnaby in by the arm. "Look who I found downstairs picking through tonight's dinner? I hope your hands are clean, Barnaby."

"Clean as a freshly shampooed poodle, Mother."

"Tell your sister what men like, and while you're at it, tell her what they don't like. They don't like girls who look like boys."

"You just answered your own question,

Mother. Answered it with your own opinion, I might add."

Barnaby turned to leave, but Deborah elbowed him back into Robbie's room. "Go on and tell her what men like, Barnaby. Your sister is clueless."

Barnaby sat at the edge of Robbie's bed and rubbed his chin. "Well, let's see," he said. "To be honest, men like kinky sex, sports bars and a good cigar." He looked up at his sister. "Do you smoke?" He heard his mother gasp a huge intake of air.

"Teasing your sister is not being fair to her." She stomped her foot and left the room but not before telling Robbie she would be an old maid.

"Your beau is downstairs," Barnaby said. "He looks good for a short fellow, very appealing, got great hair."

"Is Mindy here?"

"My date, or should I say, the love of your life, is downstairs wearing some sort of vest that appears to be from an Indian reservation, lots of beads. Oh, and Birkenstock clogs that make her look like a hippie and shorts that are far too high on her thigh for Mother's taste. You should have seen the look poor Mindy got. Mother certainly doesn't hide her feelings. She gave me a rather scathing grimace, as if I were the one in the short shorts."

They were all out on the porch as she and Barnaby approached, sipping sweet tea. All except for Deborah and Dickie, who were drinking a rather delicious-looking pink daiquiri with lots of ice.

"I'll have one of those," Robbie said as she pointed to her father's drink and smiled at Deasia.

"You can get sweet tea, chile, but you get no kick in your sweet tea and when you turn eighteen, you still get sweet tea and no kick."

"And when I'm forty?"

Deasia grinned. "Still sweet tea and no kick long as I'm here waiting on you."

Robbie smiled despite herself; the day Deasia let her have alcohol was not on anyone's calendar.

"And when you're fifty, I'll make you a pink peppermint cocktail. I put a bit of sugar in it for the kick." Deasia smiled as she retreated toward the kitchen and Robbie called out to her to hold the peppermint and add the kick or she wouldn't drink it.

"When hell freezes, I'll add the kick," Deasia called back. "You can't hold a teaspoon of gin, girl."

Robbie made a face at Deasia's back and shrugged her shoulders.

She heard her mother laugh, and as she turned to Kenny, she said, "My daughter doesn't drink, smoke or cuss. What more can you ask for in a lady?"

"It's what I love about her, Mrs. Darling. She's more of a lady than the Queen of England."

Robbie caught Kenny's wink from behind her mother's back and gritted her teeth. She wondered how she would get through this dinner party, listening to mundane chatter, accepting Kenny's flirtations with good humor, and keeping her eyes off Mindy's bodice, which bounced from her white pinot noir blouse like mounds of freshly whipped cream.

Suddenly, Deborah grabbed her daughter by the elbow and whispered in her ear. "How old is that man, Robinette?"

"Kenny? Oh, he's under sixty for sure, Mother."

She felt her mother's squeeze on her elbow and let out a sharp cry.

The dinner conversation began with talk of Princess Diana and how she sued a newspaper over photographs taken of her at a gym. Barnaby said he hadn't seen them but was sure she looked lovely in workout clothes. Kenny agreed and mentioned his crush on Mia Farrow while Mindy and Robbie raised their eyes.

"Do you think Mia Farrow is pretty, Daddy?" Robbie asked.

"Personally, I prefer Natalie Wood... she looks

like my wife." He smiled at Deborah who sat at the opposite end of the table, smiling back.

"But is she as proper as your wife?" Deborah smiled. "I mean, she is an actress, and they can be well, you know, less than proper."

"What a proper observation, Mother," Barnaby said. "What does it mean to be proper?"

"Why, Barnaby, surely you know."

Barnaby looked around the table. "Surely I don't."

Deborah looked at Kenny. "What a kidder." She laughed self-consciously.

"And so?" Barnaby leaned forward and stared at his mother, demanding an answer.

"Why, it means, Barnaby, to be a good Christian, faithful to your spouse and nurturing to your children." Deborah grinned while she sipped a glass of water.

It crossed Robbie's mind that she looked like the cat who had swallowed the canary, satiated on her own inflated opinions.

After they all had coffee and some of Deasia's home-baked pecan cookies in the parlor, Robbie found herself alone with Kenny and Mindy while Barnaby excused himself, most likely to report back to Prissy, who was waiting for him at the cottage.

"I want to take you somewhere special tonight," Kenny said, looking at Robbie. "How late can you stay out?"

"Where do you want to take me?" she asked.

"It's a surprise, but you're going to love it." He looked at Mindy. "You, too. Trust me, this place is like nowhere you've ever been before."

Robbie brushed her hand up against Mindy's. "What do you think?"

Mindy hiked herself up on the porch railing and gave Kenny a puzzled look. "Why would you want to take us anywhere?"

Kenny grinned at them. "It's over in Greenville on a secluded road you need radar to find. You'll be able to kiss each other right out in the open. It's a gay bar buried in the thickest of brush, in the darkest part of the forest. I suggest we take our flashlights." He grinned.

"How would you know about a place like that?" Mindy asked.

"My mother has a friend, a drag-queen artist. He's putting on a show there at midnight." Kenny stared at them with a wide grin. "Will your mom let you go?"

"Hell, no," Robbie said as she hiked herself up on the porch rail next to Mindy. "But I could say I'm staying at Mindy's." She looked at Mindy. "Do you want to go?"

"Hell, yeah, I've always wanted to go to a gay bar." Mindy was just about to put her arm around Robbie's shoulder when Deborah walked out on the porch.

"Where is my son?" she asked, smiling at

Kenny.

"He said he forgot something." Kenny winked at Robbie.

"We're all going to meet over at Mindy's later. I think I'll just sleep over."

"You do that, honey." Deborah reached out and clasped Kenny's hand in hers. "It is so nice to meet you, Kenny. You come on back now, you hear?" Then she reached over and whispered in his ear. "I think you need to date girls your own age."

Chapter Seventeen

Dickie

Dickie sat at the bar with a fingernail at his lip. He smiled at Lottie, who brushed back some hair from his blonde wig. His legs crossed behind his skirt, the low black blouse he wore had ruffled sleeves and showed off the cleavage that separated his very adequate breasts, not too big, not too small.

"Where in God's name have you brought me, Lottie. I think I'm surrounded by queers," he whispered.

Lottie laughed and stirred her scotch and soda, sucking the swizzle stick like licorice. "I swear, you're prettier than any woman in here, but those drag queens are giving you a run for your money." She rubbed his leg. "Aren't they gorgeous?"

"They think we're lesbians, don't they?"

Lottie gave him one of her large guffaws. "No labels here, my love. Just be."

"Isn't that the mantra of some cult or other?"

"I think it's a Buddha mantra, darlin'."

Whitney Houston's "I Wanna Dance with

Somebody" was playing out loud and strong and there were women in tuxedos dancing on top of the bar.

"This place is wild," Dickie said as he kissed her cheek.

"So nice to be out in public with you, my sweet."

Now it was Dickie's turn to laugh. He put his hand over hers. A woman in a suit crushed him at the bar and offered him a cigarette. He shook his head. "This lady prefers pipes," he said.

Lottie grinned and looked the woman in the eye. "She's with me," she said with a wink.

"Oh? You don't look like her type." The woman ordered a screwdriver and left.

"God, what the hell does she think your type is, some female lumberjack?"

"I guess anything goes in this place." Dickie looked out over the very varied crowd. He didn't necessarily feel connected, but he was having fun. He'd never seen Ginger's show, so he was looking forward to it. Somehow Ginger found out he liked to wear women's clothes and ingratiated himself in Dickie's life. Though Dickie was polite, he never reciprocated the obvious request of friendship. He kept a polite distance but always conjectured how Ginger found out about him. Ginger had approached him as if they were best friends and offered one of his hand-me-down dresses.

"Can't get into this one anymore," he'd said. "It's Dolce and Gabbana. Hate to part with it, but it will look smashing on you."

Dickie had been somewhat appalled but not in the least embarrassed. The only other person who knew about his cross-dressing aside from Lottie, was Leah. He didn't think Leah knew Ginger, so he questioned Lottie about it incessantly, demanding to know how she could reveal something so intimate. Lottie finally refused to see him if he didn't stop hounding her about it.

"I'm not saying this again, Dickie," she said." I didn't say a word to Ginger. Ginger's got radar so just shut up about it, or I swear you'll never see me again."

Close to midnight, the noise level intense, the bar had filled with people. Dickie noticed a teenager in the crowd, a friend of Robbie's. She looked right at him without recognizing him, or so he hoped.

Relieved, he whispered to Lottie, "Dickie Darling does not exist tonight." The last thing he wanted was to be outed.

"That's good, darlin'," Lottie said. "But Deedee does. She deserves to be seen."

The drag queens were stunning, certainly rivaling the female population of Pickens. There were the most ordinary-looking men there, not necessarily attractive but with obvious interest in scoring an evening with one of the most beguiling drag queens, perfectly duplicating actresses like Vanessa Williams or Penelope Cruz. And of course, there were the men with chiseled faces and effeminate affectations, who appeared to be as perfect as a Ken doll but with sarcasm dribbling on their lips as salient as their good looks.

"They're all here to see Ginger. What a diverse following she has." Lottie looked around the room, admiring the crowd.

Dickie turned to Lottie. "None of these drag queens are ugly," he said. "Why is that, they're really men? Men who look like men underneath all that makeup, men with face stubble and jock straps."

"Men with an artistic flair for making themselves beautiful." Lottie kissed his cheek. "Like you, and personally I prefer that to the real thing. I'm going to give you a makeup lesson."

"I am not a drag queen," he said indignantly. "I am the real thing, and I don't need a makeup lesson."

Lottie smiled and kissed him again. "I have the best of both worlds, don't I? I have my man and the woman behind my man."

The music stopped, and Garland's Trolley song came blasting out of the speakers. A few seconds after that, Ginger emerged in a pair of black netted stockings and a tuxedo top. He danced all over the stage with a cane, exactly like Judy herself with his dark wig and his large dark eyes.

Dickie laughed loudly. "Is that him singing?" He asked Lottie but when he turned to her, she was ashen, her face frozen in an odd expression.

"What is it?" Dickie asked. "For God's sake Lottie. You're scaring me. You look like you're staring into the eyes of a tiger."

"Don't look now, Dickie, but your daughter is sitting in a booth across the room."

"What?" Rigid, he stood perfectly still while the room was singing along with Ginger. "We have to get out of here."

"I don't think we can get out of here without being seen by her."

"Shit," Dickie said.

Lottie lit a cigarette while Dickie turned his back to the stage, hoping that would hide him from his daughter's eyes. In the mirror in front of him, he saw her falling into Mindy with affectionate strokes to her cheek.

"Kenny O'Neill is heading over here," she whispered in his ear. "What next?"

"Oh, my God," he said. "I just had dinner with the son of a bitch."

Kenny inched himself in next to Dickie, who remained in profile. After Kenny ordered a gin and tonic and three screwdrivers, he leaned in over Dickie and spoke to Lottie.

"I see there are some straight people in here tonight." He winked at her.

"Hello, Kenny," she said. "Your mother know you're here?"

"Old enough to go where I want." He laughed. "I see your sense of humor is intact."

"Didn't think you'd have any interest in a place like this," Lottie said.

"Ginger is a friend of my mother's," he told her. "What about you, what are you doing here?" Kenny stared at her and raised his eyebrows, as if disentangling his confusion.

"Ginger is my friend too."

"Oh."

Although visible in the mirror behind the bar, Dickie feared if he turned around, his daughter would be more likely to notice him. Kenny was smiling into his image, staring at him in a most unusual way. Dickie had no place to hide.

"This is Deedee, she's from out of town." Lottie put her hand on Dickie's shoulder. "I wanted to show her our most amusing sights."

Dickie held out his hand, his skin on fire. Kenny gave him a brief handshake.

"Ginger is quite good, don't you think?" He looked at Lottie in the mirror as well and when his drinks came, he asked the bartender to have them brought to his table. After he took a few bills out of his wallet and left them on the bar, he leaned into Dickie.

"I won't tell anyone," he said.

Dickie watched him walk off and then put his

face in his hands. "I need to leave."

Lottie took his hand. "Come on, walk on my right side. I think it's crowded enough to make it to the exit without being seen by Robbie. She might not recognize you, Dickie."

"Why did I ever let you talk me into this?" He scowled at her. "I will hate you till my dying day. Of course, she'll know it's me."

"Pull yourself together, Dickie. The world is not black and white, and neither are the people in it." She pulled him close. "Trust your daughter a little more than this. Who we love is a little more complicated than Deborah thinks, but your daughter has an open mind. She won't judge you."

"Shut up, Lottie, and get me the hell out of here. And make sure my daughter doesn't see me. I don't give a shit how open her mind is, I can't let her see me like this. I will call that man a liar if he tells her."

"This is the perfect opportunity for you to be honest with your daughter."

"That little bastard will tell her, won't he?"

Lottie didn't answer, just guided him out of the door as quickly as she could.

Dickie and Lottie entered the dark parking lot and got about halfway to their car when Dickie saw a fist come at his face. It was so quick and as he fell back, he saw Lottie shoved into a car with some man yelling, "Faggots, fucking faggots." The man was punching Lottie hard in the stomach. Dickie called out to her and the fists pummeled him again and knocked him to the ground. He tried to reach Lottie, but the man pounded him repeatedly. He tasted blood in his mouth. A man was holding up his wig and kicking him in the gut. Dickie tried to crawl away, but was pulled up by his neck and slammed back on the ground, once, twice, and then three times.

Someone was screaming, it pierced the night, and the men ran away. The screams kept coming and he called for Lottie. He couldn't see her. But he thought he saw his daughter cradling his head in her arms and crying. He must have passed out.

He awoke only moments later when he felt himself lifted into an ambulance. The sirens were still going off. "Lottie," he called. His daughter's tears fell on his face. His blood was everywhere, his pretty blouse torn to shreds. His breast forms were around his neck.

"Shush, Daddy," he heard his daughter say. "Don't speak."

"Lottie?" he asked. "Have to help her. I have to help her."

"They took her to the hospital. That's where they're taking you."

He closed his eyes. He thinks he must have slept for hours, either that or they knocked him out with the syringe they stuck in his arm, and he slept for just minutes. The next thing he remembered was the white room, the white robes of the doctor, and his wife Deborah, weeping in the corner of the room. He closed his eyes and pretended to sleep.

Chapter Eighteen

Robbie

Robbie looked around the waiting room because she heard her mother screaming but she didn't know where the screams were coming from. They reverberated off the walls. Her mother must have been at the front desk intimidating young nurses and infuriating older ones. She was screaming so loudly, Robbie heard the rawness in her throat. Robbie put her hands to her forehead and scrubbed until her skin felt as if it had been scrubbed away. She was sure she'd been sitting in that waiting room for hours, but it was all a blur. She had no recollection of walking into the waiting room. She must have been led in and helped to sit, soothed with the soda bottle she found in her hand. She was so shaky. Someone must have called her mother. Robbie certainly hadn't. She didn't know what to do. She felt Mindy reach for her, squeeze her arm tentatively.

"I think your mother is here," Mindy said.

"No shit," Robbie said.

Kenny had followed the ambulance to the hospital with his wife, Sandra, and Mindy. He kept saying he felt responsible, but he had nothing to do with those men hiding in the parking lot to beat up "freaks." The three men had been caught by the police not long after the ambulance arrived at the hospital.

Dickie and Lottie had been wheeled off, rushed down the hall as if at any moment they might expire. They were both covered in blood and neither were moving. Robbie couldn't get any information at all from the nurses, and she hadn't seen the doctors.

She didn't blame Kenny, he hadn't done anything, he just came back to the table saying he'd been right about something. He'd looked around the bar as if looking for someone. Then he leaned into Robbie and told her to tell her father she was gay. She looked at him as if he had two heads, not comprehending what he had said. She had just seen a girl she'd known from school with a lanky brunette throwing herself at her and it had distracted her. The blonde was Pam Tilly and Pam had been a real sore spot for Robbie; she had turned away quickly and looked back at Kenny.

"No, I mean it, Robbie," he'd said. "Look, your father is a very unusual man. He'll get you."

"What are you talking about, Kenny?" she'd asked.

"Look, look up, that couple leaving?"

Robbie couldn't believe what she was looking

at. Her Aunt Lottie was slinking out the door with some woman.

"My Aunt Lottie is gay?"

Kenny shook his head. "Shit, Robbie, that woman she's with is your father."

Robbie remembers the confusion. She didn't understand what he was talking about. She had to run after Lottie, confront her. *My mother's best friend is a lesbian? Of course, she never married, she didn't date. What would she be doing in that bar if she weren't gay?* Robbie had sprung out of her seat and pushed herself through the crowd. She heard the screaming the minute she got to the parking lot. Some men were yelling "faggot." Barely visible in the dark, she saw a fight going on. As if she were watching something unfolding before her eyes through a wide angel lens, the figures were absurdly distorted.

Then she saw her Aunt Lottie and the man punching her. She screamed and screamed at the top of her lungs for him to stop, until she saw the man run off, followed by another man, and then another. She looked to the ground at the man lying nearly naked at her feet. She screamed out again and dropped to her knees. She cradled his head in her arms. "Daddy, Daddy," she kept saying until someone pulled her away. She grabbed his wig off the ground. She had no idea why she did that; it was instinctive. They let her get in the ambulance with Dickie. She took his hand and brought it to her lips. *Oh God, don't die, don't die, Daddy.*

She went to Kenny. He was on the other side of the waiting room. She hadn't spoken to him since they'd arrived. She sat beside him.

"Look, Kenny, you probably saved his life. If I hadn't gone out to that parking lot, no one would have screamed and brought the police. I mean, everyone was watching Ginger's show. Please don't feel like it was your fault."

He squeezed her hand. "What are you going to tell your mother?"

Robbie shook her head just as Deborah showed up like a burst of lightning. She ran over to her daughter. "My God, my God, what happened?" she screamed. Robbie looked away.

"You were with him when this happened? You were with him?" Deborah looked around the waiting room, her eyes landing on Mindy. "What are *you* doing here?" she asked.

Mindy stared at her, her eyes wide, but she said nothing.

"What are you people keeping from me? Is my Dickie alright?"

Robbie took her hand. "The doctor hasn't been back. We don't know anything."

Deborah shook her head frantically. "What happened, Kenny, why was Dickie with you?"

Kenny clearly didn't know what to say. "Ah, we ran into each other."

"Where?" Deborah asked.

Kenny just looked at her with wide eyes and took his wife's hand, an action that did not go unnoticed by Deborah. "Who are you?" Deborah asked, the perplexity in her expression blatant.

"Oh, I'm Kenny's wife," Sandra said. "I'm Sandra."

The perplexity transformed into shock. Deborah glared at her daughter and whispered in her ear. "You are dating a married man?"

Robbie stood up and walked to the window. She had to get away from her mother, staring at all of them like someone who'd just finished off a pint of Cutty Sark and about to pass out. The doctor finally walked into the room with an expression of doom on his face.

"We'll speak about this later," Deborah snarled at Robbie and turned her attention back to the doctor. "How is my husband?" she asked loudly.

"Well, he's got a concussion, two broken ribs and a horrible black eye. The good news is he'll live and he'll heal." The doctor's serious expression cracked, and he smiled.

"Thank God," Deborah whispered. Her entire body limp, as if she might fall.

"Miss Lacock did not fare as well, however." The doctor reached out to support Deborah but upon hearing that news, Deborah jerked, erect, as if pulled straight up by string.

"Is she a relative?" the doctor asked.

"Lottie?" Deborah uttered.

"Is Miss Lacock a relative?" The doctor flinched at Deborah's shocked expression. "I assumed she might have been when she was brought in with Mr. Darling."

Deborah, looked dumbfounded at her daughter. "Lottie? Lottie was with Dickie when this happened?"

"She's my aunt," Robbie said to the doctor. "My Aunt Lottie."

"What was she doing out with your father… what do you all know that I don't? Why am I being kept in the dark?" Deborah stood in the middle of the room, intent on the floor, as if the answer was written somewhere in the shiny tiles, and all she had to do was follow the script.

The doctor went right on talking as if Deborah's mumblings were superfluous.

"She has a few pretty painful bruises on her legs where she was kicked," he continued. "There may be internal bleeding and we need to check for brain trauma. We'll be keeping her here for a few days. You can take Mr. Darling home. He is sedated and I've prescribed pain pills to administer three times a day for the next week."

"I want to see my husband. "Kenny, will you take Robinette home?"

"Of course," Kenny said.

"No, I want to see Aunt Lottie." Robbie looked at the doctor. "Can I see my aunt?"

"You can see her," the doctor said. "She's sedated, but she can speak to you."

"After I see Aunt Lottie, I want to see my father." Robbie looked fixedly at her mother. "Then you can drive me home, Mother."

Deborah sighed, "Then you can tell me what this little outing was all about and why I wasn't invited."

Kenny went to Robbie and took her arm. "I can wait," he said. "Then I can take you home."

"You'll do not such thing," Deborah said. "See to your wife." Deborah glared at him. "And drop that hussy off as well," she said through her teeth, loud enough to travel across the room.

"Is she calling my wife a hussy?" Kenny gave Robbie a dumbfounded look.

"She's referring to Mindy," Robbie said and shook her head.

Lottie looked nearly dead. She was lying very still, but her eyes were open.

"Aunt Lottie," Robbie said quietly.

"It hurts when I turn my head. Come closer."

Robbie walked to the bed and touched Lottie's arm. "You don't look too badly hurt. Pops looks worse."

"My God, how is he? How is Dickie? Please tell

me he's okay?"

Robbie felt something click inside her. "He'll live."

Tears rolled down Lottie's face. "He's all right then?"

Robbie nodded though she wasn't quite sure Lottie could see her. "What were you doing in that bar?"

"Ginger is a friend of mine." She said it nonchalantly. Everyone knew Ginger was a drag queen.

Her Aunt Lottie was friendly with a drag queen? Confusion washed over Robbie, as if she were bathing in it. She handed Lottie a tissue from the bedside table.

"Oh, I never knew that, that you knew Ginger Tea."

"You okay, honey?" Lottie was still sniffling and blowing her nose.

"No."

"What were you doing in that bar? That's the last place I expected to find you. You're underage."

"What's with my father, are you going to tell me? What were you doing out with him in a gay bar?"

Lottie reached her hand out from the sheets and took Robbie's. She squeezed it. "He's a very unusual kind of guy, your father. But he's never been to a place like that before."

"He's gay?"

Lottie shook her head. "Nope."

"You're gay?"

Lottie smiled. "Nope."

"Then what? Kenny said that was him that left with you, but it was a woman that left with you, wasn't it?"

Lottie didn't answer her right away. Robbie waited silently until Lottie finally spoke. "It was your father that left with me."

"You left with a woman."

"Your father is a cross-dresser, honey. Doesn't make him a bad person, not even a gay person, just a cross-dresser. That was the first time he ever went out in public like that."

Robbie couldn't say anything for a while, but she had to know. "How long has he been a cross-dresser?"

"All his life, I suppose."

"Does Mother know?"

"God, no."

"If he's not gay, then he must be straight."

"He is straight. Yes."

"You and my father, you're not having an affair, are you, I mean, if he's straight? Why else would you be with him at that hour of night?"

"Yes, he's straight. Don't jump to conclusions, Robbie."

"You and my father are close then? I can still see the look on his face when he tried to help you, when he knew you were hurt. God, that look was painful to see. I saw both love and fear in it. Is he in love with you or something?"

"Or something," Lottie said.

"What is that supposed to mean?"

"We're pretty close, yes."

"How close?"

Lottie looked away. "Close."

Robbie squeezed Lottie's hand. "All right, don't tell me." Robbie pulled her chair closer to the bed. "I think you're kind of unusual too, more so than I ever would have guessed."

Lottie inched her head enough to the right to find Robbie's eyes. "I'm not a cross-dresser." She smiled.

"Just in love with one, huh? I can see it on your face the way I saw it on his. How long have you been having an affair with my father?"

"Don't over-dramatize things."

"You're too close to him, Aunt Lottie. Are you having an affair with my father?"

"Don't tell Deborah," Lottie whispered.

"Don't tell her what? That he's a cross-dresser or that you're in love with him?"

"Take your pick, honey. You choose. And then take cover."

The waiting room was empty except for her mother. Robbie felt oddly sorry for the woman who stood in front of her, with a women's dress in her hand.

"They lost his clothes," Deborah said and threw her arms up in the air. She seemed exasperated.

Robbie stood very still. Kenny had gone, along with Sandra and Mindy. Now it was just her and her mother. She wondered what to say.

"We have to bring him some clothes. He can't leave here in a hospital gown. Come on."

"But I want to see Daddy."

"He's sleeping. You'll see him when we get back here. They must have given him a sedative."

Robbie followed her mother out of the hospital, guessing her father must have feigned sleep. Robbie was sure the last person he wanted to see was her mother. Deborah hadn't asked about Lottie and Robbie didn't volunteer anything. She listened to her mother rant and rave about the hospital giving her women's clothes. She had screamed on the way out, screamed at the women at the front desk about losing her husband's clothes and replacing them with a skirt and a blouse.

"Those fools," she said. Robbie felt for the wig inside her purse. She touched the hair softly. She wasn't sure what a cross-dresser was, and she felt quite sure her mother hadn't a clue either.

Chapter Nineteen

Barnaby

Barnaby looked across the table at Jeremiah, impeccably dressed, like a movie star waiting to get his picture snapped. His shirt was a beautiful shade of blue and his suit grey, with tiny stripes that ran through the material. He reminded Barnaby of his latest client, a shipbuilder with a Sea Ray 550 and a beautiful blonde wife with the classic appeal of Grace Kelly.

"You look rather smashing tonight, Mr. Lennox."

"Call me Jeremiah, please." Jeremiah sat back and scanned the menu.

Barnaby had dressed down so he wouldn't intimidate Jeremiah. He now saw how ridiculous that was. He had brought him to Sassafras in Greenville, an upscale fine dining favorite of his parents. He assumed Jeremiah would be impressed. He realized now that this man was doing the impressing and Barnaby was the shocked recipient of his demeanor, a demeanor that didn't seem likely for a man who had just spent nearly thirty years in prison.

"Shrimp and grits, now that sounds good." Jeremiah looked up and smiled. "That used to be one of my specialties."

"You're a cook?"

"A chef, Barnaby. A chef is an artist, a cook boils water and throws something in the pot."

"You cooked in prison?"

Jeremiah nodded. "And before prison."

Barnaby smiled. "Will you cook for me sometime?"

"What do you like?" Jeremiah sat back and observed Barnaby. "Are you a steak lover? I bet you are a lover of fine, rare steaks."

"Sure enough."

"Then I will make you Filet Mignon with porcini mushrooms and compound butter. After that, I'll introduce you to my original Southern delights. You like spicy?"

"Boy, I'll bet you'd give Deasia a run for her money in the kitchen."

Jeremiah sat forward. "Deasia? You know Deasia?"

"Yeah, you know her too? She's been our cook for years."

"She's my neighbor, still works for you, huh? I should say she *was* my neighbor. One of the few people who visited me in prison."

"Deasia visited you?"

"Deasia, my brother, a few friends."

"You still live in the same place you lived in

before you went off to prison?"

"Should say I *will* be living in it. But it's mine. I own that house and my brother lives in it now and pays the taxes. But I'm moving back in soon as I can. Two more months is all I got fore I can leave my reentry program. My house is mortgage free. Deasia lives across the yard."

Jeremiah leaned back and smiled at Barnaby, showing his white teeth like something he was proud of, like a perfect poker hand. "Tell me about yourself, boy. I want to know who you are."

Barnaby started talking, he wasn't sure why, but eager to gain Jeremiah's trust. Maybe he knew more about who killed Fletcher than he had ever revealed. He was in the alley that night. He might be protecting someone. If Barnaby could charm him enough, gain his trust, he just might reveal some incriminating truths.

Barnaby talked about his childhood, his parents, and his success as a financial adviser, like his father. He talked about his new Camaro, his sister and what a talented artist she was. He told him that he played baseball on weekends, but he stopped short of talking about Prissy, even though Prissy was what he was most proud of. He should have known Jeremiah would pick up on that.

"No women in your life, boy? A good-looking kid like you?"

Barnaby leaned back as a waiter placed his shrimp and grits before him. He took a sip of his wine. "Great Chablis," he said.

"Why are you avoiding telling me about your girlfriend … you into boys?"

Barnaby laughed and shook his head. "No one knows about us, especially my parents, not yet, anyway."

"So, what's the big secret, she married?"

"She's Black," Barnaby said softly.

"Oh," Jeremiah sat back.

"I'm sure you've come up against prejudice before."

"What do you care about what people say?"

"Not people, my parents, specifically my mother."

"Deborah?"

Barnaby stared at him until Jeremiah started laughing, laughed so much and so loud that people turned and stared. Barnaby was a bit shocked at his reaction: what did Jeremiah know about his mother that he didn't?

"Sorry," he said, finally. "Tell me about her. Ah, not about your mother, about your girl."

Barnaby started talking then, told him all about Prissy, the way he had just talked about himself, how beautiful and smart Prissy was, how she was Deasia's only daughter and how she was going off to Tulane University to become a lawyer and how he wanted to give her his grandmother's engagement ring but once his mother saw that on Prissy's finger, she'd collapse on the floor and die.

"She won't die," Jeremiah said.

Barnaby looked up. "She will, or she'll come close to it."

"How come your mother didn't get your grandmother's engagement ring when she married your father?"

"I don't know, maybe Grandmother didn't approve of my mother." Barnaby sat back and laughed. "Maybe she just didn't want to part with it till I grew up."

"Maybe." Jeremiah sat back and neatly wiped his mouth with the soft white napkins. Then he looked Barnaby right in the eye.

"So, you want to let that beautiful woman go off to New Orleans without your ring on her finger? Don't be a fool, boy. You did say she was beautiful?"

"Oh, yes." Barnaby smiled. "Inside, too."

Jeremiah drummed his fingers on the table. Barnaby finished his shrimp and grits in silence, thinking Jeremiah was right and he was being a real pussy about it. The fact was he and Prissy were getting married, but he'd never made it official. He'd never gotten down on his knees and asked her.

"Deborah Darling is a hypocrite, forgive me for saying, but she's only prejudiced when it suits her. When your mother wants something, she takes it, makes no difference what it is or who it is. Don't let her browbeat you into letting that girl get away."

"How do you know so much about my mother?"

"Grew up in this town just like her."

Aware he had a very confused look on his face, Barnaby said, "Are you saying she's a hypocrite, my mother is a hypocrite?"

"No, I'm saying her passions are ineluctable, that's all."

Barnaby smiled; he'd have to look up that word when he got home. "What would you know about her passions?"

"I'm just saying that the passion of being prejudiced is as complex as sexual desire. It's based on something purely mental, deep DNA shit."

Barnaby nodded. "You mean like my ancestors hated you, therefore I see you from my privileged White-DNA-controlled perspective in which I am king, and you are servant?"

"Something like that."

Barnaby rubbed his forehead. "I probably should ask Prissy to get engaged, cement our relationship. I don't know what the hell I'm waiting for."

"If she's as wonderful as you say she is, you best keep the wolves away."

"I don't even know why I haven't asked her to get engaged. I mean, it's a given that we're getting married, but I haven't cemented it with my grandmother's ring." Barnaby put his head in his hand. "What the hell am I waiting for? Am I afraid of Mother's reaction? That's no damn reason."

"I suggest you pay a visit to your grandmother, son."

"Hell, yes," Barnaby said. "Hell, yes. I am getting that ring for Priss." He jerked his head up. "Do you know my grandmother?"

"Hell, Lillian knows everyone whether they know her or not. So, yeah, you could say I know her."

On the drive home that night, Barnaby realized he hadn't talked about Fletcher's murder at all. The only thing he'd learned was that Jeremiah Lennox was as much of an enigma as whoever killed Fletcher Smith, the answer to which he might never know. However, Jeremiah was right about Prissy. He had to put a ring on her finger, specifically his grandmother's ring. She'd been promising it for his bride since he was in knee pants.

Chapter Twenty

Lillian

The grand parlor was hardly ever used, just for large dinner parties, but this morning, Lillian opened the organza floral drapes and let in the sun. Today was going to be a special day and she knew it. The room gave every impression of overflowing in friendly warmth and only a modicum of dust sprayed into the room from the swish of fabric. Shame on her for keeping this magnificent front room so dark for so many months, but she never entertained anymore, never played the grand piano. Or saw the room filled with waiters and silver trays lined with fingerling potatoes topped with avocado and smoked salmon and her favorite of all, goat cheese poppers with honey. She always catered from Feasts and Fetes, well, after Jeremiah went off to prison, that is. He always catered her affairs back in the day. And he would do so again, she would see to it.

She expected Barnaby any moment. He was bursting at the seams to ask for her engagement ring; she'd heard the excitement in his voice when he'd called her that morning. He had been his own worst enemy, cowering in a corner because his mother would be appalled at his choice of a bride, a Black girl! Heavens! Even though he was Black in some capacity, maybe as much as fifty percent for all she knew. She was hoping he wouldn't back down, lose his nerve, and let Deborah make mush out of him.

Deborah was most likely to object, until Lillian gave her a gentle talking to, a warning of sorts, a threat perhaps. And she would go through with it, despite Deborah's protests; she would apprise Barnaby of his lineage if her daughter-in-law didn't allow the wedding and allow it with great gusto. This was so unlike her own reaction to Dickie's choice of a bride.

It's not that she didn't like Deborah back then, it was more of an agitation around Deborah. Deborah was superficial and Lillian saw it right away. She was intellectually starved. She lived in a void, in a world created in her own image, a vacuous girl and now a vacuous woman. Sanctimonious, pious, and unforgiving. Deborah, with her strict aversions to anyone who didn't look like her or think like her. It never seemed to bother Dickie though, for her son liked pretty things and so, that's what he had, a pretty thing.

Lillian had received a call from Jeremiah that morning as well. He told her that he'd been out with her grandson the night before and he thinks he talked him into asking for Prissy's hand in marriage before she went off to New Orleans and left him wondering if anyone would notice what a catch she was.

Jeremiah had called her the moment he awoke in that place they had him staying in, it was quite horrid, but he only had a few weeks left before he could return to his home. Lillian still cringed when she thought about what she'd done to him, but she'd had to protect her son. Good Lord, it wasn't only her son, it was her grandchild as well. She imagined it must have been at one of her glorious dinner parties back in the day when she was still young and considered witty. Jeremiah must have served Deborah a tasty tidbit off his silver tray and met her eyes and possibly held them a moment too long. Deborah had absolutely no self-control. The man had sex appeal and her son… well, Dickie was so perfectly refined-looking that it just knocked the sexuality right out of him.

Dickie was smitten with Deborah at the time — who wouldn't have been smitten with such a vivacious young woman? But she strayed, had a hot appetite for sexy men. Well, Lillian took care of it all, just as she took care of that nasty mess Dickie had gotten into in high school. Paid that family a bundle to move to Charleston, to keep their mouths shut. She'd known Leah Warren's mother quite well and it was she who came knocking, not necessarily to berate Dickie. She'd told Lillian it took two to tango, so she wasn't blaming Dickie, but she certainly let it be known she'd leave town with her pregnant daughter with some financial help, and Dickie would never know about his child.

However, Dickie found out eventually, not about the way his mother had saved the day but that he had a daughter, an adorable little girl that Lillian couldn't help picking up and kissing in parks and stores and anywhere else they happened to run into each other. Crazy old woman, the child must have thought. Her granddaughter for God's sake — why shouldn't she pick her up and kiss her? Of course, when the child got older, Lillian only hugged and kissed her cheeks over and over, until Leighton blushed and moved off.

So many secrets, and so burdensome to be privy to all of them. She financed Jeremiah's restaurant back then, and it was quite successful until they pinned that murder on him, which he didn't commit. True, he was in that alley with Deborah that night, most likely pumping up against her and demanding to see the White son he'd fathered. Lillian was sure Deborah had told him that night that Barnaby looked like a White baby. Jeremiah was likely to brag about it. Would have gotten himself lynched and poor little Barnaby ostracized forever. How foolish of Deborah to want him to continue that affair, to love his son from afar and never say anything about it or claim the son he'd fathered. Deborah had just given birth to Barnaby and the child needed to be protected.

Lillian offered Jeremiah money to leave town. Surprisingly, he refused to leave, even refused the money. What else could she do but tell Deborah what to say, and pay off the jury that convicted him.

Unfortunately, she had to do it. She had to get rid of Jeremiah. Her status in Pickens would always pay off. When she told the police it was Jeremiah who killed Fletcher because he was in love with Rhonda, Fletcher's wife, the police didn't bat an eye. They didn't even investigate whether the two even knew each other. They would have accepted any excuse to arrest Jeremiah. My God, who wouldn't be in love with Rhonda? She was gorgeous. No one knew she was a lesbian, except Lilian, of course.

She never meant for Jeremiah to go off to prison for so long and over the years she tried to get him out. It was she who found the innocent project that eventually got him freed. No one knew of her behind-the-scenes activities. Jeremiah still believed it was Deborah who got him locked up. Lillian smirked. Deborah had wept for months after Jeremiah went to prison. She was mad for the man. Lillian felt terribly guilty, but now that he was out of prison, she planned to finance another restaurant for him, the same way she got him those new suits and that spiffy car he drives.

He didn't have to know it was she who made sure he disappeared back then. She did it to protect her grandson from his biological father, who might have told everyone the truth, might have embarrassed Dickie, and endangered her grandson. Deborah's marriage would have been ruined. Lillian had to get involved.

Barnaby walked in through the door and took her breath away as he always did. Her wonderful, smart, and handsome grandson, whom she adored. He would have everything he wanted, most of all, the woman he loved, and she would do anything for him, even if it meant blackening her soul to protect him.

"Grandmother," he said as he kissed her and took her hand. "How ravishing you look."

"I dressed up for you. I even opened up the front room for you."

"What is the occasion?"

"You are the occasion."

"I see," he said and led her into the magnificent room with its tall windows. There was such a softness to it. "I love this room." He smiled. "Now, will you tell me the occasion?"

"You tell me." She smiled and her once quite beautiful face was alight with the sunniness, her eyes were less pale, her skin aglow.

"Well, in fact, I do have something to ask you."

Lillian sat forward; her long thin legs crossed at the ankles. Her gnarled fingers caressed his hand. She glanced at the drawer that shielded the ring.

"I want to ask Prissy to marry me." He grinned sheepishly, the little-boy grin of his youth.

Lillian's face glowed like the moon. She jumped up and held him. "I love that girl."

"So do I," he said.

She had brought the ring down from the upstairs bedroom because she knew this was coming. She went to the drawer where she had placed the ring in a velvet box and held it out. She briefly remembered her husband, the handsome self-made billionaire, Richard Darling Jr., Dickie's wonderful father, who had provided a life of absolute joy until his untimely early death at the age of fifty. She wiped a tear from her eye.

"You could not have made me happier." She looked at him with a brilliant smile. "I'm sure Prissy will say the same."

"What about Mother?"

"Leave her to me." She sat beside him and stroked his shoulder. "We'll have the most wonderful engagement party. I'll have Jeremiah cater it. Would you like that?"

Barnaby snapped his head up. "How do you

know that I know Jeremiah?"

"I know everything, darlin'," she said.

"How do you know him?" he asked her with a curious smile.

She flipped her hands in the air, "Small town, honey. Everyone knows everyone. He used to cater for me. Lord, how many parties I had back when I still had a skip in my step." She winked at him.

Barnaby kissed her on the cheek and then opened the box and held the ring up. "This will look beautiful on Prissy's finger."

Lillian smiled. "Not a woman alive that doesn't look good in diamonds."

The phone rang loudly, and Lilian got up to answer it before her maid got to it. After a moment or two, she returned.

"Your father has been in an accident. Come, drive me over there."

"An accident?" Barnaby said as he got his car keys out of his pocket and helped his grandmother to the door. "Is it serious?"

"I doubt it. He's propped up in the sunroom with a few crime novels, drinking an Alabama Slammer."

Chapter Twenty-One

Deborah

Deborah sat staring at Dickie. He was so quiet. She had set him up in the sunroom on the chaise and he just lay there looking out at nothing.

"Cat got your tongue, darlin'?" she asked.

"Hurts when I speak," he said softly.

Deborah nodded. She wanted to ask him what the hell he was doing in that nasty bar, but she was putting the pieces together. How foolish of her not to have known years ago that her husband and Lottie shared their strangeness, or should she say *their perversions*? Oh, how that made her shudder. Well, she knew about her Dickie, had always known. One doesn't plant a peck on the cheek of a transvestite unless one has bonded with said weirdo. She even told Lottie she saw Dickie do that, plant a kiss on Malcolm's cheek when he was sashaying around town as Ginger Tea.

Deborah didn't care, not really, and she had no actual proof of it, but she knew. Dickie simply dressed too well and took too many damn walks not to have some perverted sexual secret. How chivalrous of him to have never told her about Lottie, that Lottie was one of those women, that strange assortment of mannish females who pair themselves off with like kind. But then again, Lottie did not have a pair, a mirror image of herself. Well, not as far as Deborah knew. Maybe if she had admitted to Dickie that she knew about his appetite for deviant sexual behavior, he would have shared that Lottie was a deviant, as well. Then they all could have been done with the truth.

Deborah looked up as Lillian entered with her son. Barnaby ran to his father and knelt by his side. She saw Dickie stroke his hair. Barnaby hadn't even acknowledged her.

"You look like the devil," Barnaby said, "red face and all."

"How are you, son?" Lillian asked, taking Dickie's hand.

"Hurts when I talk," Dickie uttered again and tried to smile, his mouth moving into a strange dip.

Lillian took charge, as usual, called for Deasia to bring in more ice lemonade, got her son an extra pillow, adjusted the shade to keep the light from his eyes and then sat on the other side of him and went back to holding his hand.

"I'll have another Alabama Slammer," Dickie managed to get out.

"You certainly will not," Lillian said,

punctuated like a hammer coming down on a nail.

Lillian always took control and that was both a good and a bad thing. Lillian had certainly gotten her out of that mess with Jeremiah. Deborah knew Lillian liked Jeremiah; they were strange pals, bonded, Deborah believed over their passion for food. Lillian liked all that spicy stuff that Jeremiah excelled at: Thai mussels and red chili peppers that burned your tongue, and that spicy bean dish he made with eggs that made Deborah choke and cough so much she nearly expired. Thank God she didn't have to be served that nonsense anymore.

Jeremiah wouldn't take money for his silence. Deborah knew Lillian offered to pay him off. He didn't want anything except to bury her baby six feet under and pretend it never happened. They were both afraid for Barnaby. Jeremiah had been so adamant that the baby would be Black that he threatened to kill it. He said it was him or the baby because when the town found out he'd bedded down with Deborah Darling, they'd lynch him.

Whether he meant it or not about doing away with Barnaby didn't matter, it had scared her to death. She didn't know what she would do if the baby was born Black. She didn't know what Lillian would make her do. But by the grace of God, the baby was not born Black, and she tried to tell Jeremiah that. She tried to tell him there was no reason to feel threatened by his son. That Halloween night in the alley, that's all she'd wanted to do; tell him that Barnaby was born looking as Caucasian as she did. It was as if she'd told him God had come to earth the way he smiled and relaxed and moved back into her with the same sexy rhythm that had always taken her breath away. She assumed everything would be alright after that.

But then Lillian put the fear of God into her, kept telling her that Jeremiah might claim Barnaby as his son, he might blab all over town that he was the father of a White baby. They would have lynched him, just for claiming that. Lillian told her to tell the police that she saw Jeremiah leaving the alley the night of Fletcher's murder, even though Deborah didn't see Jeremiah *leave* the alley. Only thing she saw was him grabbing her arms and holding her close, his breath on her face and his lips so near her mouth. No, he was having too much fun to leave the alley.

He was just about to kiss her when they both saw that woman *whish* past them, her high heels clicking. They even heard the shot as they stood embracing in the dark with his sighs of relief about the baby and her thinking she wanted him to take her right there in the night, quickly and discreetly. "Was that a firecracker?" he had asked. She remembers laughing, telling him it was her heart popping over him.

Well, her telling the police she'd seen him leave the alley drove them apart, of course. But she got nervous, couldn't let anyone tie them together. Lillian figured the best way to get rid of Jeremiah was to involve him in Fletcher's murder in one form or another. A Black man seen in the same alley where a murder took place? Had to be the Black man committed it.

Deborah smiled as she watched Lillian with her son, coddling him the same way she coddled Barnaby and Robinette. Damn woman coddled everyone but her. "I care very much for Jeremiah," Lillian had said. "But I am going to protect my son and my grandson. I need to see him put away for a few years." A few years? The poor man spent nearly thirty years behind bars. Deborah, too guilty to write to him, and didn't dare visit him. Lillian organized the group that got him freed and she paid off his house and sent him all sorts of things in prison, everything they allowed him to have, Lillian sent him. Guilt drove her, Deborah surmised.

Every time Dickie made love to her, Deborah thought of Jeremiah. But that didn't suit her at all. She didn't look the part of a Black man's mistress, so she had to erase his image from her mind. She looked perfect with Dickie; he was her handsome, rich White husband, so who cared what she thought about when he was pumping away at her? That's the thing. You might be in a hundred people's fantasies and never know it. Well, she certainly didn't fit the part of Lottie's fantasies either, but you can't control how other people think. How disgusting not to be able to control other people having fantasies about you. Deborah rose to her feet.

"I'm going to the hospital to see Lottie, make sure she's alright."

Dickie jerked his head up to her. "Tell her that if there's anything we can do—"

"Of course, Dickie. Goes without saying."

Deborah didn't expect to see Lottie looking quite as banged up. It startled her. "My Lord, they got you pretty bad."

Lottie didn't smile, just tried to nod her head.

"What were you doing in that place?" Deborah pulled the chair close to the bed and watched Lottie turn her head away. "I know what kind of bar that is. Kenny came to the house to see Dickie and I asked him. He told me straight out. He told me it was great entertainment. Yeah, right, great entertainment if you're a pervert."

Lottie stared at the wall.

"So, what were you doing there with my husband?"

She saw a blush come to Lottie's cheeks as she turned back and met her eyes.

"You don't have to answer that, I know."

Through Lottie's frozen expression, Deborah saw the tears form in her eyes.

"I'm sorry," Lottie said.

Deborah squeezed her hand. "Oh, don't be sorry. You can't help what you are, I would imagine."

Lottie looked at her, quizzically, oddly. "What do you mean '*what I am*?'"

Deborah sighed. "It's okay. I know you share Dickie's perversion. You're one of those women just like he's one of those men, every now and then, of course. When the mood hits him, I imagine. Are you that way, too?"

Lottie nodded her head for want of anything else to do and remained silent.

Deborah let out a short laugh. "I put it together, your bond with Dickie. I know it's some sort of sexual perversion with him, but women are more complex than men." Deborah paused and looked off. "I don't understand things like that, but I'm sure you couldn't tell me how you felt. But you could have, you know. I would have been okay with it. However, Lottie, dear, I am so in love with my Dickie and certain I could never look at a woman the way I look at him. I'm a very normal woman. You understand?"

Lottie remained silent and Deborah continued. "I love you like a friend. You're my best friend and I've known you for years, but I would appreciate it if you kept all this lesbian stuff out of our friendship?"

Lottie stared at her.

"I understand your friendship with Dickie now. You're alike. It's okay, but please don't speak to me about it. I need to think about it as little as possible."

Lottie nodded.

"I just need to think of you both as being normal."

Lottie nodded again.

"When do you leave the hospital?"

"Tomorrow."

"Well," Deborah patted her hand. "I'm going to send Heaven over to your house to help you out. I can spare her a few days a week. How's that?"

"Not needed."

"Oh, *pshaw*, Lottie. You never say what you really mean to say."

Leighton was just turning out of her drive when Deborah got home. Lillian had gone off to the guest house with Barnaby, and Dickie was in the same place he'd been when she'd left.

"I just saw Leighton leaving, what did she want?"

"DNA samples."

"What?"

"She intends to test the DNA of everyone she can round up from the night Fletcher was shot."

"What for?"

"Apparently, they have the DNA of someone who was very near the body, could be a witness, could be the killer."

"Nothing like beating a dead horse."

"I gave them hair samples from your brush. I didn't think you'd mind."

"Of course not. I didn't kill him."

Chapter Twenty-Two

Dickie

Dickie was up and about in only ten days or so, taking his walks and doing some mild exercise, the kind of gentle muscle stretching he remembered doing back in college. Today he would visit Lottie, and then he'd visit his mother and thank her for giving Barnaby her engagement ring to give to Prissy. Barnaby had whisked Prissy off to Chez Duo, the most expensive restaurant in all of South Carolina, Dickie was sure.

Barnaby lured his lover with Champagne and lobster and some oysters to start and after the rib eye steak for two, the waiter cleared the table and Barnaby reached into his pocket for the ring. He'd gotten down on one knee before her and she squealed so loudly when he popped the question that every head in the restaurant turned. Then they all clapped. Barnaby laughed when he told his father, laughed with misty eyes. The restaurant sent congratulatory drinks, and naturally, Prissy was on cloud nine and hadn't yet come down from it.

Deborah was still unaware even though Prissy wore the ring now and Barnaby walked around with a grin as wide as the Atlantic Ocean. Deasia was constantly laughing — why, her toes didn't even touch the ground, Dickie thought. Priss had made a catch, but his son was the real winner. That girl was as smart as she was sweet and as loyal as she was lovely. Dickie was quite fond of her.

Well, they'd have to tell Deborah that evening before she found out on her own and hit the roof. It wasn't fair not to tell her. He didn't want to see her hurt by their silence, and he knew she would be hurt, not joyous, but hurt. That was the problem for Dickie, that she wouldn't be overjoyed to have Prissy as a daughter-in-law, ecstatic that her son was making such a good choice. But if they didn't tell her soon, she'd be angry, and no one wanted to see Deborah angry.

But Deborah was full of surprises. Dickie was sure his marriage would be over after she discovered that he had been beaten to within an inch of his life in front of a gay bar. Certainly, the papers would have a field day over his being in a dress that night. But the papers didn't print it. He was certain his mother had intervened and had made sure it was hushed up. He thought his affair with Lottie was obvious. Deborah was sure to put the pieces together after they were caught out in a bar, except Deborah didn't discover anything, she misinterpreted what was right in front of her eyes. Lottie couldn't get over it.

"She thinks we're gay, Dickie. She doesn't even have an inkling that we've been screwing each other for thirty years."

Poor Deborah, he thought. Perhaps it was time he drew back the veil of misconceptions and revealed the truth. "I think we should marry," he said to Lottie, but all she said back to him was, "In your dreams."

Dickie leaned back in one of the white wicker chairs on the back patio of Lottie's house. Having the shit kicked out of him had messed with his brain. He'd been doing a lot of deep thinking lately. He didn't know where that would lead him, but he felt differently. He wanted truth in his life. He was being buried in bullshit. Living at home with Deborah made him feel suffocated by the lies, by all the pussyfooting around by everyone to keep Deborah from the truth about everything.

"I'm serious. I want to marry you."

Lottie stared at him. "I've been having an affair with you for so long that I can't think about being serious with you."

"Marriage is serious?"

"Of course it is." Lottie leaned back and sipped on her cocktail. "We don't need to act like we're young, Dickie."

He reached out for her hand. "You know, I was in love with Leah McNeil once, long time ago.

I never told you that."

Lottie turned to him. "Can't picture you with Leah."

"Oh, I was quite in love with her."

"Are you still?"

"A little."

Lottie sighed. "She's a lesbian, Dickie."

Dickie sat up quickly and stared at her. "What? I don't believe it. Leah, a lesbian? Don't fool with me, Lottie."

"Malcolm is my friend, tells me things. She's been in a relationship with Rhonda Smith as long as we've been getting it on, maybe longer."

"Oh, my God."

"Malcolm knows Leah, they're friends. They're all queer as a three-dollar bill, Dickie. Leah, Rhonda, Malcolm, all queers."

Dickie put his head back. "The truth is out there, isn't it? Leah? A lesbian?"

"I don't want you to divorce Deborah, don't want you to hurt her. Besides, you know marriage is not for me."

"She'll survive, and by the way, marriage is not for you because I'm the only man for you and I'm taken, so to speak. There's no other man for you but me, Lottie. That and only that is why marriage is not for you."

"We wouldn't be able to stay in this town if we married. We'd be hated for carrying on an affair all these years right under Deborah's nose."

"It was just a thought, just a thought, Lottie."

"Tell me something you never wanted me to know and if it shocks me enough, I'll think about marrying you." Lottie grinned at him.

"I have to shock you enough to get you to marry me? Wasn't telling you I was in love with Leah shock enough?"

"I'm looking for a reason to actually do it, to actually … do it."

"The reason is that we belong together, and Deborah needs to live in the real world without me in it. Maybe find herself a man who is just like her."

"Clueless?"

Dickie smiled. "Exactly."

"I can't do it to her, Dickie. I just can't. So please don't bring it up again."

Dickie got out his pipe and lit it. "You know she had an affair?"

Lottie nodded her head. "She tells me everything."

"Why didn't you ever tell me?"

"Not my place to, Dickie."

Dickie suspected that Barnaby was not his biological son. He'd suspected it for years. He didn't know who the father was for sure, but he knew Deborah. It was right before she became pregnant, a year or so before. She came home reeking of another man. She was like a cat in heat, walking around the house pretending sex with him was enough, was the thrill it was supposed to be. He knew it wasn't. He saw that private distance she took from him. After Barnaby was born, she changed, acting the role of wife and mother as if meant to play it. But that wasn't the real Deborah. He had no idea in hell who the real Deborah was. He went along with it; why not? He had the perfect family and he had Lottie.

"I don't know what I'd do without you," he said and brought her hand to his lips. "You are *l'amour de ma vie.*"

Lottie turned to him and smiled. "You're going to tell her about us, aren't you?"

"No, of course not," Dickie said. "Not unless you agree to marry me."

Lottie took a sip of her gin martini and looked off.

Chapter Twenty-Three

Dickie

It's not that Deborah didn't know her daughter, she simply didn't *want* to know the many facets of her. Deborah's picture of Robbie's life was like a PG-rated television script in which her daughter was completely one-dimensional. Problem was, the real script of Robbie's life was R-rated, much more complex than Deborah could have ever imagined.

Deborah should be accepting the truth about her daughter, but truth was so far out of Deborah's grasp. Dickie couldn't go on pretending that they were Ozzie and Harriet, and their children were products of the 1950s. Dickie wondered how Deborah would interpret that truth. *Our daughter is not a lesbian, Dickie. She doesn't know what the word means. She's still a tomboy is all.* Deborah would most likely think that Dickie was projecting, thinking that just because he has those 'leanings', his daughter did as well. Oh, he knew that Deborah thought he was as fey as fairy tale elves and he let her. What did it matter, really?

He'd make his wife as relaxed and comfortable as he could that evening, but he had to give her a jarring dose of reality. He'd ply her with alcohol. Then he'd tell her that he wanted to support his daughter's passion in life, which, unbeknownst to Deborah, was art, and by the way, Robbie was a lesbian. He'd start there, then he'd tell her about Barney's engagement to Prissy. Well, maybe that was Barney's responsibility, so he'd tell Barney to come to the house with Prissy and dangle the damn ring in front of Deborah's eyes. And his affair with Lottie. Maybe he could get Lottie to tell her.

Dickie sighed. He was a coward. He was the one to face her. He alone.

He was proud of his daughter's talent. His mother had forced him into acknowledging what she called a "diamond in the rough." "There's greatness in her, Dickie," she'd said. So true that he hid his head in the sand. He was no better than Deborah when it came to supporting his children. Deborah had ignored Lillian with a noncommittal shake of her head when she went on and on about how talented Robbie was and Dickie had done the same. Robbie had mentioned how much she loved to paint, she'd mentioned it casually over the years, so it really didn't have any more punch than saying she loved to ride horses. She had brought home her paintings to share with them and he had to admit, he was lukewarm about those paintings at the time. The art had looked juvenile to him.

Unfortunately, Dickie's ignorance of art prevented him from seeing a likeness to the artist, Rothko. Deborah was downright disinterested. Robbie's talent had significantly developed in high school and her art teachers wrote glowing reviews of her work that her parents smiled over with noncommittal remarks.

Discovering her parent's disinterest must have been disheartening, so Robbie went to her grandmother for support. Lillian was enthusiastic and proud and provided her attic room for Robbie with its grand skylight. Lillian raved about her granddaughter's work and talked her into applying to the Fine Arts Department of New York University. They were both thrilled when she was accepted and had a little celebration of fried mushroom appetizers and Champagne.

Lillian finally told her son that she intended to support his daughter's passion and would pay for her four years of college. She told Dickie that it was despicable of him not to recognize his daughter's ability. Dickie was shocked when she revealed Robbie's art studio up in the attic and told him that his daughter had been going there for years, escaping everyone's disinterest, and throwing herself into what she loved. Looking at his daughter's work, Dickie finally realized that Robbie was gifted. He stared at some startling paintings he had never seen before or ever imagined his daughter could have created. Ocean paintings of stark bungalows and sand shells that looked as if they'd fallen from the sky, shadows of women in colorful headdresses wearing the whimsical hats that looked like the hats she kept in her bedroom.

"Your daughter is extraordinarily talented," Lillian had said. This talent of Robbie's was never mentioned at home. Deborah would have thought it superfluous.

His life was a sham, and it would continue to be a sham until he told his wife everything he knew, and she didn't know, including his desire for cross-dressing, and his commitment to support his daughter, and his son's engagement to a Black girl. Maybe Deborah would say, "Oh, what cute idiosyncrasies our family has, darlin', let's acknowledge them and then ignore them. They'll go away."

"Hello, sweetheart." That evening he had gone into Robbie's room and sat at the edge of her bed.

She looked up and smiled faintly.

"I know how much going to Europe means to you," he said.

She continued to look at him as if curious about what he'd say next.

"I'm going to give you the money to go to Europe this summer and when you're ready, I will give you the money for New York University. Grandmother tells me you've been accepted into their fine arts program. She and I will both help you financially."

Robbie's mouth nearly fell to her chest. "I was going to tell you."

"And your mother?"

"She's never thought much of my choices, but I guess I have to tell her too."

Dickie sighed. "I won't take this away from you and I won't let your mother do it, either."

Robbie gave him a beautiful smile. "You don't know how relieved I am. I thought I'd have to run away and starve in New York. I would have gone no matter what, you know."

Dickie winked. "Your grandmother would have bailed you out of anything." Dickie took her hand and kissed it. "We have to support those we love. We have to." He looked at her with a great deal of intensity. "Thank you for being there the other night. If not for you, those hoodlums might have killed me."

Robbie looked away. "Has Barney told her yet?"

"About Prissy?"

Robbie nodded.

"Tonight is the night of reckoning for your mother. I shall tell her everything. I'll tell her about you, about Barney, about me ..." He raised an eyebrow at her.

Robbie smiled. "Then be prepared for a hurricane."

Dickie sat back and looked at his daughter, her youthful loveliness. "Is there anything you want to ask me?" he said. "I know you must be wondering ... about my secret."

"Only if you want to tell me."

He took her hand. "I cross-dress ... sometimes. It's no big deal. I enjoy it."

"I'm gay, Father." She looked at him sadly. "It's no big deal, is it?"

He squeezed her hand. "I don't want who we really are to be our secrets. There is nothing to hide or to be ashamed of ... or to feel terrible about. Other people's opinions do not have the power to diminish us."

"Mother?"

"Oh, yes, Mother ... well, I'm afraid Mother is in for a shock tonight, isn't she?"

"Lottie? Are you having an affair with her?"

His head snapped back, and he stared at her. "What makes you think that?"

"Well, you were there at The Red Lady with her. You obviously trust her. And she looks at you like you've been married for years."

Dickie reached out and kissed his daughter's hand. "I love Lottie, yes." he said. "I love your mother, too."

"We all just need to be happy, Daddy. What are we doing to ourselves if we can't even accomplish that? We're living in the dark, in other people's illusions. I want to live in *my* reality. I want to own who I am with all my heart."

Dickie squeezed her hand. "Yes, darlin'. Let's be true to ourselves. 'To thine own self be true.' Hamlet." He smiled. "Remember? I read you the play when you were only a little girl."

"Well, you told me the story of Hamlet. And thank you, Polonius," she said. "I still remember it."

Dickie brushed two strands of hair that had fallen into her eyes. "I never want to hurt anyone, most of all your mother."

"But she has no idea who any of us are."

Dickie sighed. "No, darlin', she hasn't a clue."

Chapter Twenty-Four

Deasia

1963

Deasia looked across the yard and watched Jeremiah pack down the dirt for his geraniums.

"Can't afford a gardener?" she called out in her most teasing way. Teasing Jeremiah was what they all did. He was just so conceited. She walked over to the fence and watched him ignore her. She yelled out again. "Hey, didn't you hear what I said, Black boy?"

Jeremiah looked up and smiled. He walked over to her, shirtless, showing off his fine muscles.

"Jackson see you out here flirting with me, he gonna whip your ass."

"No, he gonna whip yours."

Jeremiah laughed. "You sassy little girl. I just might have to whip your Black ass instead and spare Jackson the exertion."

"Anybody's ass deserved to be whipped, it's yours."

"And why's that?"

"You think you Sidney Poitier."

Jeremiah laughed. "Well, we got a few things in common, three at best."

"Oh yeah? What's that?"

"Good looks, good looks and good looks."

"Oh Lord," Deasia laughed so much she fell back. "I sure fell into that one." But she couldn't argue with him there and far be it from her to tell him that.

"I wonder if Sidney Poitier fools around with White women as much as you do."

Jeremiah cocked his head. "What you talking 'bout, girl?"

"Guess what?" She wondered how he'd take the news. Good for him if it made him squirm. "I just got hired to work in that White woman's kitchen, the one you been screwing."

"I ain't screwing no White woman. I got enough Black ass to keep me busy."

"Ha, she White and she rich and she over here 'bout three times a week thinking no one know, no one hear the screaming coming out of your bedroom."

"Screams of delight are you saying?" He winked at her.

"I won't tell no one."

"Don't care if you do. Black people do not tell the truth, don't you know that? Who'd believe you?"

"Yeah, I know it, don't know how I'm gonna look that woman in the eye without laughing my head off thinking of you and her riding each other like Broncos. She getting it on with a Black boy? Lord have mercy. Lord have mercy. She a rich, White bitch, Jeremiah. She gonna do you in."

Thinking back on that, Deasia smiled. Life was so uncomplicated back then. Jeremiah was a good man, didn't deserve the fate he got. But he out now. She snapped back to the present as she watched the young man through the blinds. He was walking up to her door very professional like. She knew she'd be questioned again. Damn, she'd told that woman detective all she knew; why did she have to repeat it all?

She heard the doorbell ring and went to answer it, letting herself have one long sigh and hoping her nerves wouldn't show.

She let him in, a pleasant young man with too much hair.

"Thank you for seeing me, Deasia. I'm Detective Martinelli. I just have a few questions about that night Fletcher Smith was murdered. My partner said that you knew the Smith's house woman?"

"That a long time ago, he was murdered in 1963. Lord, that thirty years ago. How I be expected to remember back thirty years?"

Mart nodded. "Did you know the Smith's

house woman?"

"Grayson? Yeah, I known her for years. Still know her."

"Did she ever speak to you about their relationship, Fletcher, and his wife?"

Deasia nodded. "He was violent, used to beat her. But everyone in town knew that. Her arms were always purple."

"Purple?"

"Yeah, bruised."

"Oh. Was she ever violent with him, you think?"

Deasia shook her head. "Grayson never told me that. Lord, she never told me anything like that."

"What kind of secrets did she tell you, Deasia?"

"No secrets."

"Perhaps you're just not remembering?"

"No, no secrets."

Mart sat back. He drummed his fingers on her table. "What about the lady you work for now, Deborah Darling? Did she have any secrets back then?"

"What you mean secrets?"

"Oh, you know, things you don't want other people to know."

Deasia shook her head.

"How well did she know Jeremiah Lennox?"

"I wouldn't know that. I wouldn't know anything about that."

Mart suspected she was lying. He pressed a bit harder. "Did you ever see Jeremiah and Mrs. Darling together?"

Deasia knew she'd have to lie. She couldn't tell this man about them riding the bronco over there in his bedroom. She couldn't do that.

"Maybe once or twice," she said. "In town. Maybe in town."

Mart got up and looked around the room. He noticed a photograph of Deasia, Barnaby Darling, and Prissy, her daughter.

"Your kids grew up close, huh?" he asked, studying the photograph.

Deasia nodded her head. "They engaged, my daughter and Barnaby Darling."

Mart took the photo up close and stared at it. "Wow," he said. "Barnaby looks like he could be Jeremiah's son. They look so much alike." He opened his eyes wide. "You ever think that, that they look so much alike?"

"No, sir."

Deasia's heart was going a mile a minute. Anyone looking close enough could see it. She saw it almost immediately when Barnaby started walking. She remained silent and let the detective stare at her. He shook his head for a bit and put the picture back.

"You think she was raped? I mean there's DNA now, we can find out if they're related."

Deasia jumped to her feet, her anger giving

her fuel. *Why every White man think Black men got to rape White women. Hell, many White women are there for the taking.* "What you saying? That woman wasn't raped! Jeremiah didn't need to rape her. She over here three days a week in that man's bed of her own accord. Jeremiah not a rapist."

Mart smiled. "I see."

Deasia fell back. "Oh, Lord."

"No need to worry. It doesn't matter. We just needed to know if she had a reason to frame him. She might be lying about what she saw in the alley that night, covering up for someone."

"She was in love with him. She wouldn't frame him."

"In love?"

Deasia's face was a furious beet red. "It a long time ago, pay me no mind, I don't remember much. Why you want to know all this? Jeremiah out of prison."

"I don't really care if Deborah Darling had an affair with Jeremiah. We're just looking for the man or woman who killed Fletcher Smith. If Deborah is lying about seeing him leave the alley, she could be lying about not seeing the murder. Any suspicions?"

Deasia shook her head. "No, sir."

1963

Deasia had just percolated herself some coffee and the aroma was intoxicating. She was rested because she hadn't cooked the night before. They had all gone off to a Halloween party looking like slave owners, and all she had to do was serve drinks and light hors d'oeuvres and tell everyone how good they looked. Deasia didn't understand the fascination White folks had with slavery. It was as though they all had something taken away from them and were trying to get it back. She knew Jeremiah was going to that party. Everyone invited Jeremiah everywhere because he had White manners and he was ambiguous looking, like the puppy dog that grows up to be a wolf.

That knock on her door startled her. She hoped it wasn't some misguided confederate soldier from the night before who'd lost his way, had too much to drink and needed to murder a slave to ensure the glory days of the old South. She was relieved to see Grayson beyond the glass.

"I hope you've got a pot of coffee on, girl."

Deasia smiled. She was always happy to see Grayson though they hadn't been that close growing up; they'd renewed whatever friendship they'd had when they both took on domestic duties with the White and wealthy and moved only two houses down from each other.

Grayson walked into the kitchen and went

directly to the coffee.

"Not making coffee at your house anymore?" Deasia asked her with a smile.

"You put chocolate in the filter like I told you?"

Deasia laughed. "Pecans," she said.

Grayson poured herself a cup and sat at the table. "You hear the news?"

Deasia shook her head. "What news?"

"Fletcher Smith was murdered in the alley behind Smith's Bar last night. Shot to death."

Deasia's mouth dropped. "No? His meanness finally caught up with him?"

Grayson shrugged her shoulders. "I guess you could say that."

The two women drank their coffee in silence. The tension cloaked Deasia, she knew Grayson was having one of her moments when she opted for silence rather than saying what was on her mind.

"What's up with you?" Deasia finally asked.

"Miss Leah come back from the party with her face all beat up."

"You don't work for Miss Leah, how you know that?"

Grayson looked away. "She stays with Miss Rhonda sometimes. They went to the party together. I watched her little girl."

"Leah's little girl?"

Grayson nodded.

"Did Fletcher beat her up, so she killed him? You think that's what happened?"

"Don't jump the gun."

"What you trying to say, girl?"

"They had blood on them."

"Who? Who had blood on 'em? Did Rhonda kill Fletcher?"

"I can't say no more, but just telling you that makes me feel better. If I hold this in any longer, I'm going to explode."

Deasia put her head in her hands. "Bastard deserved to die. Don't care who killed him."

"They're gonna blame Jeremiah."

Deasia's eyes opened wide. "You got to tell him what you know then, about the blood on those White folks. Jeremiah didn't kill anyone."

"I can't. I can't say anything. Miss Rhonda, she treats me good. I don't ever want to lose that job. I love Miss Leah and Miss Rhonda. You can't say anything, but Deborah Darling said it was him. That's what I heard. She said Jeremiah left the alley right after the shot was fired. No one is going to disbelieve that White girl."

"Then he's doomed. Oh my God. We got to do something. I bet there was no blood on Jeremiah. Why that woman do that?"

"Who is going to believe anything we say?" Grayson laughed. "We just have to watch it all play out before us. We need to keep silent, or we lose everything. You hear me, Deasia? We lose everything. If we rat on a White person, no other White person will hire us. They'll think we're untrustworthy."

"There are still other White people in this town we can work for."

"I just told you, we betray one White family, we won't be trusted by any White family."

"She wouldn't blame Jeremiah for a murder, she sleeping with him, why would she do that?"

"All the more reason to get rid of him, acts too White for a Black man. She married to Dickie Darling. She can't mess with that. Anyway, she said she saw him leave the alley, that's what I heard."

"But Jeremiah is an innocent man."

Grayson raised her eyebrows. "And that matters because…?"

"Lord have mercy," Deasia said and put her head in her hands.

Chapter Twenty-Five

Leighton

Leighton watched Mart drag his feet as he walked around the back of her house and entered from the deck. Aspen let out two barks until he realized who it was.

"What's with you?" she asked as he came into her kitchen. "You look like you don't want to be here. Here or anywhere else."

Mart smiled. "Never feel that way, Leighton."

"That's good, because I was going to suggest we throw some steaks on the grill and have ourselves a party."

"Sounds mighty nice."

"So, what's the good word?" Leighton walked to her freezer, took two steaks out and placed a bottle of white wine in. "Let's give the wine ten minutes," she said.

"Good word is that Deborah Darling did not kill Fletcher Smith, she was too engrossed that night with Jeremiah. She didn't see him leave the alley because he was with her and never left her. She lied. She was having an affair with him, and she was the woman he was meeting back there.

She protected her ass by ratting him out."

"She fingered a man she was having an affair with?"

"A Black man she was having an affair with. She didn't want anyone to know that. She was married, just had a baby. She didn't want it obvious she was meeting him that night, so she got nervous and lied. Made it sound as if they were just two strangers in the night passing each other in a dark alley."

"And he never mentioned to the police that it was Deborah Darling he was meeting in the alley?"

Mart shrugged his shoulders. "Who'd believe him?"

"She was questioned, said she never heard anything but some woman's heels clicking past her and the shot, she heard the shot, and after she heard the shot, she said she saw Jeremiah leave. Whether it was intentional or not, she put suspicion on Jeremiah."

Leighton held the back door for Aspen who bounded outside. Mart and Leighton followed, each taking a seat and putting their feet up over the rail.

"She was having an affair with Jeremiah. Deasia told me." Mart grinned. "She didn't mean to tell me, but it came out. I think Barnaby Darling is Jeremiah's son." He looked at her and shook his head. "Doesn't anyone in this town but me notice how much they look alike?"

"People often don't see what's right in front of them. Anyway, Jeremiah isn't exactly strolling around town. Well, that's not going to solve our crime," Leighton said. "It's their problem."

Mart got up and ran around the yard with Aspen, who chased after the sticks Mart threw. Aspen bounced in the air, his wide mouth in a grin. Leighton was sure Mart was avoiding conversation.

"Dickie Darling is a cross-dresser," Leighton suddenly called out. Mart stopped throwing sticks and walked back to the deck slowly.

"Oh, so you know?"

"Got beat up outside The Red Lady wearing a dress. Yes, I heard."

Mart let out a long sigh. "Yep."

"Probably a joke. Doubt if he's a cross-dresser."

"Yep."

"Not too talkative today, are you? Why didn't you tell me? I had to learn about it at the station."

Mart nodded and looked off.

"Papers didn't print it," Leighton said. "Money talks, I guess."

"Yeah, I guess."

"Hear anything about the DNA tests?"

Mart remained silent and then stood up and went into the kitchen for the wine. He handed Leighton a glass and stood before her. "The results of the DNA are in, Leighton. Came in yesterday.”

“Why the hell didn’t someone tell me?” She jumped up. “Whose DNA was on the cup?” she asked.

“Dickie Darling,” Mart said quietly.

Leighton’s jaw dropped. “Dickie? He must have seen something that night. He must have been in the alley.”

“Coulda been the killer,” Mart said.

Leighton shook her head. “I don’t think so, he’s not a killer, but he might be protecting someone who is.”

“I have to tell you something, Leighton.”

Leighton studied him: he was serious, perplexed even.

“Yes, Mart?”

“Remember that we had to add our DNA to the database a few years ago?”

Leighton nodded.

“You’ve got Dickie’s DNA, he’s your parent. I’m sorry Leighton. I wouldn’t let anyone else tell you. I’m really sorry.”

Leighton sat back and the wine glass in her hand fell to the deck and shattered.

Leighton saw her mother at specific times. There was little spontaneity between them. Sunday night dinners were usually at Leighton’s childhood home, where Leah made either meatloaf or Spaghetti Carbonara. Wednesday nights had always been at Beau's restaurant, where Leighton told her mother about her latest cases. Since Beau's death, though, Leah visited Leighton at home and they threw steaks or chicken on the grill and Leighton tried not to show how miserable she was without Beau, and no, she wasn't getting over it. Leighton talked about mundane things, her latest shopping spree, or she'd hand her mother a video of a movie and suggest they watch it.

This Wednesday night, however, there would be no video, no entertaining chatter, nothing but the steak, the bottle of wine and the uncomfortable silence.

"You're angry at me," Leah finally said. "Do you want to tell me why you're being so cold, why we are struggling to make conversation?"

Leighton regarded her mother, wondering in that moment who the hell she was. She had always looked upon her mother as being the put-upon wife of a man who'd had one too many affairs. She'd assumed her father was her father, though he'd always treated her as if she were from another planet and the only thing they had in common was their passion for crab cakes and war movies. She decided she would not accuse; she would simply inquire.

"Why do I have Dickie Darling's DNA,

Mother?"

Her mother paled, stopped breathing, her eyes vacant, her body rigid, time suspended. Leighton feared her question had placed a garrote around her mother's neck to extinguish her.

Leah looked off.

"Why aren't you giving me an explanation?"

"He's your biological father." She turned back to her daughter. "That's why you share the same DNA."

Leighton raised one eyebrow. "That means you had sex with him?"

Leah remained silent.

"And when did you and Dickie Darling create me?"

"When I was in school. I was young. Dickie and I were close. You might say we were boyfriend and girlfriend. In high school, we got a bit too close and I became pregnant. That's when we moved away from Pickens. My parents didn't want anyone in Pickens to know I was having a baby out of wedlock. I hadn't even finished school."

"But you moved back to Pickens. Were you hoping to reunite with Dickie?"

"No, of course not. I was married to Walter by then and Dickie was married to someone else."

"Then why did you move back?"

"That's another story."

"I wish to hear it."

Leah sighed and took Leighton's hand. "I moved back because Rhonda Smith lived in Pickens and wouldn't live anywhere else."

What in God's name would Rhonda Smith have to do with any decision her mother made? Leighton was nervous, afraid of the truth, but she needed the truth. She had to hear it. "And why, pray tell, would you care a rat's ass where Rhonda Smith lived?"

"Because I was in love with her."

The world spun around Leighton, sucking her into some hole in the earth that led somewhere sane. "In love with her?" Leighton stammered. "I didn't even know you knew her."

Leah kept her daughter's hand in hers. Leighton did not move away. She had no will, incapable of resisting anything.

"We went to great lengths to protect you from any gossip. Rhonda and I were very discreet, still are. We're never seen together. We still make it a point not to be seen together."

"Still?"

"Yes."

"I think this calls for another glass of wine." Leighton got up and poured her mother a glass and then herself. She wanted to start talking about the wine, how it came from Oregon, one of Beau's favorite whites. How he used to compare it to a French Chablis and how it went well with blue cheese. But circumnavigating this fascinating past was impossible: her mother had emerged like Aphrodite from the sea, with all the secrets of the deep.

"And here I thought you were dull, worthy of all my love but dutiful and dull."

"I'm sorry if I've disappointed you, Leighton."

"Quite the contrary, you've shown me my blindness, my unfair judgments."

Leah took her daughter's hand again. "I loved Dickie once," she said. "I was absolutely crazy about him in school."

Leighton was surprised. "You were?"

"Oh, yes."

"He was arrested outside of The Red Lady for being in drag. Some thugs beat him up."

"Oh my God, Is he alright?"

"He'll live. Did you know he cross-dresses?"

"Yes, I did."

Leighton sighed. She didn't want to go there. She didn't want to know anymore. She wouldn't ask if her mother had ever loved Walter. Instead, she said, "Dickie's DNA was identified on a cup found near Fletcher Smith's body. Dickie must have known who killed him."

"He didn't know."

Leighton's head jerked up. "Why do you say that?"

"Because he wasn't there when Fletcher was killed."

"How do you know that?"

"Because I was there. Dickie had left and never saw anything."

It started to make sense; her mother had to protect Rhonda. The hole in Leighton's stomach magnified. "Did you kill him because he used to beat Rhonda?"

"No," Leah said. "I did not kill him. Rhonda didn't kill him either." She turned to look at her daughter. "It was an accident, a terrible, terrible accident. He didn't know there were any bullets in the gun. He wasn't even supposed to have the gun."

Leighton sat back. Her hands trembled. She watched her mother as if she'd never seen her before. This stranger had, in the last twenty minutes or so, shattered every illusion Leighton had about her.

Chapter Twenty-Six

Leah

Halloween 1963

The Angel Oak tree spread its branches over the ground like the knurled hands of an old man. Yet it was beautiful and so commanding, so interesting, one never noticed anything else on the property until the house appeared at the end of the drive like something out of an old film, *The Horse Soldiers*, perhaps, or of course, *Gone with the Wind*. Rhonda had told her that the tree was over five hundred years old.

Rhonda's family house, better known as "The Plantation," was large and white and imposing, how she assumed a Southern general would be, guarding the old world of slavery and the Southern way of life. Leah did not like the house. It stood for the past. She wanted something for the present for her and Rhonda, something cozy and warm that took a friendly stance, a welcoming stance. Their house would stand behind its lack of history, its small porch and paned windows would be a clean slate for the future. Rhonda's house was not welcoming. It was demanding. It did not appear with open arms, it manifested, like omens and curses, like those limbs of the Angel Oak that grasped the earth with audacious reach.

Fletcher was not there. He was never there. He refused to live in it, refused to settle into his wife's fortune and take credit for it. It wasn't his, it was hers, hers and that long line of ancestors who had owned hundreds of slaves. "Your family was the reason we fought the Civil War. All those lives lost because of you and your goddamned cotton fields and darkies and fancy-pants ways." That's what he'd tell her. That her ways were fanciful, and her motives were tarnished, as if Rhonda had owned anything other than the inheritance she was bequeathed.

Fletcher had bought the largest house right outside the town of Pickens and had moved Rhonda into it after their marriage. He was from Minnesota and had a certain disdain for Southerners and their pride in the war they'd lost. There were monuments to Civil War generals all over the place in Pickens. Confederate flags lined the lanes and the streets, proudly displayed from front porches. But it had been a job that had brought Fletcher South, so he'd basically had no choice, not if he wanted real money in the bank. But he'd gotten the ultimate opportunity when he married Rhonda. He could then afford all those storage units now that he had the freedom to dip into his wife's assets. No sense managing a chain of home goods stores when he could own his own business and expand on what he owned until he was almost as rich as his wife.

He was successful. That was for sure. Rhonda used to say it went to his head and that's when he started womanizing and beating her up, drinking as if entitled to every bottle of gin in Pickens. Maybe he hit her because he was drunk, but he hit her when he was sober, too. He hit her because she was there, reminding him of good breeding and fine manners, of college educations, aquiline noses, and refinement, what wine goes with what and a taste for fois gras on those awful sour fruit berries. He could go on. She turned heads, so then she must oblige the heads she turned, must be a whore, mustn't she? But then Fletcher found out his wife was perverted, preferred the ladies. Fletcher didn't get it, but maybe a few knocks to the head would cure the bitch of desires that Satan had surely planted in her soul.

He had beaten the crap out of his wife earlier that day, so she'd come to her family plantation with its imposing columns to hide away, to protect herself from Fletcher's red raging face. She'd called Leah and told her to bring her children and they would go to the party together from The Plantation. Rhonda said she couldn't bear to go to the party alone and face Fletcher's obnoxious bravado and his perpetual leer when he looked at women. No one would notice that she'd come with Leah. Grayson would watch Leighton, and Kenny had been promised he could attend the party so long as he didn't try to buy any beer or act up.

Leah looked at Kenny in the back seat of her Buick. He was happy; he'd begged to be allowed to go to the Halloween party. Leah surmised that some girl he liked was probably going to be there. He seemed to be getting his shit together after so much turmoil, so many fights with other boys who just might have looked at him the wrong way. And that horrible shooting at the gas station. Kenny spent a few months in a detention center after that. The man he shot recovered and Kenny ordered not to go near him. Since he'd been home, he'd been acting like a model citizen. "I never want to go back there, Mom," he'd told her. "They make me eat when I don't want to eat and do what I don't want to do." Well, in any event, being locked away seemed to have worked. His grades were high, and he was happy to be home, playing football and chasing girls. She assumed he still carried a lot of rage at both Walter and his natural mother, but to all appearances, he'd found a way to deal with it.

She was sorry for Kenny, and she loved him, not the way she loved Leighton, but she loved him, a sweet kid who'd been abandoned by his mother. That pain must be deep, so Leah didn't mind that he clung to her, perhaps a little too much. She knew he needed her. Walter wasn't the greatest father in the world, so she tried to be both mother and father to Kenny, to support him, be there for him.

Leah did not expect to find Rhonda hobbling around when she got to the house. Grayson let her in and anger inside her grew in monstrous proportions. "What the fuck did he do to you?" The bruises on Rhonda's legs graphic evidence she'd been viciously kicked into sempiternity.

Rhonda smiled and kissed the top of Kenny's head. "He looks great. Billy the Kid, you are bad. You are more bad than any of them. You are the baddest outlaw for sure."

Kenny beamed and headed for the kitchen, where he was sure to coax some of Grayson's Southern Pot Roast from her.

Leah fumed, her anger a forest fire, fueled by the sadness in Grayson's eyes before she averted them, and found refuge in some tiny spot on the floor.

"Grayson, would you take Leighton to her bedroom. I'll be up to say goodnight." She watched Grayson take her daughter up the stairs and then turned to Rhonda. "What did he do to you?"

"Beat the shit out of me. What do you think?"

"That son of a bitch."

"Told me I think I'm better than anyone else because I happened to mention that his costume was kind of mundane and did he want me to spruce it up a bit?" She laughed. "Jesus. The man is out of his mind. He'll beat me for saying 'pass the sugar.'"

"Are you alright? Are you sure you want to go tonight? Does it hurt?"

"I'm fine. Hurts only when I walk. "Bastard is not going to keep me from living my life, Leah. We're going to that party and tomorrow we will talk about divorce, in front of an audience, that is."

"He will contest it."

"Worth a shot," Rhonda said.

Johnny Cash and "Ring of Fire" reverberated on the jukebox at Smith's as Leah walked into the bar. She had just taken Kenny outside where the barbeque was and told him to stay put.

"I don't want to see you inside. Minors are not allowed. You've got some friends out here, Kenny, so stay put."

Kenny grinned. Leah thought he looked adorable in his outlaw get up but then noticed the gun.

"What are you doing with that gun? Didn't I tell you that you couldn't take your father's gun?"

Kenny put his hand on the handle of the old Smith & Wesson and grinned. "I doubt it has bullets, Mom. But I can't be an outlaw without a gun."

Leah smiled. "I doubt if your father would have kept a loaded gun in the house but don't use it anyway. Don't even pretend to use it. It's just for show."

"Right, Mom," Kenny said and watched her ease back inside the crowded bar.

Dressed as Ashley Wilkes, and next to Scarlet O'Hara at the bar, Leah mischievously stayed in character to have some fun with Dickie's wife, disguised behind the mask. She flirted with Deborah, who clearly had no idea who Leah was behind *her* mask. Also somewhat drunk. Deborah checked her watch and then slid off the barstool and weaved out back to the alley. As Leah looked around the bar, she saw Fletcher, spilling all over a brunette like rain. She walked over and hit him in the side —hard —so hard he said "*Ow*" and turned around.

"What the hell is the matter with you?" he said, rubbing his side.

"You're the matter with me. You know, Fletcher, I am not afraid of you," she said as the woman he'd been spilling over threw her eye-daggers, "therefore I am taking Rhonda to the police tomorrow and I'm telling them that you beat the shit out of her, and you need to be locked up."

"Keep your voice down," he said in a fierce whisper.

Leah met his eyes. "It can't go on, Fletcher. You can't keep hitting her. You might kill her one day. We can show the police the bruises."

"Get the hell away from me."

"I'm doing it, Fletcher. I'm turning you in. There's me, there's Grayson and there's Rhonda herself. We're witnesses to your beatings. That's got to mean something."

She studied the look on his face and knew she'd frightened him. She slid off the bar stool and went outside to get some air and lit a cigarette with shaking hands. Someone else was out there and she turned, just as Dickie grabbed her arm. At the same time, Fletcher came at her, saying he had to talk to her … she was so angry she stubbed out the cigarette on Fletcher's hand as he reached for her. He yelled out. Dickie was still pulling her away, she guessed without any idea of what she'd done to Fletcher. She told Dickie to get away and go back inside. She watched him walk off and disappear into the darkness. Almost immediately, pain ignited on the side of her face. Fletcher had hit her, punched her hard. She stumbled and then saw Kenny.

He screamed at Fletcher, "Get out of here or

I'll shoot you," holding the gun up.

Fletcher told him to piss off and grabbed Leah.

"Let my mother go," Kenny yelled again.

Fletcher grabbed Leah tighter around the neck and she yelled in pain, kicked him, and broke away, perhaps a foot or two from him.

At the shocking and earsplitting sound, blood seeped from Fletcher's head, splatter saturating the front of her shirt. Frozen before the body, she stood still for barely a second before leaping into action.

Everything flew by as if time ran in front of her at double the speed of light. She grabbed Kenny, rushed him out of the alley, and pushed him back to the car while he cried, saying repeatedly that he hadn't meant to do it. Calming him as best she could, she sped around to the front of the bar. By some miracle, Rhonda was there.

She rolled down the window and called to Rhonda over Kenny's tears. "I didn't know it was loaded. I swear I didn't know it was loaded. I just wanted him to stop hurting you."

"I came out here to look for you. Everyone is saying they heard a shot." Rhonda peered in the car and noticed the blood on Leah. "Shit," she said.

"Get in the car, Rhonda," Leah said, and as Rhonda threw herself into the backseat Leah sped off, fast as she dared. The pulsing wail of sirens sounded seconds later, audible until they were way past town limits.

Leah will never forget the look on Grayson's face when she saw the blood on the front of her shirt, and the horrible burn on Kenny's hand.

"Oh my God," she said.

"Help him get cleaned up," Leah said. "Give me back his clothes."

Leah had picked up the gun, taken it away from Kenny after he'd dropped it on the ground. Now Rhonda held it. "What will we do with this?" she asked.

"Give everything to me. Any blood-stained clothes and the gun. You stay here and deal with the police."

"Look, Leah, we can say it was an accident. He's just a kid and everyone knows about Fletcher, that he's a monster."

"A monster who owns this town." She took Rhonda's hand. "Look, I can't let anything happen to Kenny. He was only trying to protect me. Everyone thinks of him as a delinquent and he shot that guy at the gas station last year, which looks bad for him. They won't believe a word he says. They'll throw him back in reform school and he'll never get his life together. He's doing so well now." Leah cried large, choking sobs. Rhonda held her.

"No, we'll protect him, Leah. Nothing will happen to him. I swear."

Leah drove out in the dark past the Angel Oak tree. She drove until she got to Walter's boat at Lake Keowe; a small boat that he rarely used for fishing, she often let Kenny use it with his friends. Leah pushed it out on to the river and paddled to the middle of the lake. The night was covered with stars. She listened for the sounds of people, but the silence was all-embracing. She tossed the gun into the river and watched it sink. She built a fire onshore and burned her clothes and Kenny's clothes, and then put the fire out. Despite her exhaustion, she would not let herself rest or cry until she was back in Rhonda's arms.

At Rhonda's sprawling mansion, she realized she had been gone for three hours. She found Rhonda in the parlor.

"Have the police been here yet?" Leah asked as she walked in.

Rhonda went to her and took her in her arms. "Your face is swollen," she said.

"What did the police say?"

"Nothing. Just that he was dead. They asked me where I was. I told them I was at Smith's, but I hadn't seen Fletcher. I asked them if they knew who killed him and they said they didn't. That's it.”

"I passed Ginger's car on the way here. He didn't see me, but I think he's headed in this direction. He lives in the opposite direction. Where else would he be going at this hour?"

"We'll deal with him."

"Grayson?"

"We're safe with Grayson. She won't say anything. Kenny is safe. I promise."

Chapter Twenty-Seven

Dickie

Dickie watched his mother walk toward him from the hammock in the back yard, one of his favorite spots. It looked out onto Deborah's garden where color abounded in a striking, resplendent palette.

Lillian took a seat next to him and the hammock swayed in gentle acceptance. She took his hand. "Deborah spotted my ring on Prissy's finger," she said.

Dickie closed his eyes. "We should have told her."

"Well, Barnaby should have told her, but she intimidates everyone in this family but me."

"Well, then you should have told her."

"It is not my place to tell your wife that her son is engaged."

Dickie let out a long sigh. "I guess you're right."

"It's ludicrous, you know."

Dickie sighed again. "He's not mine, is he?" Her cheeks flushed pomegranate pink. "I mean, biologically he's not mine."

"That has never mattered to me."

"Nor to me, Mother."

"She had an affair. You know that."

"With that Black man, Jeremiah?"

Lillian nodded her head. "You did the right thing, ignoring it."

"Yes, I suppose I did. It didn't matter, Mother. I loved Barnaby completely."

"And I love him completely, as well. He will not be denied his happiness."

"He doesn't need his parent's permission to marry whom he chooses. This isn't the eighteenth century. But his parent's blessings would be nice."

"If Deborah does not accept Prissy as her daughter-in-law, Barnaby will never have her blessings. He'll be hurt by it forever. He's always needed his mother's acceptance, though he doesn't show it."

Dickie turned to her. "We have to tell Barney the truth. I don't know why it matters to Deborah. The boy's biological father is Black, and she knows it. She should just let it be."

"When have you ever known Deborah let anything just be?" She put her hand over his. "You leave this to me, son. It's got to be done. I'm afraid it will be harsh, but it's got to be done."

"Always to the rescue, Mother."

"Thank you for inviting me to dinner." She grinned at her son.

He raised an eyebrow. "Did I invite you to

dinner?"

"You most certainly did."

"So be it."

"His mother's disapproval will not stop him from marrying Prissy, but her disapproval will make him very sad."

"You going to tell Barnaby the truth?"

"The truth is necessary," she said.

"There, then, let the truth be known and let Deborah make peace with it." Dickie took his mother's hand as they walked back to the house.

Dickie walked through the sunroom and into the living room, where Prissy and Barnaby watched Deborah pace before the large windows that looked out onto a row of red Crepe Myrtle trees. The sun was a warm yellow and the sky was blue and benevolent, in sharp contrast to the angry expression on Deborah's face. She stilled, a human statue, as Dickie walked into the room. His mother had retreated to the back where the kitchen was.

"Did you know about this?" Deborah shouted.

Dickie took in Prissy's pained expression and the rage on his son's face. He went to Deborah and tried to take her hand.

"Get away from me," she shouted. "You kept this from me, Dickie. You knew about it and you kept it from me."

Dickie looked at his son. "I'm sorry, Barney."

"Don't apologize. Mother is having a meltdown because Prissy and I are engaged." He rose from the couch and walked to his mother. "I believe I was way over twenty-one on my last birthday, Mother. I believe I can marry whom I choose."

"You can't marry a Negro. Please come to your senses, Barnaby. You can't marry a Negro in South Carolina." Deborah looked at Prissy frantically. "You can't let him do this," she said.

"I most certainly can marry Prissy, Mother. I do hope you'll come to the wedding. Oh, and Grandmother is throwing an engagement party for us next month. You're invited, of course."

Lillian appeared from the kitchen. "I've been invited for dinner. I could not refuse. Deasia has just given me a taste of the most delightful Shrimp Scampi." She sat on the couch next to Prissy and took her hand. "How beautiful the ring looks on you, dear." She looked up. "Now, what was everyone screaming about?"

"You can't possibly be supportive of this." Deborah glared at Lillian.

"And why wouldn't I be?" Lillian looked at her innocently. "I assume you're speaking of my grandson's engagement?"

"How dare you give her your ring without consulting me first." Deborah put her hands on her hips and glared at Lillian.

"I didn't know I needed your permission to give away what was mine." Lillian frowned. "You're disappointing me again, Deborah."

Deborah shook her head from side to side. "I'm not supportive of this," she said. "I don't support this at all. I will never support it. I will not come to the wedding."

"Then you owe your son an explanation," Lillian said. "There is no reason to deny him his happiness. He loves this girl. He always has."

Barney sat beside Prissy and took her hand. He looked at his grandmother. "She says that Prissy is a Negro and therefore not appropriate to become my wife. I can't see why that should make a difference. I've never looked at Prissy as anything other than the woman I love."

Lillian went to Dickie and smiled. "Well, Barnaby has Negro blood, so why should it matter if he marries Prissy? Isn't that perfect?" She now smiled at Barnaby. "But I believe that 'Negro' is no longer appropriate. I believe we say African American now." She looked back into their shocked faces. "I really don't believe it matters, though."

Lillian watched as Dickie slumped into a chair and Prissy looked at Barnaby, incredulousness adorning her face. The look on Barnaby's face was one of pure shock.

"We have Negro blood?" he asked his father.

Dickie remained silent so Barnaby turned to

his mother. "Would you care to explain?"

Dickie got to his feet. He went to Barnaby and put his hand on his shoulder. "Your mother had an affair, son. I forgave her. It was a long time ago." He turned to see the look of horror on his wife's face.

"You knew she had an affair?" Barnaby asked. "Who with?"

"Your grandmother and I knew she had an affair." Dickie kept his eyes on Deborah now. "She was young, son, don't judge her."

"You bastards," Deborah shouted. "You bastards." They all watched as Deborah ran from the room and up the stairs in tears.

"Jeremiah Lennox is your biological father, Barnaby," Lillian said softly after Deborah left the room. She took in his dazed expression. She hugged him close. "Your father and I thought you should know. Your mother is still denying it. But it's the truth."

"I love you more than my own life," Dickie whispered. "You are my son. Blood does not determine that. Love does."

Barnaby collapsed into his grandmother's arms. "I can't believe this," he said.

Dickie slowly climbed the stairs and knocked lightly on the bedroom door. When he received no answer after several more knocks, he turned the knob and let himself in.

Deborah sat at the edge of the bed; mascara smeared her lovely face.

"Deasia has brought out the most delightful coconut shrimp hors d'oeuvres. Can you pull yourself together and come downstairs?"

"I will not come downstairs."

"Don't do this to our son. This should be a happy occasion. We all love that girl."

"Lillian had no right to tell my son that he isn't yours," she screeched.

"Perhaps she didn't, but he needed to know. I needed to know. For God's sake, it was your responsibility to tell me, Deborah. What difference does it make now if he marries Prissy?"

"She's far blacker than he is. My God, Dickie, look at Deasia and Jackson. Their children will be black as the night."

"You should have thought of the consequences before you slept with Jeremiah. Besides, what does that matter?"

"God, Dickie. You can't blame me for what I did so many years ago. I was so young and inexperienced, and then to find out I had married a bisexual. It was a shock to me. You can't blame me."

Dickie looked at her for a long time and then he walked over and stood before her. "You think I'm bisexual?"

"Oh, Dickie don't deny it. I knew. I saw you

kissing that she-man on the street, unabashedly placing a kiss on his cheek. He might have planted a kiss on yours, too, for all I know."

"Malcolm?"

Deborah nodded. "I never said anything to you. If you needed some sort of perverted fling with a man, then so be it. I didn't want to know. I still don't. But I needed a real man, Dickie. I needed a real man. I was young and foolish, and Jeremiah was there, throwing himself at me."

"I am not bisexual, Deborah."

She looked up at him. "Don't deny your affairs. I should not have denied mine. But you were the only man for me. You still are. Do you think I love anyone else but you?" Deborah got up and walked to the dresser. She took a tissue and wiped her eyes. "Don't deny your true self and all those superfluous rendezvous. It happened so long ago for me. You still go out prowling the streets for men."

Astonished, Dickie sat in the small club chair beside the bed. He put his face in his hands before addressing her. "I will not deny anything. I have never been with a man in my life. I had an affair with a woman, not a man."

Deborah got up and went to him. She took his hair in her hand and jerked his head back. "What? Are you telling me you had an affair with a woman?"

"I'm telling you I am *having* an affair with a

woman." He grabbed her hand and removed it from his hair.

"What woman?" she yelled. "What woman?"

Dickie got to his feet and walked to the door. "What difference does it make?" He turned to her. "Pull yourself together, Deborah, and come downstairs."

Chapter Twenty-Eight

Deborah

Lottie empathized with her tear-stained friend, black lines of mascara smeared across her cheeks and upper lip, resembling a raven on a perch.

"I'll have another martini," Deborah whispered.

"Deborah, you can't drink yourself into oblivion. You must face what is happening. Learn to accept what is happening."

Deborah let out a short cry. "Easy for you to say. You have no responsibility. You don't have a son who is marrying beneath him. Nor do you have a husband who has been cheating on you for god knows how long."

Lottie looked around the room for a waiter, called him over and ordered Deborah's martini and a mint julep for herself.

"We're going to get some food after this drink. You can't get in a car and drive after you've had three martinis."

"Stop mothering me, Lottie."

Lottie sat back. Her discomfort showed. In a

gesture to convey concern, she reached out and covered Deborah's hand with her own.

"Everything we do has consequences, Deborah."

"Oh, stop acting so pious. You must know who he's having an affair with."

"He's still having an affair then? That's what he told you?"

"Yes, he said he was. He just didn't tell me who with." She leaned across the table and found Lottie's eyes. "You must know. He talks to you."

"Not about that, Deborah."

Deborah sat back. She'd conjured up every female in Pickens but not a one of them registered as Dickie's type. She was Dickie's type and there was no one else in Pickens who fitted the bill, who was even as remotely attractive as she was … except if she still had the bloom of youth on her cheeks … well, youth is everyone's type.

"That detective?" She peered at Lottie. "Recently widowed. Young. Blonde. Could it be her?" Deborah peered at Lottie again. "What do you think?"

"Oh my God, Deborah, it's more likely to be Leighton's mother than Leighton."

"Leah?" Deborah perked up. "I never thought of her. I mean, she's so unfeminine."

"She's very attractive," Lottie said softly.

Deborah's expression suggested all the pieces were falling into place. "Yes, in a very modern way, I suppose. She could be his type. She does have a certain buoyancy about her."

"They used to go together in school."

"What? He never told me."

"He told me." Lottie looked frantically for a place to rest her eyes, anywhere but on Deborah. "Look, Deborah, I'm famished. I'm going to order lunch."

Deborah was livid as she took the back roads home. She'd offered Prissy fifty thousand dollars to break off the engagement. Prissy had left the room in tears after she called Deborah "a horrible woman." She'd offered Deasia the same fifty thousand to talk her daughter out of the marriage and Deasia very quietly had refused. Defeat threatened to overwhelm her. She might have to just live with it. But she still had to deal with her husband. Perhaps she could control that. She certainly couldn't offer him money to end his affair, but she had ammunition, weapons made of silk she was sure would force him to his knees.

She put on her sheer black negligee that evening. It showed off her breasts and made her look taller and thinner. She spent an hour applying her makeup. She dabbed Channel behind her ear and on her wrist. She found him in the den reading one of his crime novels.

"Darling," she said. "I know who this woman

is. You've had your fun with her and now I want you to end it."

Dickie looked up. "Deborah, I'm sorry. I never meant to hurt you, as I'm sure you never meant to hurt me, but this affair has been going on for as long as I have been married to you."

Deborah's lips quivered. "Thirty years?"

Dickie nodded his head. "Something like that."

"Then why haven't you left me? Why did you find it necessary to betray me like this? Though I would not have given you a divorce. For God's sake, we have children."

"I had no reason to leave you. Everything seemed so perfect. I had you. I had her.

"I will divorce you now, though."

"If you must."

Deborah's legs almost buckled. "You want a divorce?"

"She understands me."

"Leah? Leah understands you? You don't think I do?"

Dickie shook his head in disbelief. "Leah?"

"Yes, she's your lover, isn't she?"

"I loved Leah once, but for the last thirty years I have been with my soul mate. Unfortunately, that has never been Leah."

"I hate when you lie to me. Then who is your soul mate, Dickie? Who the fuck is your soul mate? I am not afraid of competition."

"I cross-dress," he said. "I want you to know that, Deborah. I cross-dress."

"What is that?"

Dickie laughed. "You see? I want to be understood."

"I understand you."

"No, you don't."

"Then who the fuck does, Dickie. Who is your fucking soul mate?"

"I think it's best we end this conversation. I don't wish to hurt you any further."

Deborah stood in the middle of the room, quivering with anger. "I am going to bed, and you are not welcome beside me." Deborah slammed the door on her way out, setting off a flutter in Dickie's heart. He took his hand and wiped away the one tear that escaped from his eyes. Where to go now, he wondered.

Chapter Twenty-Nine

Leighton

Kenny did not deny that he shot Fletcher Smith that night in the alley in 1963. Leighton had gone to his house accompanied by her mother. Kenny must have known by Leah's expression why they were there. He put his hands out in a joking manner. "I won't resist," he said.

Leighton did not cuff him; he went with her willingly as Leah held his hand.

He signed a statement at the station saying he had shot Fletcher by accident. He'd tried to frighten him, tried to protect his mother. Many people would testify to the bruise on Leah's face that night — Malcolm, Grayson, and Rhonda, but no one had seen Fletcher strike Leah. But perhaps there were others who had seen her swollen face, black and purple bruises, that Fletcher beat up women was common knowledge. Leighton assumed that based on Kenny's age at the time, and that he had no idea the gun was loaded, he wouldn't serve time. They had to prove it was an accident, but Leah had no doubt he'd be doing community service, perhaps lecturing kids on the danger of firearms, rather than serve a prison sentence. Rhonda would get him the best attorney and the whole sordid wretchedness of that night would be behind them.

Leighton loved Kenny for sure, and was sorry for him, but there was no real sibling closeness; they were nothing alike. As for their looks, Kenny's hair was the color of milk chocolate and Leighton was a strawberry blonde, like Leah. Kenny was built like his father, short and muscular, whereas Leighton was long and slender. She'd always towered over him. He had his father's eyes, a warm brown, and Leah's eyes were an unusual blue, as salient as a blue orchid. Sometimes, they struggled for conversation: he was full of bravado when he was young and teased her about boys, to the point of obnoxiousness. He could be less than gentle about her choices, but it didn't really bother her. She was so like her mother, secretive and quiet. She was athletic and a bit of a bookworm just like her mother. Kenny could barely throw a baseball and the only thing he ever read was the parking tickets he'd accumulated. She'd never felt they were connected. They were such different people. It had always been extraordinarily difficult to find common ground with Kenny. However, she loved her brother, as did her mother.

As they grew up, she never doubted they were related by blood. She believed that Walter had fathered them both. Now, knowing the truth, the similarity she shared with her biological father was shockingly apparent. She thought back to when Lillian Darling used to grab her out of nowhere and kiss her cheeks. Her mother just stood by with a smile. Of course, she did, she was Lillian Darling's grandchild and Lillian must have known the truth. Her mother certainly knew it.

"Mommy, why does that lady like me so much?" she'd ask and Leah always answered, "Because you're such a darlin' little girl."

Then, when she was older, too old to kiss and hug, Lillian would hug her anyway. Leighton would feel the squeeze and the peck on the cheek. "What a beautiful girl you've turned out to be," she'd say and wander off after stuffing a twenty-dollar bill into Leighton's pocket.

Leighton never really thought much about it. Old women often love children was how she interpreted it. Now, with the truth, she was aware of missing pieces, and a void she never felt before. Nothing was ever missing before. Now it was.

She turned into the parking lot of Beau's old restaurant. Dickie's car was there already. He's early, she thought. He'll think I want to speak to him about Fletcher's murder. She smiled. She was always early to meetings, too.

She'd gotten the broker to open the restaurant for Dickie and not bother to wait for his arrival. The broker mentioned a buyer for the restaurant who seemed serious.

When she walked inside, Dickie was sitting in a booth, which saddened her for a moment. Beau would have made him coffee and brought rolls and jam to the table. It was a perfect time for brunch. The restaurant looked so barren except for Dickie's presence. He looked despondent and distracted. Beau's presence in the background, giving her an encouraging smile, was almost tangible.

"Mr. Darling," she said as she slipped in opposite him.

Dickie raised his eyes. They were identical to hers, that striking blue orchid color. Why had she never noticed before that their eyes were the same?

"You've got me over here quite early," he said. "You must have solved the crime."

"I didn't want to bring you to the station for this."

Dickie smiled and she noticed a dimple on the right side of his face. "This sounds intriguing," he said.

"Your DNA was found at the scene, on a cup on the ground approximately five inches from Fletcher's face."

Dickie had no memory of that. "Really? That's odd. I suppose I may have dropped it. I had a lot to drink that night."

She leaned forward. "How well did you know

my mother?"

Dickie leaned away from her. "What an odd question."

"How well?"

Dickie thought about his wife, her accusation about Leah. If she only knew how much he had loved her. But that was years ago. It seemed now like it never happened. It was so youthful and so innocent. What he had with Lottie was as deep as the ocean floor.

"Pretty well … once. We went to school together. Did you know that?"

"I know it now," she said.

Something had changed: Dickie picked up a certain sarcasm in her tone. "You think I killed Fletcher because of the DNA?"

She shook her head. "I know you didn't kill him. My brother did. He was trying to protect my mother, thought he'd frighten him away, but the gun went off. It was an accident, but I guess I'll have to let the courts decide."

Dickie was shocked by the news. Then why am I here, he wondered. "I'm happy to hear you've solved your crime. But your brother? Sorry about that."

"You were trying to protect her too, weren't you? You thought my mother had killed him."

"Why would I want to do that?"

"I don't know, maybe because you loved her."

Dickie scrabbled for the right words. "Well,

yes, as a kid, I loved her."

"You loved her as a young man, too." She looked into his familiar eyes and put her hand out to touch his. "I know I'm yours … biologically speaking."

Relief enfolded him and he sighed deeply, his heart pounding. "Yes, I've known for years. I wanted to claim you, but it would have been too confusing for you and would not have looked good for your mother." He was rambling and tried to smile. "I'm sorry," he said. "You know how people are. She would have been the brunt of gossip."

"No need to apologize," she said and squeezed his hand. "My youth was full of mistakes, too."

They looked at each other awkwardly for a moment before he spoke. "Can I tell my family about you? Is there really a need to keep it secret anymore? I've never wanted to keep you secret; you know."

"Well, your mother knows. She used to pick me up and kiss me all the time."

Dickie put his head back. Yes, of course his mother knew; she knew everything.

"Well, now that you're a Darling might as well get to know what you're in for."

"Your wife?"

"Oh, she'll be fine with it. It was so long ago. Deborah will be thrilled I'm sure."

Out of nowhere, the phone rang, the shrillness

startling Leah. She didn't think the phone should ring without Beau there to answer it.

"I believe your phone is ringing." Dickie smiled. "Go on and answer, I'll be fine. I'll wait right here."

Leighton got up and picked up the receiver on the counter. Dickie watched as a large grin broke out across her face. It must be good news, he thought.

"Someone has made an offer on the restaurant." Leighton put her arms out. "And what an offer it is."

"Congratulations," he said.

"Your mother has offered me a fortune for this place."

"My mother?" Stunned, Dickie gaped, lost his breath, and quickly recovered. "What the hell?" he said.

Chapter Thirty

Lillian

Proud and delighted with herself, she had just signed a contract on Beau McArdle's old restaurant. A wedding gift of sorts — oh, not that she wasn't going to get something special for Barney and Priss — this was something she wanted very much to do for Jeremiah. Well, if truth be told, it was for Prissy's mother, Deasia, as well. What perfect partners they would make, Deasia and Jeremiah. Oh, not in the romantic sense. Deasia loved Jackson to death and Jeremiah loved women in the plural sense. But she had always known they were friends, Deasia, and Jeremiah. Jeremiah had told her when Deasia was first hired to work for the Darlings, when he told her that Deasia cooked even better than he did, and her family would not be sorry and for sure, they haven't been. Lillian would take ten percent of the profits and her partnership guaranteed the restaurant's success.

Lillian was putting money in Leighton's bank account, too. It made sense all around. Leighton needed to get on with her life and Beau's restaurant was a constant reminder of her loss. She could use that money to put away for the child she was sure to have one day, or she could just go wild on a new wardrobe.

Lillian had discussed the business proposition with Deasia and Jeremiah, whether it was something they genuinely wanted. Turns out they were overjoyed at the prospect of a partnership with her. Both had tear-filled eyes as they cranked her hand like a car jack. Deasia needed persuading not to turn her back on such a golden opportunity, which hadn't taken more than thirty minutes. They said they used to fantasize they cooked together when they were young, and they'd talk about it for hours and argue about who was better at cooking what. Besides, Lillian wanted to do something for Prissy's mother.

Deasia needed the independence and, plainly, it would not look good to have her new granddaughter's mother working as a domestic. She owed Jeremiah more than she could ever repay him, but he always appreciated everything she did for him, so innocently unaware of the part she had played in his destiny. "You are like a son to me," she'd tell him.

Lillian liked doing things for other people, she couldn't help herself. Nobody in her life was as dear to her as her son Dickie and his children. That's why she'd protect them at any cost. She'd eliminate any threats. She was happy that Dickie was bringing Leighton home to meet his family. Now it wouldn't look so strange when she kissed and hugged her.

Deborah was livid, though, still having heart palpitations over everything that was happening around her. Her son's marriage, her husband's affair. Then Dickie announces that Leighton is his biological daughter. Poor Deborah almost fainted. Now she cries every day over her husband's indiscretion that not only spawned a child but is continuing to darken her life. It's unfortunate she's blaming Leah when Dickie got over Leah years ago, right around the time he started going to bed with Lottie. Deborah is screaming divorce as well as Dickie, but Deborah didn't mean it, she's just trying to force Dickie to his senses.

Divorce was out of the question. Lillian would certainly have to put an end to that. She had no loyalty to Deborah and less love for her than for someone who stole her pocketbook or beat up on dogs and children, but nothing was going to change her status as Lillian's daughter-in-law. Divorce was a dirty word, a very dirty word.

It would be detrimental for her son to divorce Deborah. They were the couple everyone loved. The couple everyone invited everywhere. Dickie didn't know his own mind and as much as he thought he was in love with Lottie, it was for the sheer thrill of it. Truth be known, he loved his wife. He loved that she was scatterbrained and ridiculously opinionated but turned heads everywhere they went. He loved that she attracted clients to him with her pretty smile and her very Southern charm. He liked beauty. Lottie didn't have that, but Deborah had that in spades, even at fifty-five years old.

The only thing Lottie had was the same quirky gene her son had. Quirky doesn't mean much, not when you set it against children and thirty years of marriage. Lottie didn't have much in the way of loyalty, either. Her son must have thought about that when she threw herself at him despite her friendship with Deborah.

Lillian didn't like disloyalty. That's why she never forgave Deborah for carrying on with Jeremiah. She thinks that's why Dickie strayed. He sensed it. No sense being loyal to a woman who's taking her pleasure elsewhere.

Well, now it was his turn. Dickie had made a fool out of her for thirty years sneaking around with a woman that liked him dressing up in high heels. Maybe getting away with something like that was enough to hold a marriage together. Much as she disliked Deborah, she admired her willingness to turn the other cheek to what she surmised was her husband's proclivity toward men. Foolish woman. That had never been Dickie's interest. Deborah would protect her marriage at any cost. She would no more divorce Dickie than chop the head off a chicken.

Lillian understood that in his heart, her son was the most loyal man on earth, loving Deborah despite everything, but he was very vulnerable to Lottie. Lottie was one of those women who gets you good and then throws you out when you've spent too many nights boring her to tears. Lottie didn't like men: she liked the idea of a man liking her. Lillian's intuition said Lottie could ruin her son's marriage and be sorry for it later.

Lillian pulled up in front of Lottie's house, nice and early. Most likely, Lottie thought she was there to impart her blessings now that Dickie was free to marry her. "Over my dead body," Lillian uttered. Money talked and she would make it easy for Lottie. A new job, a promotion, a new town, maybe even a new man with an unusual predilection. That's what Lottie liked, not to be bored and certainly not to be wed, the two don't mix.

Chapter Thirty-One

Deborah

Dickie had moved his things into his son's old bedroom. Quite serious about the divorce, he was oblivious to what people would think of him taking up with Leah. Everyone's hearts would go out to Deborah. Poor put-upon wife. Oh, the sympathy she'd get from every damn soul in Pickens.

Deborah didn't think people thought that much of Leah. Dickie would have to bear the brunt of his choices. The woman wasn't all that friendly, never entertained and never remarried, so who the hell wanted to socialize with some old prune like that. Well, at least now Deborah knew why she'd never remarried. She couldn't have thought that much of herself to play second fiddle to a woman who had it all. Deborah puzzled over why Leah had never demanded that Dickie get a divorce years ago and take up with her. What the hell kind of woman puts up with a married man? She enjoyed only a small part of Dickie. Deborah had all of him. They had a full life, children, popularity, success. They had always been invited everywhere. How did Leah tolerate the respect his wife received from all of Pickens? Leah McNeil was a disgrace. Deborah had nothing to be jealous of.

Still, Leah had a piece of him, something of Dickie that Deborah didn't have. What the hell was the attraction between them? What was the bond that held them together for more than thirty years? Dickie still desired her even if he desired Leah as well. Deborah had to admit that she was the one who initiated intimacy between them. Dickie could take it or leave it. But whenever Deborah desired sex Dickie was always ready, always able to please her. But did he please himself? Was he fulfilled or would he lie in bed afterwards wishing it were Leah beside him?

She had to make sense of this. It didn't compute for her. She had to tell that woman she would not give Dickie his freedom any time soon: she intended to fight back. It's true their children were grown now. Robinette was going off to college at the end of the summer and Barnaby would be married in the fall and probably get Lillian's house. Her mother-in-law had mentioned it, how she wanted to move into the guest house on her property and give the family house to the children, meaning Priss and Barney. Deborah shuddered. She dreaded to think what the town would say once her son sired little Black babies. Well, maybe she'd get used to it ... and maybe she never would. There she'd be, living alone in the house she had shared with Dickie while her children humiliated her. She was sure her daughter would be an old maid, but at least she'd be free to take care of Deborah once she shriveled up into a little old lady.

Robinette came into the room just as she was devising what she'd say to Leah when she confronted her. She would not agree to a divorce, and she would threaten to expose Leah all over town as a withered old prune who couldn't get a man of her own. She'd ruin her reputation for good.

"Hello, Mother," Robinette said. "May I speak with you?"

Deborah was terribly distracted, but shrugging off her daughter would only give her more reason to be upset with her. Robinette had told her she was absolutely the most bigoted woman in the world and should be thrilled Barney was marrying Priss. She most likely heard that before the news of her mother's affair with Jeremiah. She'd bedded down with a Black man, there, how bigoted could she possibly be? Far be it from Deborah to mention that she slept with him because she thought he was White. Well, was he White or not? And besides, she didn't marry Jeremiah. She married Dickie.

"I asked if I could have a word with you, Mother?"

When Deborah turned, her daughter was sitting down, looking as nervous as a long-tailed cat in a room full of rocking chairs.

"Of course, darlin', what is it?"

"I like girls."

"Of course, you do, and I hope you have at least four of them, four beautiful little daughters for your grandmother and I to spoil." Deborah laughed and then reached for her purse. "I really must go now, dear. I have an errand."

Robinette rose to her feet. "I don't think you heard me, Mother."

"I did, I did, you like girls. So, do I darlin', not as easy as boys, but you know what they say, a daughter is a daughter for the rest of your life."

Deborah took her car keys from her purse and started outside. No way in hell was she going to let that wench of a woman share her husband one moment longer.

Chapter Thirty-Two

Leah

Leah packed with great precision, labeling every box, carefully laying out her casual clothes and her personal mementos and photographs. She wanted to make sure she didn't forget anything of value. She wouldn't be taking the furniture. She felt the house would show better with everything in it. Rhonda had finally decided to move Grayson and her family into The Plantation and make Charleston her permanent home. Leah could not have been happier. Finally, she and Rhonda would live freely together as life partners. Maybe it was the relief of putting Fletcher's murder behind them. It had haunted their lives until Kenny was arrested. The attorney Rhonda had found for him had assured them there would be no prison time and that Kenny's reputation would hardly be marred. Kenny had carried that around with him all these years and when Leighton had been assigned the case, they'd all been nervous wrecks, though no one wanted to admit it. They would have preferred to delude themselves that night in '63 never happened.

Now, their lives would not be marred by any dark clouds hovering over them. Having Leighton know the truth about her relationship with Rhonda was a relief. Her daughter didn't harbor any prejudices about people of a different sexual orientation, although it was probably rather jarring when it came to her own mother. Leah would never forget the shock on her daughter's face when she learned that her mother was a lesbian.

Leah happened to glance out of the window just as Deborah Daring drove up in her fancy Cadillac. Surprised to see her, Leah opened the door before Deborah could ring the bell. "I saw you drive up," Leah said.

"This won't take long," Deborah announced as she stood on Leah's porch and gave her a steely stare. Leah stepped back from the palpable tension.

"Can I come in?" Deborah asked with a certain detachment in her tone.

"Yes, come in, Deborah. I'm in the middle of packing, so I can't offer you coffee. My cups are all in boxes." She smiled.

"You're moving?"

"Yes."

"Where?"

"Charleston."

"Alone?"

"Please, sit." Leah said. "I'm not taking the furniture, just the cups and some dishes."

Deborah looked as if her heart had dropped to the floor. "Dickie has agreed to that?"

"Dickie?" Leah looked at her in utter confusion.

"Yes, well, I can assume that, can't I? After all, you've been screwing my husband for thirty years. I assume he'll move over to Charleston with you, though his business will suffer for it."

"Where in God's name did you get that idea?" Leah asked. Did Deborah honestly believe she was having an affair with Dickie?

"Well, I mean Leighton. She's Dickie's daughter and your daughter, he's screwing someone, been screwing someone all these years. It must be you. He never got over you. It's clear to me. There is no one else in this town that's more appropriate than you."

Leah sat back. She didn't want to be in this position. She knew exactly who Dickie had been having an affair with. Malcolm had told her years ago.

"It is not me, Deborah." Leah got up for a cigarette and then sat back down. "We went out together in school and yes, we had sex in high school, but it was over between Dickie and I when I moved to Charleston years ago."

Now it was Deborah's turn to look confused

and at a loss for words. Leah anticipated she would be called a liar.

"You expect me to believe that?"

"It's the truth."

"Then who? Who could he possibly be sleeping with if not you?"

"Look, Deborah. I wouldn't worry too much about it anymore." A somewhat contrite and superfluous suggestion, but it had the ring of truth.

"Why not?"

Leah sighed deeply. She wanted to make Deborah feel better, but didn't want to reveal what she knew.

"Dickie loves you. He won't leave you. He'd never live in Richmond." She'd said that to console Deborah but just as she said it, realized that Deborah might not have heard the news about Lottie yet, that she'd gotten a job offer she couldn't refuse and was moving to Richmond.

"Richmond?" Deborah's head came up quickly. "She lives in Richmond?"

It had just come out. She hadn't meant to say it. Just the other day, Malcolm had told her that Lottie Lacock was moving to Richmond.

"I hear she got a job offer there. It was a quick decision."

"Who are you talking about. Who is she? What the hell 'she' are you talking about?"

Backed into a corner, Leah had to admit what

she knew. She had to tell who the hell it was moving to Richmond.

"Lottie," she said softly. "Lottie Lacock."

Deborah stared straight ahead of her for several seconds. "Lottie?" she whispered, her confusion tangible. She turned back and looked at Leah as if she'd been struck by lightning.

"I'm sorry, Deborah, really I am."

"But I don't understand. She's a lesbian, isn't she?"

Leah was somewhat amused but not altogether. Deborah was clearly trying to process the possibility that it might be true.

"She isn't, Deborah. She's had affairs with quite a few men in Pickens, all of them married. Dickie was the longest, though. She probably really cared for him."

"I care for him."

Leah nodded and in a gesture of sincere pity, she took Deborah's hand in hers and held it. Deborah shrank into the folds of the couch, speechless and shocked. She let Leah hold her hand for a few seconds and then stood up. "Thank you for telling me," she said.

Leah watched as Deborah made it to her car. Leah watched her clenching the wheel, crying. She watched as the car sped off, and then walked back into the room and reached for the phone to forewarn Dickie — she owed him this warning. He had to be prepared for Deborah's anger.

Instead, she called Malcolm.

"His wife knows about Lottie," she said. "She's pretty upset."

"You talking about Dickie Darling? How do you know that?"

"She came over here to accuse me of being Dickie's lover for the last thirty years. I couldn't let her think that. She was so upset. I told her I doubted he'd move to Richmond, so she shouldn't worry. The affair was probably over. Dickie isn't going to leave Pickens. She didn't know who the hell I was talking about at first. She didn't know anything about Lottie moving to Richmond."

"I guess it wasn't your place to tell her, but she would have found out eventually. You were backed into a corner, Leah."

"I feel sorry for Dickie, her too."

"It's okay. It's not your fault. She would have found out soon enough."

"Is there anything I can do to help him? You think I should forewarn him that his wife knows who he's been sleeping with?"

Malcolm shook his head. "She might change her mind and not move."

"There's a 'For Sale' sign on her front lawn."

"Money talks, I guess."

"Well, I am moving to Charleston with Rhonda and the only reason I'll come back to Pickens is to visit my grandkids."

"I'll miss you girls," Malcolm said. "Don't

worry about Dickie. He can take care of himself, and he always lands on his feet. His wife will forgive him.”

“You need to befriend him, Malcolm. He needs a friend.”

“He’s not one of us girls.”

“Oh, what the hell difference does that make? He’s different, just like you, Miss Ginger Tea.”

Chapter Thirty-Three

Deborah

Deborah drove around for what seemed like hours, so angry, her entire body shook the whole time. She had to think clearly. She would never forgive Lottie and most certainly, she would never forgive Dickie. Without intending to, she found herself in front of Lottie's house, staring at the "For Sale" sign on the front lawn. Would Dickie move with her? Well, at least she hadn't moved yet, her car was still in the drive. The temptation to ring the doorbell and beat Lottie senseless was overpowering, but Southern ladies do not raise their fists in rage. The urge to drive her car into the pristine white front porch until nothing was standing but the splinters of its former glory almost won, but she would not tarnish her Cadillac for the indiscretions of that tawdry, cheap woman.

She got out of her car and walked to Lottie's garage. Something in the garage would give her an idea.

The kerosene, neatly stacked on the side, was the answer to her prayer. Her thoughts tumbled like scrabble squares falling into place and forming a word. She took one can of kerosene and went into Lottie's backyard. Deborah had always admired it, the way the trees yielded her so much privacy. She spread the liquid at the back of Lottie's house, back where she was unlikely to be seen. She took a match from her pocket and lit it, then tossed it on the ground. It took to the kerosene with a hiss, a big, powerful raging hiss. She lit two more matches and tossed them toward the kerosene.

Deborah ran back to her car and watched for the fire, unable to see it from the front of the house yet. A few neighbors ran outdoors. She watched as one of the neighbors studied the Cadillac. That was good, her car seen by someone was good. Her tinted windows would shield her identity and she was happy Dickie had talked her into tinted windows. "For Christ's sake, Deborah, if you want to be seen put the top down," he'd told her.

She suspected she'd hear the fire engines before long, so she started her Cadillac and drove off.

Chapter Thirty-Four

Lillian

Lottie had changed her mind, said she didn't want to move to Richmond, said she didn't feel like ending her affair with Dickie. Lillian was livid. She'd have to apply more pressure, sweeten the deal somehow. She drove over to Lottie's house and smiled when she noticed the "For Sale" sign, standing sturdy on her lawn. Maybe she's changed her mind again, Lillian thought.

Lillian was about to turn into Lottie's driveway when she noticed Deborah's Cadillac. She accelerated and drove on by: it was either one of Deborah's friendly visits or she had found out it was Lottie who'd been screwing her husband for thirty years and she was there to make mince pie out of Lottie.

Lillian turned onto the street behind Lottie's house. She didn't want Deborah to see her and wonder what the hell she was doing there. Lottie's move to Richmond had to be Lottie's idea and not hers, though why would it matter, she thought with a smile. Deborah would be forever indebted to her if she knew, but still, best to keep her daughter-in-law in the dark.

Lillian felt it might be a good idea to go in the back way and warn Lottie that Deborah was sitting outside, most likely plotting her demise. Then she thought she might be too late and poor Lottie was lying up there with a black eye. She pulled the car right onto Lottie's back lawn where it would be hidden if Deborah turned on that street — likely since it was on her way home.

The fire was beginning to engulf the back of the house. "Oh, dear God," Lillian said as she got out of her car. She ran as close as she could get to the house without filling her lungs with smoke. It looked as if the fire had caught onto the curtains on the other side of an open window and the inside of the house was now an inferno. Lottie was trying to get out of a second-floor window.

"Jump," Lillian screamed.

Lillian heard the glass break and then saw Lottie climb through. She slid down the roof and fell. She landed on the grass and Lillian hurried to her. She looked a mess and moaned something about her leg. Shards of glass pitted her hands and legs, but she wasn't bleeding too badly. "Hold on, I'll get you a doctor."

"It was Deborah," Lottie said. "I saw her from the window. I saw her. Didn't know what she was doing at first, but she had kerosene. I saw her. She set this fire." Lottie tried to scream it out, but her voice was hoarse and soft.

"Don't talk now, Lottie. I'm going to take you home. You're going to follow my instructions to the letter. You hear me, Lottie? To the letter. Now, can you make it into my car? I'll take you to my house and call you a doctor."

Lottie nearly collapsed in Lillian's arms, but Lillian helped her to the car and sped off toward home.

Chapter Thirty-Five

Deborah

She drove out to Powdersville and parked across the way from the garage. She hoped no one would see her in such a shady part of town. She knew that's where Jeremiah worked, at the one and only gas station in Powdersville. She sat outside the station only minutes until she saw him emerge, jump in his Mustang, and drive off. She followed behind until he stopped in front of an old two-story building. When he got out of the car, she sat on the horn until he turned. He didn't know who was honking at him, not at first, but then he walked up to the open window.

"Deborah?"

"Get in," she said.

"Well, I'll be a son of a bitch." He opened the door and slid inside as Deborah sped off. "To what do I owe this honor?" he asked, his manner caustic. "You know I got nothing to say to you."

"Barnaby knows you're his natural father."

"Oh." Jeremiah put his head back on the seat. "He's a fine boy."

"He'll want you to be in his life."

"I'd like that." He turned and looked at her. "What are you up to Deborah? You didn't come to this shady part of town just to tell me that? Ever hear of a telephone?"

She reached out and took his hand. "It wasn't me that turned you in. I did what Lillian told me to do."

"It's water under the bridge, Deborah. It's over. I want to concentrate on the present."

She drove out to a place they used to go, at least a thirty-minute drive. She stopped where they used to stop, on the old, abandoned property of the Sutters, who had gone bankrupt years ago.

"No one has bought this place yet?" he asked.

"Too near the swamp," she said. "The house is falling down. Nothing but swamp land now. It was bought and sold twice in the last thirty years, but it's deserted as the planet Mars."

"*Phew*, stinks like Pluff Mud."

"Good to see you."

"Why'd you bring me out here? You going to put a bullet in my brain?"

She laughed and then reached over and put her hand between his legs. She stopped the car under a Maple tree. "You still got a hold on me," she said as she rubbed him until his penis was out of his pants and in her mouth. He pushed away from her for just a moment, but stayed until she had sucked every inch of him, and he exploded all over her, himself, and the leather seats.

"I won't be able to stay away from you," she whispered in his ear.

"Take me back where you found me, Deborah. I have a curfew."

"Ever drive a Cadillac?"

He shook his head.

"C'mon then, take the wheel." She got out of the car and walked to the passenger side. He was eager to feel that beauty under him and she knew it. Who wouldn't want to drive a Cadillac?

"Don't drive too fast," she said.

He turned the car around and drove back the way they came. They said little on the drive back and Deborah knew he was wondering if she wanted to continue seeing him. She smiled. Highly unlikely she'd want anything to do with him.

"You're still as handsome as ever," she said.

He turned to her. "Stay away from me, Deborah," he said. "I was twenty-five back then, I'm fifty-five now, old enough to know better."

Deborah laughed as she dropped him off and touched his hand. "That was nice," she said. "I expect you to return the favor."

"Not interested." He smiled and closed the car door softly.

Deborah drove back into town, into the parking lot of a supermarket her side of town never used 'cause it was in the poor section. It was deserted and nearly dark. She pulled the car into a spot, got out, and walked to the police station about a mile away. She avoided people on the street, but didn't have to worry, there were very few.

She reported her car stolen right about the time the police were taking a statement from one of Lottie's neighbors, the one who had seen the Cadillac outside Lottie's house.

Dickie wasn't home when she arrived back, even though the sun was falling in the sky in a burst of brilliance. She took a nice long bath. He was in the sunroom when she emerged from her bath full of warm scented bath bubbles and body oil. He seemed nervous. She walked to him and gave him a kiss on the cheek. "Hello, darlin'," she said. "Had a ride home earlier from your daughter. Such a lovely girl."

"Why'd Leighton drive you home?"

"My Cadillac was stolen. Can you imagine? Someone stole my Cadillac. I went to the police station and she was there as I was leaving."

"Hope to God we get the Caddy back." His mouth fell open as his body tensed, sweat on his forehead and under his arms from the exertion of burying a trunk in a goddamn swamp.

"Your shirt is wet with sweat, Dickie," she said.

"I hope we get that damn car back without a scratch."

"Oh, I imagine we will get it back. Can't hide a car like a Cadillac, it stands out. As for any scratches, we can only pray."

He mumbled something and watched her settle in a chair opposite his. She talked about the wedding and how she wanted to help Prissy with the guest list. "So many people leaving town," she said. "Leah is going off to Charleston for good, but if you'd like me to, we'll send her an invitation. I know you'll want to invite Leighton. But it's not up to us, we'll let Prissy approve our decisions. I think three hundred people will be fine, what do you think?"

"You've had a change of heart?"

"Of course, darlin'. Why darken my days with disappointment?"

"And where will this wedding of three hundred people take place, in the town square?"

"Lillian is giving them her house. Didn't she tell you? Prissy wants the wedding there. I mean, it's the prettiest place in town."

"Definitely prettier than the town square."

"I'm so excited."

"You are in support of the wedding now? Just the other day, you were trying to pay Prissy to leave town."

She gave him a coy smile. "Well, a girl can change her mind, can't she? I was being unfair, terribly unfair. And I told you, life is too short for disappointment."

"I suppose so."

"I doubt whether Lottie will come all the way from Richmond to attend, but you know we'll invite her."

Dickie's head shot up so fast he might have caused a crimp in it. "Of course."

"Seems she was offered a job in Richmond, Virginia. She's taking it too. I like Richmond … remember that summer we went up there with the children?"

"I didn't know about the job offer."

"Well, darlin', you know now."

She watched as he picked up another one of his God-awful crime books. Experience told her he would run to his mother and threaten to join Lottie in Richmond, but they would be empty threats. Lillian, — who made it all happen of course — would never approve of a divorce and certainly not of a marriage to Lottie Lacock, who still looked like Bella Lugosi as far as Deborah was concerned. Obviously, she hoped Lottie had gotten out of the house in time, but truth be told, Deborah was grateful she'd had the opportunity to burn Lottie's house down while she was in it. If she got out, so be it and it she didn't, oh well.

Deborah went back to the kitchen and got Deasia to make her some iced tea. She knew Deasia was furious at her, but that would pass. "So thrilled and excited about the wedding," she said while Deasia gave her an odd look. "Are you as excited as I am?" Deasia gave her another odd look and went back to throwing ice in the pitcher like she was hitting golf balls.

Chapter Thirty-Six

Dickie

He stood in front of Lottie's house and felt like dying. There was hardly anything left of it. How was he to cope without her? He learned she'd been napping in her bedroom when the fire started but managed to get out of the house. Dickie hoped she hadn't hurt herself, but there had been damage, terrible damage. He drove to his mother's house at her request and that's when she told him that Lottie had cuts and burns all over her. He didn't want to see the body, relieved his mother didn't let him open the trunk. He didn't want any knowledge of what she might have gone through.

A neighbor had seen Deborah's car in Lottie's drive but turned out Deborah's car had been stolen. When the police impounded it, they found Jeremiah's fingerprints all over the steering wheel and semen on the car seat. They surmised that Jeremiah had burned down the house and wanted to incriminate Deborah in retaliation for fingering him for Fletcher Smith's murder. Deborah certainly had motive, her husband's thirty-year affair with her best friend. His wife certainly deserved the sympathy. Leighton told Dickie that Jeremiah stole her car and set the fire. As for the semen, it was just like Jeremiah to pick up some woman in the Cadillac and have sex with her before dumping the car. Dickie wasn't quite sure what he believed or what he didn't believe.

Jeremiah's trial was set for the following month. He declared that Deborah Darling lured him into her car, lured him into having sex, and even allowed him to drive the car so his fingerprints would be all over the place, just so she could frame him for the fire she set. "My wife would never let anyone drive her car," Dickie said, but as an afterthought he added, "but if it benefited her in some way, she would have."

He knew Deborah was aware of his affair with Lottie now, and that it was Leah that had told her. Malcolm had called him about it. Malcolm told him that Deborah had confronted Leah and she'd spilled the beans. "Oh, not on purpose," Malcolm had assured him. Somehow Malcom had it in his head that he and Dickie were best friends.

Dickie refused to believe his wife would ever set fire to Lottie's house. It had to be Jeremiah seeking revenge. But his mother told him the truth, that it had been Deborah. Then Deborah dropped a bombshell when she told the authorities Jeremiah had raped her in 1962 and he was Barnaby's real father. The town rallied behind Barnaby and were he ever to run for mayor, Dickie had no doubt his son would get every vote. Sympathy was on his side. Poor bastard, innocent little Barnaby deserved support, by-product of a terrible act of rape.

Dickie kept his mouth shut —it was never rape — but Deborah was protecting her son, to justify marrying a Black woman, and Dickie would defend her decision. However, the town, skeptical that Deborah was raped, remembered the teenager she had been, wild as a tiger and more than capable of bedding down with a sexy man like Jeremiah.

When Dickie found out about Lottie's job offer in Richmond, he planned to ask his mother what the hell she thought she was accomplishing by running Lottie out of town. But then he learned Lottie was lying inside a trunk in the back of his mother's car.

"I was driving back to apologize'" Lillian told him. "She gave me such a hard time about it. She kept saying she wasn't going to leave you. When I got there, I saw the fire and Lottie in the backyard, screaming. She'd escaped out of a window. The ambulance was taking too long. I got her in my car before anyone noticed her and drove off and called you. But the smoke took over her lungs, Dickie. It killed her."

"What have we done, Mother?"

"Nothing could have saved her, son. She was

gone."

"Did she suffer?"

"Deborah did it. She set the house on fire. If Lottie had lived, she would have turned Deborah in to the police. She was furious."

Dickie put his head down and sobbed in his mother's lap. "What have we done?"

But Lillian just shook her head. "Sent her to a better place, son. We must protect your wife, now. We have to think of Deborah. Let Lottie disappear. No investigation that might threaten Deborah. Let it go, Dickie."

Whether he would ever get over it made no difference. He had to stand tall and be the man Deborah had married. Maybe someday it would be different but for now, it was more of the same. He stopped mentioning divorce and so did she. No reason to divorce, they had a marriage set in stone now that there was nothing there to threaten it. Lottie was buried in swamp land out there by Sutters. Isn't that where he took her? "No, no, no, I didn't," he told himself.

But he did: she was at the bottom of the swamp because he'd put her there.

Epilogue

Five Years later

Halloween 1998

Jeremiah was never tried for the murder of Lottie Lacock. There was no body when the fire was finally extinguished. Without a body or enough evidence, a murder conviction was not likely. The police concluded that Lottie had disappeared, made it out of the house, made it to safety, but where she had gone was a mystery. She hadn't reappeared anywhere, not in Richmond and not in Pickens. The disappearance of Lottie Lacock was never solved and now, after five years, people assume she was murdered, her body buried somewhere. Leighton McArdle and Joe Martinelli have been investigating but the file finally wound up in cold cases.

Jeremiah had an alibi for the time the Cadillac was seen in Lottie's drive. Several people had seen Jeremiah at the gas station in Powdersville at the time the car was spotted in front of Lottie's house. Deborah Darling's Cadillac was returned to her after forensics found no other prints but those of

Jeremiah Lennox, Deborah Darling, Dickie Darling and the children of Dickie and Deborah Darling. The semen found in the car was hushed up and as far as the town knew, Jeremiah had stolen the car for a joyride. Deborah did not press charges. Jeremiah was given a slap on the wrist and told to stay out of trouble.

"Dickie can you fix my mask? The damn thing isn't tight enough. It keeps slipping." Deborah turned around but not before giving Dickie that smile that used to melt his heart.

Dickie tied the strings of her mask into little knots while his two grandchildren nearly toppled him in their game of "catch me if you can."

"Those boys will be the death of me," Deborah said in her exasperated breathy voice, commonly used around Calvin and Malcolm, Prissy and Barnaby's two sons. Prissy was pregnant now with a girl. She had just found out the sex of the baby the other day and glowed with the news. "Oh, I've wanted a girl," she told her guests while Barnaby beamed at her side.

"Little Deasia," he said. "After Priss's mother. That's what we're going to call her." He winked at his mother, who quickly turned her head away.

The last thing she wanted was a little granddaughter with her ex- cook's name. Dickie caught the face Deborah made and gave her a grin. She quickly recovered but did not grin back. As she passed through the kitchen in her elaborate costume as Queen Mary, often known as "Bloody Mary", she overheard someone remark how dark Barney's children were. "And are there any more beautiful boys in the entire state of South Carolina than my blessed grandsons?" Deborah asked demurely, to which the ladies replied, sweet as molasses, "I'd say the whole United States," they giggled. "Most assuredly."

All the food for the Darling's Halloween party had come from the River House, as it had for the last several Halloween parties. The River House was Deasia and Jeremiah's Cajun French restaurant, the once-famous possession of Beau McArdle and the investment of Lillian Darling. River House was enormously popular, and Deasia and Jeremiah recently had to hire three new waiters. The servers at the Darling's Halloween party were all White. "Times certainly have changed," Deasia said to Jeremiah. "White people serving while we're earning." She broke into a grin.

Barnaby walked up to Deborah and planted a kiss on her cheek. "You look ravishing tonight, Mother."

Deborah smiled and kissed him back. She caught Jeremiah's eye and winked at him. He gave her a smile as difficult to interpret as Greek.

Dickie went to the door to welcome his

daughter Robinette and her partner, Gillian Hathaway. He kissed both girls. "Darlins', so good to see you. How long will you be staying?"

"All week, Daddy, I want to show Gillian how good the food is here, how sophisticated." She smiled up at her father. "She is, after all, a graduate of the New York Culinary institute."

"I hope you'll be cooking for us then." Dickie winked at Gillian.

Gillian laughed. "I'm looking forward to it. I hope to knock your socks off."

"Take your things upstairs, girls, and then come back down to the party before these savages eat all our food." Dickie kissed his daughter again as he went off to find Deborah. "Oh, and don't forget your costumes," he called back.

"Robinette has arrived with her partner," Dickie said to his wife.

Deborah's face turned red as a basket full of ripe strawberries. "How nice," she said.

"I want you to be gracious." Dickie squeezed her hand.

"Is that what they do in New York, popularize perversion?"

"Be civil, Deborah."

"Of course. I'll accept the girl as what? My new daughter-in-law?" She glared at Dickie. "What absolute bullshit."

Dickie walked away when Leighton arrived, with her husband, both dressed in eighteenth-century attire. Tom was a formidable figure. Appropriately running for mayor of Greenville. The man adored Leighton and she finally allowed herself the happiness she deserved, especially after Beau's death and that brief affair she'd probably had with Sean Dowd. Leighton has been happily married for three years with a two-year-old daughter and a new baby on the way but still works her cold cases.

"Hello, darlin'," he said as he put his arm around Leighton's waist.

"Dickie," she said and kissed his cheek.

Dickie smiled. It had not been easy, his life, none of it, but it was done and in his own way he was happy. He told Leighton and Tom to help themselves at the bar, that the waiters were slow. Then he walked through the French doors and out into the night. Now he needed aloneness. He needed to be himself.

It was almost cold, and the stars were abundant. It was so clear. The air in his lungs was a blessing, a feeling of life filling him. He thought of Lottie, but he always thought of Lottie. He wished she had gone to Richmond. He would have joined her eventually. Dickie resented his mother for all that drama around Lottie. He hated his wife for setting that fire, but he'd never seen Lottie's dead body, so he kept telling himself she wasn't dead. He kept telling himself that one day she'd appear. One day he'd learn that it had all been a horrible joke, and he'd buried an empty trunk out at Sutters.

It wasn't far to the guest house, under a five-minute walk. He was happy his son had Lillian's house now, it was perfect for Barney's family, and it freed up the guest house on his property for him. His mother was quite content in the guest house on her property, happy to see her great-grandchildren so often. She told him that if she ever needed anything, Prissy or Barney could be there in two shakes of a lamb's tail.

You couldn't see Dickie's guesthouse from the road, and you certainly couldn't see it from the main house. That's why it didn't matter that he kept the lights on to guide him to his sanctuary. It looked so warm and cozy. He'd told Deborah he was using it as his office. Deborah would never walk or drive to the guest house anymore. She had absolutely no interest in it since Barney had moved on. Dickie was careful not to make her suspicious, though, not to make her think he was keeping a mistress there. But every day he came. Tonight, his absence was sure to go unnoticed. It was, after all, a Halloween party back at the main house and Deborah was playing hostess to the hilt."

He walked in and stared at the cut-out skeletons and a lit-up pumpkin. "Ginger," he called. "Place looks great, spooky enough." Ginger Tea came from upstairs and flowed down the staircase like some marvelous, sultry actress with great sex appeal, a true siren from the 1940s, wearing bright bracelets and a crimson dress, almost see through. How fine she looked, Dickie thought.

"Your dress is lying across the bed, Dickie boy. Don't be long."

Dickie gave her a wink and a smile before he gave into the glee of adorning himself in the scintillating evening dress. He had also bought the most alluring diamond necklace and he couldn't wait to see how the sparkle brought out his eyes. He was overjoyed. By the time he got downstairs, after dousing himself in his wife's Chanel, Ginger had the fire going and the Champagne corked. "I've also made hors d'oeuvres," she said.

"Delightful, my dear," he said as he kissed her hand.

They put on some jazzy music, and they sang along to Cole Porter and Ella Fitzgerald. But the music always made Dickie cry. The fantasy turned empty and Ginger had to soothe him, assure him that this is the closest he could get to Lottie, having a good life, making her proud.

"Not good enough," he whispered.

"Look, Dickie, I know a woman who likes drag queens. She's into them."

"I'm not a drag queen," Dickie said indignantly. "I'm not a drag queen," he repeated.

"Besides, I don't like cheap women or bizarre women. I'm a married man."

"Yes, of course you are, Dickie. Of course you are."

"My time is up, must get back to the party. Where's my Dracula costume?"

"Why don't you just go back as you are? I mean, you've hardly had time to wear that gorgeous dress. It seems a shame."

Dickie paused for a moment. "I should, shouldn't I? I don't really like the Dracula suit."

Ginger looked at him. "Go for it, Dickie. No one in that room is more beautiful than you."

"I should go back to the Halloween party like this. My wife would have a hernia, though."

Ginger jumped up. "Well, she deserves a hernia."

"No, I'm going to do it and I'm going to do it alone. It will be my moment." Dickie got to his feet and went to the door. "I must do this. I can't live with myself any longer if I don't. I'm doing it for Lottie. She would be proud of me."

"Are you sure you don't want me to come with you?"

"Most sure," Dickie said.

"Alright, then I'm going to Miss Tangerine's party. I did promise I'd show up."

Dickie waved him on and walked out into the night with its blinking stars and its chill. He knew he looked beautiful. Who could resist him?

He saw them all through the glass doors. How they laughed and chatted. He didn't see Barney's little boys; they must have been put to bed. Deborah was clearly flirting with some big muck a muck who was running for some office or other. Dickie thought he was a pompous ass, but Deborah once remarked that he was charming.

"Ha, charming," Dickie whispered. "More charming than I with my beautiful buttocks and my full red lips? My long thin legs? Ha, I doubt it."

He went to the doors and turned the knob, his heart beating dangerously. Perhaps he'd expire right then and there, but so be it. If a heart attack were to happen, so be it. He entered the room with great flair and posed before the doors.

How they stared at him as he stood there smiling. It was if the entire world went quiet. "Get me a cigarette, darlin'," he said to his wife, who had approached him with resolute steps.

She didn't move once she reached him. She stood in place like a goddamn statue. At last, his daughter, Robinette, dear Robinette, walked up and took his hand. "I'm Robinette, she said. "who are you?"

"Deedee." He heard a hush fall over the room. "Can someone hand me a glass of Champagne?"

"It was his son, Barnaby who handed him a glass. "Drink up, Deedee," he said. "You look like a million."

"Well, I have to make a toast first," he smiled at Deborah, who still hadn't moved, who did not even appear to have taken a breath.

It was Leighton who said, "To you, Deedee." She raised her glass in a toast. They were all raising their glasses to him, presidents of banks, senators, businessmen, so many upstanding citizens were in that room. Tom Hart, next new mayor of Greenville stood next to his wife with his glass in the air. Their smiles were genuine, a bit confused but certainly amused.

"And to all of you," he said. "My friends, my family, my wife."

Deborah was laughing hysterically. "Dickie," she said. "You went to sleep with your clothes on. I didn't even notice. I must have been exhausted. You passed out in your beautiful dress. Where on earth did you get it?"

He opened his eyes and looked around. He was in his own bed. His wife was lying over him with that wonderful smile. "Where am I?"

"Here, give me your dress."

He slipped out of it and tossed it to her as she gently placed it over a chair. He was relieved to see her smiling.

"You were loaded last night. I was a bit loaded myself. There were so many people to amuse but it was a great party. Just a wonderful party. You were the pièce de résistance, though," she said.

"Oh, my God. I feel like I've been asleep for years."

"You're going to miss the birth of your next grandchild, Dickie."

"No, I won't. I promise."

"Well, I like Gillian. She's quite funny."

"Are you being serious?"

"She needs a man, like my daughter. They both need men but she's nice."

"They like each other, darlin'."

"Oh, Dickie, don't be ridiculous."

"Surely I died last night. I barely remember a thing."

She looked at him oddly. "You didn't die, Dickie. You came alive. They all loved you dressed up like a woman. Whatever possessed you? It was hysterical. The best costume ever."

"You like me in women's clothes?"

"I'm not saying that. I liked you charming all our guests. They just thought you were the living end. I married such an eccentric, such a life of the party. But if you run around town in dresses, Dickie, I'll shoot you where you stand."

Dickie smiled to himself. "Our parties are the best, aren't they?"

"The best, darlin'."

He turned on his side to stare at her. "I forgive you, Deborah," he said softly. "For anything and everything."

She didn't take her eyes from his for several moments. "I forgive you too, Dickie."

He got out of bed and opened the windows. It was a new day. The sun had risen like an orchestra introducing its music.

"It's a new day, darlin'. A new darlin' day for the Darlings."

"Isn't it, though?" she said as she lay across the bed in her most alluring way. Dickie's dress from the night before had been thrown across the chair, casually, as if it belonged. As if it belonged as much as the honeysuckle air he breathed in. As if it belonged as much as the mist that floated off the swamp like a rising ghost. As if it would remain unchanged forever, unnoticed for years, but not forgotten.

The End

Watch for A Saffron Sun in 2023
Sequel to The Darlings